ONE THIRD
OF
PARADISE

Also by Julietta Harvey
Familiar Wars

For John, for Katerina,
for Julietta and Eleni

Julietta Harvey

ONE THIRD

OF

PARADISE

Polar Books

First published in 2015
by Polar Books UK, Greenways,
Bowbridge Lane, Prestbury, Cheltenham,
Gloucestershire, GL52 3BL, England

Typeset by M Rules, London
Printed in Great Britain by
Berforts Press, Stevenage

ISBN   978-0-9536309-6-7

CONTENTS

1

DUTY FREE

The Greek drama unfolding in front of the Olympic Airways desk gave the vast hall a centre – a large indignant heart. Its accents were foreign, its music familiar. Eleni joined the silent chorus of bemused travellers watching – a woman in furs, voluminous in flesh and voice, gesticulating at the unperturbed young woman behind the desk.

"Where is your superior? We travel Athens London all the time – regular customers, and they are charging us for excess luggage!" She heaved up with difficulty a large suitcase, and let it fall with vengeance on the scales. Drops, rivulets of agony ran down her forehead.

The dialogue was in English, but Eleni heard her native grammar commanding, demanding – and she had no defence.

The young woman remained unmoved. "I am sorry, you will have to pay for excess luggage."

"I travel once a month. Do I want to? No! But it is necessary. I have my child, my son, studying in London. He will be a doctor next year."

Beside her a well-groomed young man stood straight, staring at the luggage, avoiding all eyes. The peach bloom of a blush rose into his cheeks. He looked uncomfortable in his leather jacket, tight around his midriff.

His mother looked at him with pride. "A young man in his prime." The word "prime" reverberated through the bewildered silence. "I am a mother! I am tired! Do I have to pay for excess luggage on top?"

The employee shrugged: "It's regulations."

"Regulations!" The hall shook with the crescendo of motherhood.

"Mother, please!" the son pleaded – in Greek.

"Mother, please." Eleni also pleaded mutely, to her own mother, in Greek. It was a general plea, open-ended, and made no sense since her mother was now dead. If Eleni could ask her for anything it would be – please, don't be dead.

How could she unhook herself from the tangled dead-ends of her feelings? She followed her compatriot with fear and longing. Longing to be part of her story – full of life's routines, like travelling and shopping and saying good-bye – knowing that the good-bye will not be for ever or for long.

So, her eyes followed the large woman battling, protecting, wanting. She watched mother and child with envy and revulsion, wishing to move away from that smothering mothering. Yet she fed on the melodrama. Because it was her native language, threading unseen and unheard between those two, that made her own loss so essential and intimate – as her mother's scissors, cutting the mysterious strings that tied mother and daughter, were now tearing into her own flesh.

She was a translator by profession, but this kind of translation played with life and death. She dwelt for a moment on the word orphan, very similar in both languages. And during that slow uttering of the word a long shadow of desolation passed slowly over her head, separating her from others.

Her attention returned to the woman considering with pain her mute and still luggage. She pushed with her foot a swollen bag – "Take back grandma's thermals."

Her son picked up the bag. As he received instructions, a glimpse of violence travelled through his face. He raised his finger to his mouth, his lips pursed in a slight sucking movement. Then instantly he hid his hand in his jacket and obeyed his mother's orders.

Eleni checked in her bag, containing lightly a hasty assortment of clothes. As the girl at the desk considered her passport Eleni watched, with a distaste that satisfied her, the mother pulling down her son for the parting embraces.

She walked round the duty-free displays half-desiring this or that good. She paused in front of the cosmetics, and deciphered expensive reassurances of beauty and youth. Perfumes. She looked for the bottle which, mysteriously, contained the invaluable extract of summer evenings in love.

A drop of this elixir on her skin might capture those warm, scented evenings – when she climbed down the wall in the dark, scratching legs and arms. Into a garden with statues and fountains and palm trees – a garden sinking under jasmine and oleander, canopied by the old wisteria year after year dislodging with its self-involving growth the stone walls. She summoned the two lovers hiding in the dark to kiss, and whisper, and kiss.

Eleni saw the woman in the fur coat reflected in a mirror. Her bosom inclined, as if to expectant babies, towards gargantuan bottles of whisky, sherry, assortments of chocolates. At the sight of the vast descending bosom Eleni felt washed back into her desolation. "What will become of me now?"

On the plane the hostess raised, for everyone to see, her life-giving utensils, her lifeless voice bringing Eleni the nausea of the knowledge of death.

In mid-air, she observed herself tearing layers of years, travelling into the rent in the wafting vaporous cloud. Born into raw sunshine, she hovered naked and exposed, lingering over the threshold of home: pulled and pushed by currents of longing and loss.

She saw clearly what waited for her in Greece. The gathered

beneficiaries. Her sisters and their husbands appropriating, blaming. She wanted to turn back, before she became entangled yet again in old, disfigured resentments.

She undid her belt and spread the Greek newspaper on her lap. She fingered the pages, searching to steal into someone else's story. But her own family map was spread on her lap. The sisters blindly occupied their allotted territory. Sophia, the eldest, was in control; Kaliopi, in the middle, coaxed, bullied; Eleni herself, late and last, was the expatriate, the pariah. And those responsible for this angry geography were no longer responsible. Her mother's will – there must be a will. Her father must now give her the dowry he never gave her. She must have her just portion of the property, and of the land – this was her motherland.

"Catching up with Greek news, I see." With patronizing affability the man next to her spoke slowly, in English, so she could understand.

"Yes," she lied, in Greek.

"The same old mess. How long have you been abroad?" Furtively he scrutinized her clothes, calculating her sexual readiness, she thought, her marital situation. He noticed the black, and became circumspect.

Appearances matter at home, she mused. She scrutinized his clothes. She guessed him to be a businessman, a rep. Word processors? Food processors? His politics, flexible.

"Where do you come from?" He took his jacket off . Old Spice aftershave, mixed with his own male smell, reminded her of dancing in a restaurant garden by the sea.

"Thessaloniki."

"A compatriot! Where was your neighbourhood?"

"Ah, it's gone. Where do you live?"

"On the New Waterfront."

"Of course!" She remembered that stretch of the waterfront, which was now a fashionable residential area. For her the place remained a growing and ageing labyrinth of huge concrete cubes, at the edge of the sea, extending into the dark. Waiting for years to become a family promenade, the concrete had aged and become its own illicit city. *Ta Blokakia.* The gigantic concrete blocks made a refuge for young and slowly ageing lovers. The paths between them wide enough for one, two if they stood close, very close, necessarily embracing, and all evening kissing, indefinitely in love, oh infinitely. Till gangs of children arrived, jumping from block to block with sticks and stones to drive love out. The police turned a blind eye. She was being airborne back into that labyrinth of first, early, ignorant love. The concrete gigantic cubes had become a concrete promenade, but ghosts of all those lovers in hiding must be hovering.

The trolley with the drinks arrived, she chose gin and tonic – a non-Greek drink, an act of forgetfulness. He joined her, explaining that he usually drank beer, although he did also like wine, especially Greek wine, but only with food. She asked him why he had come to London.

"Toys," he explained with pleasure. "I bought toys, and ideas for toys." He opened his briefcase and a rubber doll appeared round his hand, grinning and grimacing. "I have a toy-shop. It's called *Concepts* – on Egnatia Avenue." She accepted the toy-pen key-ring he offered her – as a memento, he said – before he put his briefcase away. He fell on his packaged dinner with the same gullibility and gusto. His glass of Mount Athos he sipped with restraint, felt it his duty to praise it, and all Greek wines, and olive oils, and olives.

After dinner he turned to her, his face plump and benign. "Would you like to see a photograph of me?"

He took out a photograph of himself, several years younger, in army uniform. He gave it to Eleni, and with a coy, self-satisfied smile waited for her reaction. The eyes of that young face in the photograph looked back directly and spoke to her. "Very nice!" she said, and returned the photograph. Then he took out a small travelling bag with expectation, almost with glee, to blow it up into a travelling pillow. "'Porta-pillow' they call it, the latest thing." He arranged the inflated velveteen bib round his neck, and let his head rest serenely on it as on a soft halo.

Eleni kept vigil over her neighbour's blissful sleep. His face reminded her of plump-cheeked cousin Alexandros, her gentle play-mate, who obeyed her in all their games, but slipped through her fingers when during the interminable summer siestas he was sound asleep – selfishly asleep. When she carefully lifted the soft eyelid, the eye underneath did not see her, or see anything in that room or in that world. She never told him what she did to his eyes.

The flight seemed brief, cramped and intimate – like a child-hood. Pinned down and belted up, contracted into her allotted space, she was delivered home.

The airport of Thessaloniki was small and noisy as a family business. Armed policemen eyed the few foreign girl-tourists with cool appraisal. Men and women moved before her under a fine dusty web of familiarity. Men and women of property, their tread secure and self-regarding. Their dark eyes measure and take possession, their bodies are satisfied. She looked under the layers of satiety for the lean lover of her youth, she traced dark circles under eyes, remnants of forgotten passions. A thrill – of native sensations, of voices, smells held her body. The roots of her being were stirring, searching.

She came outside and was possessed instantly by the light. Instantly it brought into focus the remembered, perhaps manufactured, happiness of home: but at its centre, always, the still desolation.

She felt on her skin the familiar warm air. She lifted her face to the uninterrupted blue, then entered her world as a child enters a familiar game whose rules she knows and accepts. A world of clear outlines and stark definitions – where words stood out, like lines of lead soldiers, without ghosts of things unsaid.

A world – suddenly she saw – not watched by a mother's vig-ilant eye. A forbidden voice called out to love to come and play hide and seek with death. Forbidden glances sought those moments which stopped on a kiss, keeping on hold future, history, the world.

Eleni." A man's voice. But not young, her father's voice.

"Baba."

She saw her father, standing forlorn in the neglected garden outside the airport building. His face preoccupied, his old briefcase, bulging, pulled down his arm. A familiar grey suit, well preserved. A black arm-band. His hair silvery-grey, in place. A bewildered face – but the body was young, the step quick. He was obviously glad to see her. He separated the oleanders savagely and stepped across, oblivious to their scent and the trespass.

They embraced. She held him with the vehemence of a vanishing daughterhood – a part she used to play with expertise and gusto.

"I'll look after you, Dad."

He shook his head – an indefinite recognition of an indefinite number of sad events. "Welcome home, my child." My child.

He insisted on taking her bag, she insisted on taking his briefcase, which he wouldn't let go.

"You are late, my child, late." He took her by the hand and hurried her towards the bus. His fingers tightened round hers, never quite at rest, or at home. But to her this restlessness was home, the one stable, familiar thing.

In the bus, he withdrew his hand from her and let it rest, half-closed, in his lap. He rubbed the palm with his other hand, and rubbed each finger separately: then sank into preoccupation.

"It is not well, my child. My hand is going bad on me."

She took his hand, gently tried to push the fingers open one by one, because she did not want to believe her father's hand could suffer. The skin of his palm pulled the fingers in together: the small finger was closed, the others less so, only the thumb was free and mobile, mocking the hand that fed it.

"Have you been to the doctor, Dad?"

"Who has time for doctors..."

7

"We'll go to the doctor now I'm here." She held the damaged hand in hers, and he said yes, doing her a favour.

A solitary villa with one palm tree in the front garden appeared, and disappeared quickly. Its windows and wrought-iron balcony were perennially overshadowed by a large sign, 'School for the Blind'.

2

MOURNING FEASTS

They entered Sophia's flat and were confronted by a roomful of relatives, the women in black. The noise stopped, an argument hung in the air. Tryphon's voice lingered on and, stretching out a legal point, it rose to courtroom pitch in order to stamp on the air the absolutely right, last word. Sophia, his wife, presided with tired indifference.

Kaliopi's sturdy maternal body rose before them. "Where were you, Dad?" She turned to Eleni and smiled at her with the pained moral superiority which by now was engraved on her face. The two sisters embraced, briefly, brushing accusation onto each other's body as they parted.

"Where is mother?" Eleni looked round the room.

"She is not here. You will see her tomorrow." Kaliopi played mother.

"She is at the morgue," Sophia cut in, matter-of-fact. Her body was small and brittle, her eyes sensuous, watching over animate and inanimate things with alertness. All three had their father's hooded-eyed watchfulness. They embraced tentatively: Eleni pulled back as she saw the piano, which had been promised to her, and had waited for her all these years – she saw her piano sitting deaf and dumb in a corner. Her eyes cast about the room, hooking onto the familiar objects glaring, blatant, out of place. The carpet from mother's living room, her decanter and glasses. Pieces of home, fragments of mother, misappropriated.

Sophia read her feelings, unperturbed, the relatives watched with expectation. The men in grey suits and black armbands slowly got up from their deep comfortable armchairs. Tryphon, Sophia's husband, the eldest of the sons-in-law and a successful lawyer, stood tall and dignified, his plump lips and wide nostrils alert to sensations, his olive-black eyes, hard lively centres in a round taut face, commanding the room. Kaliopi's husband, Koulis, still wore a drooping moustache and an expression of weary sarcasm – tired, tarnished, unconvinced. Mother's sister, Aunt Lefkothea – large-bosomed and loud-voiced – stood over her pampered husband Efstathios, spreading invisible wings of indulgence. Uncle Efstathios sat in well-fed handsomeness; his swooning blue eyes and wan smile greeted an appreciative world.

Aunt Lefkothea approached with open arms, and Eleni hung onto the consummate mother. She held the large warm body, that made her feel young and small. She held on to her for a long time, for the sake of all the years that had gone by, for the gain of so much flesh, for the loss of beauty and youth, for her own loss.

"She is relieved, my poor sister, she is released."

Eleni was comforted by the tears in her aunt's voice.

"She was young, poor Anastasia, too young, and so unprepared, so unwilling!"

Eleni turned to the chorus of relatives singing the communal sorrow. But the animation of worldly affairs, of recent acquisitions, of lost bargains or arguments still played in their eyes. Eleni read in their faces rich food, lack of exercise, lurking disease.

"She had to stay at the morgue – the heat in the apartment…" Aunt Lefkothea whispered, cajolingly. She presided over the rest of the black-clad women, who nodded their agreement with sorrowful discretion.

Mortality reached Eleni's nostrils. As she went round

greeting, embracing, she studied faces, secretly blaming those flushed, fed faces.

She looked for her father, who had been led by Kaliopi to the sofa. Kaliopi wanted to know why he had gone to the airport. "Didn't we say we didn't need to go? Why didn't you at least tell us?"

Father was restless. He turned away from her and gazed at the gathering with dislike and suspicion.

"I changed my mind! I wanted to go to the airport. I wanted to see Eleni. Are you satisfied?" His voice rose above the other sounds of the room.

The women asked Eleni about her flight, the weather, her life. Eleni's face creased in a smile, full, mute, that locked out and locked in. She said she would show them photographs, but her life out of this room seemed to be someone else's.

The women returned to their quiet lamentation, moving their upper bodies back and forth, releasing a deep sigh now and then and crossing themselves. They talked in whispers to each other about the deceased, nodding their heads in communal sadness and acceptance of the will of God. The men returned to their argument.

"Let them call it 'The Republic of Skopje', or whatever they like."

"As long as they leave the word 'Macedonia' out of it." On that they all agreed.

Cousin Apostolos, Lefkothea's eldest son, thought the Turks were behind all this. "The first chance they get they'll be in our houses – they'll have us surrounded."

"Watch out for the Bulgarians." Lefkothea's younger son, Phoebus, fanned whatever he said, however mundane, with the erotic aura of his long irresistible eyelashes. "They have a minority in Skopje. Will they just sit and watch?"

"The Jews are selling their property and buying in Athens." His young wife with blond-bouffant hair spoke with sudden confidence.

"If the Jews sell, they must know something. They smell the air of the market." Father made his quick interjection, and then, indifferently, returned to his thoughts.

"Nonsense, women's small talk!" Tryphon wouldn't let anyone else know more than he did.

Father's eyes sparkled with a flash of dislike. As Tryphon launched into a new peroration – while simultaneously swallowing a sizeable *smyrneiko* meatball – his father-in-law gazed at him, the corners of his mouth pushed down in displeasure. He surveyed the relatives with superior indifference, native Macedonians all of them, landowners. Now she was dead, he was a foreigner to them, the travelling merchant, the refugee.

Sophia got up and joined Kaliopi and Koulis. Eleni followed from a distance her sisters' converging faces and animated whispers, but could not make out the words. Father observed with agitation from his corner. Eleni moved next to him on the sofa and rested her arm around him. He gently slapped her thigh – "My girl." It was an embrace of love, and loyalty. Now, as always in this family, she needed an ally. And her father always was an instant ally – but unreliable. Her sisters were plotting, Eleni knew it, and Father knew it. She wondered if they already had mother's will – she hoped there was a will, which made good mother's promises.

"They print on their travel brochures 'Macedonia' and stick in a picture of the Salonica White Tower. And what do our politicians do? Nothing. We betray our own history! They paid this poofter, he calls himself an artist!" – Tryphon raised his voice – "they paid him a fortune to make a statue of Alexander the Great for the Twenty Fifth of March." He paused, for suspense. "On the day of the celebrations, we all waited in the freezing cold for the big moment – the Minister of Macedonia was there, and even the Minister of Culture. I was standing right behind them. They pulled down the sheet… And what Alexander met our eyes! No muscles, no stature, no greatness. Our Alexander the Great riding his scrawny horse barefoot!

Without his helmet, without weapons! Alexander the Conqueror, a puny little pacifist."

The relatives were animated. They all had seen pictures of Alexander the Great and they all had an opinion. Yes he had long wavy hair, but he had the neck and the body of an ox. Just like his horse, the ox-headed Bucephalus. Aunt Lefkothea spoke for the women: "We are simple women, we may not know all the ins and outs of politics, but when it comes to Alexander the Great, every one knows he was great." The rest of the women shook their heads in agreement.

Father, tired and dejected, made an effort to sit up tall on the soft low sofa. His eyes, red from sleeplessness and tears, leapt with minute fast movements among the relatives. "Little do they care." His mouth changed forms of distortion with increasing irritation as his tongue played secret games with his false teeth.

Kaliopi's husband called for soda water. With perverse synchronicity Tryphon put another stuffed vine-leaf into his mouth. His face went suddenly red, his eyes leapt wildly communicating alarm, helplessness, indignation. Sophia gave him a glass of water un-tenderly, then turned her attention again to her youngest sister: it was difficult to read her thoughts.

Eleni returned her gaze. Looking for sorrow in her sister's face, she saw power. She turned to Kaliopi – her stout body bending over the guests, offering them hors d'oeuvres. Eleni recreated, with art and vengeance, childhood nightmares. With mother dead, she saw herself irretrievably at the mercy of two amplified powerful mothers. She was a child when they were brides, beautiful, splendid in the midst of splendour. How could she expunge those pictures from the family album?

She sought to unearth her mother's image from beneath the clutter of bric-a-brac and blame. An image that was the remembered, unknown centre, which Eleni always sought and always abandoned. An image stamped in her mind, fugitive and perennial, from a photograph. But the smile on her mother's face – was it meant for her? The soft pleasure in her eyes – was that meant exclusively for her?

"The target is – here – Thessaloniki – the port." Cousin Apostolos tapped his finger on a particular spot of the table with sombre finality. Momentarily he was transformed into a general with the map of the Balkans at his mercy.

The more Eleni sought her mother the more she lost her. She sought refuge in her father, sitting apart, distant, distracted. But tangibly alive. She wanted, with a distorted need, the energy, the power, even the familiar anger of his youth: the tyranny, that had scorched her life. She imagined holding his hand, his hand holding hers: holding it and letting go, holding it restlessly, uncomfortingly, taking a better grasp, then playing with her fingers. His fine, sinewy hand, warm and nervous. She saw it slowly closing through the years. The tendons shrinking and pulling it shut, the muscles shortened and powerless, and he, looking at his useless right hand, tired from such avarice and hard work, the hand that had been raised – to strike? perhaps to stroke.

She had amplified him in her fear. A fear that probably concealed and protected a love: or had it been the other way round? Had love been fabricated to cover up and muffle her mortal fear? And now, could he, would he accept that potent brew that had seeped thoroughly through her life?

Like a plant to the sun, Eleni's body tended towards the things that had secret links with her mother. Her hands and eyes wished to hold on to those good things, household goods and gods, as if they were her mother's hand, or face, or the hem of her garment. The touch of garments, the slipperiness of silk, the soft depth of velvet; the patterned labyrinth of sensuousness in the rugs leading only to themselves; the fragile transparent clarity of things reflected and resonating in crystal – what music might be hidden in the mute still piano? In the tiredness of grief and change, her mind languished for the alluring silence and solitude of things. And, unseen by Mother's vigilant austere eye, she was letting herself drown into a fabricated mother – all pleasure, all trust, all sleep.

All pleasure, like the evening air of her native land coming though the balcony door – the gauze curtains hardly making a flutter – and moving her body through its roots. This temperate air, full of native noises and pirouetting movements in the dark, carrying memories and desires of young and loving sinfulness. All pleasure.

Memories of open-air cinemas and theatres, open-air dancing to melodies of seduction, open-air love – which might even disperse the fury of the three black-clad sisters. A memory of her first party dress of green velvet. Eleni could recall in detail the neck line, the tightness round the waist, the depth of green, the softness, the whisper. That remembered green velvet may hush the black of bereavement, and the clutter of family and war, absorbing all into its sea-wavy green depths – of love, probably of love – or, was it a thrill, which set their lives quivering?

They had not dared to give names and utter words, but ghosts of native seductive words, *eros, amartia,* always hovered around their half-dressed bodies. And their bodies, still sinless, unsure how to love and unwilling to part, were blindly shaping their lives.

At this proximity of death, young life and love with its inordinate desires rushed in. Her body is still young. And before she touches the cold hardness of death she must find the person, that boy who had meant to her life and love, whose body had nothing to do with death – nothing of death in that young body.

Uncle Miltiades got up and walked slowly towards the toilet. His wife, his beautiful comrade in their youth, stretched an arm to the vol-au-vents.

"What do you think of Mimi, then?" Aunt Lefkothea sat down next to Eleni. She could not hide her unrestrained approval of her son's new fiancée. "She's got a dowry" – her hand moved as if carrying handfuls of imaginary gold. "He's fallen on his feet again."

Eleni looked at the couple, nodding in agreement. Her cousin, a lady-killer with lascivious eyes, divorced and recently redundant, rested his arm with proprietorial weight round Mimi's padded shoulders. Aware of being the object of attention, she sent the room a coy, controlled smile.

"The children?"

"Their mother looks after them. Thank God he got rid of her."

Eleni remembered the fuss they had made of the first wife – she too had a dowry and youth. They told her to be quiet and patient: he was a man! Of course he would look at other women! Only with patience and good temper could she win him back.

Eleni looked away. She would like to see Nikolas. She knew the hospital where he worked. Would she re-enter those dark alleys of plotting, of secret meetings, the fear and thrill of betrayal?

Aunt Lefkothea, the consummate mother, pushed a plate of *mezethakia* in front of her son. He smiled with tolerance, and adjusted his posture to give further freedom to his stomach. His bride-to-be promptly brought cutlery and a napkin. His mother grew fat with pleasure watching her son eat. But instantly she turned to her husband, who was resting hungry blue eyes on her. She slapped her cheeks with self-blame for this harsh omission and jumped with exhilaration to her highest duty: to serve the eldest and dearest of her "boys".

The rarest of delicacies were instantly presented to Uncle Efstathios, and he smiled coyly to her and to the rest of the relatives. "How she spoils me!"

Eleni and Father exchanged looks, a sparkle of recognition for the familiar comedy.

The other relatives helped themselves to the funeral feast. Kaliopi and Eleni competed as to who would prepare the best plate for Father – who accepted it without appetite. Aunt Lefkothea, this being her sister's funeral, was the queen of the party, circulating, offering, encouraging people to eat. Sophia, the hostess, watched grudgingly, counting – Eleni imagined – the drinks, the bites. She grabbed from her husband's hands the bottle of old brandy he brought from the bedroom, and told him to calm down. With quiet agility she stopped the maid at the doorway carrying in a platter of new delights. "Later," she ordered quietly.

Sophia came to life when her son Alexis appeared, a tall, good-looking, shy young man in jeans and leather. With un-sated maternal appetite she pressed into his unwilling hands a plate heaped with the flower of the feast. He held the plate casually as he exchanged polite greetings – tossing the long hair out of his face. His father watching him with annoyance, his mother feeding on his every word and movement.

Alexis was explaining to Eleni the latest divisions in the Young Communists. His father in response launched into another anti-communist diatribe, simultaneously choosing, tasting, chewing, swallowing the tasty morsels before him. Greed and politics, paternal frustration, baby needs and male autocracy were too potent a mixture, and – his cheeks swelled, his eyes stared in new-born bewilderment. "Water" he managed to indicate, some-one offered wine, he gulped with difficulty through the tense silence, and gulped again, with greater difficulty. His wife stood over him with a glass of water.

"Either speak, or eat," she spelt it out to him as if to an illit-erate. Unable to answer her, his eyes opened further, his fist secretly clenched. Their son was quiet, but indifferent, Father looked at his son-in-law with unconcerned superiority.

Food, the comfort of the bereaved, the healer of family sorrow, was consumed. Family feelings choked on themselves. But the body of Mother, perennial food and home of all love, was not allowed in her daughter's home.

When food and wine had been consumed, it was time to talk of the dead. And the thread of history started with Uncle Miltiades, mother's younger brother, in his dark suit and old trilby hat, who looked asphyxiated by the attention of the two corpulent women in black on either side. Only now Eleni noticed the disfigured half of his face and remembered that he had suffered a stroke. It was from all the torture he had in the Civil War, the family said. He was then a real guerrilla. Now he was grey, and quiet like a child.

His wife served him food and admonitions. She had been beautiful, she had ensnared him to the mountains. With her husband's illness, the beautiful comrade – her features now coarsened – suffered from melancholia. Yet this occasion of death had livened her up, and now and then the loud laugh of her youth resurfaced, to everyone's discomfort.

Uncle Miltiades rearranged his trilby and cleared his throat. He rehearsed Mother's childhood, her cruel jokes, her clever answers. The rest of the relatives, like an experienced chorus, came up with the response – of amazement, and amusement, and laughter and tenderness – wiping at times a discreet tear. They recalled their sister's rebelliousness, her teasing, her prizes at school – stories familiar and painfully delicious to her daughters' ears.

Mother became a young daughter, her own daughters' daughter. Old photographs came to life. The dead were resurrected. Fleetingly Eleni and her sisters and Father, and the relatives around them, attended tenderly and with quiet mirth to the soul of that young girl that had departed. At last Eleni could grieve.

Eleni reminded them of how grandmother Maria stopped her from school. "Tell us, tell us what she did to her, what she said to her." Events needed a guilty party.

"Her mother said to her, 'Anastasia, now you stay home to help with housework. You are twelve, you've learned enough, now learn how to be a good housewife.'" Eleni knew the story from her mother's mouth, and had heard, in her very words, her bitterness, and longing for learning.

The relatives all shook their heads in agreement – it was a pity, a great pity. They sang her other virtues: her embroideries – done with such patience and passion. What a good cook, and wife and mother. One by one like amber beads of a *komboloi* her virtues were fingered, and felt, and left behind.

No one mentioned what else grandmother Maria had said to her young daughter when she was only seventeen. "You are plain, Anastasia. You had better become a good housewife if you want a husband – because you are not beautiful." No one mentioned this, but Anastasia's daughters knew and grieved for the harshness of those words.

Lefkothea offered Father a glass of wine, he wiped his tears. Kaliopi went and sat next to him and passed her arm around him. Sophia and Eleni held hands. Momentarily the three sisters were together. The memories of the dead meandered through the gathering, bringing tears – finally free warm tears of bereavement. Father and daughters came briefly together in their common loss.

Grief satisfied, thoughts wafted out of the fogs of the past and came to rest upon themselves. Kaliopi asked Aunt Lefkothea about her gall-bladder.

"I need to diet," she admitted. "The doctor said I need to lose kilos and kilos. But my pampered boy here needs to lose even more. Exercise, the doctor said, exercise and diet."

They talked about vitamins, cholesterol, blood pressure. Lefkothea asked Sophia to bring her new blood-pressure gauge. They asked how much it cost, argued about how it worked, finally, in respectful, hushed seriousness, they took turns in having their pressure taken by Sophia. They became devoutly absorbed in the mysterious functions of their body.

"May life be with us", they wished each other as they crossed themselves with Christian forbearance.

Thoughts of their bodies, and lurking fears of death and disease, brought them back to food. They exchanged recipes, told each other of good tavernas. They grew excited. They proceeded to summer villas, property prices. They worried about taxes – it was getting difficult to hide the odd extra. The answer was to write everything in their children's name. Sighs of thankfulness and "Glory be to God", and also "Glory be to God" that they had some property and a few investments abroad.

The family narrative moved from eulogy to elegy to the domestic banal, and almost rose to melodrama when one of the aunts asked Lefkothea in whispers whether the deceased had left a will. Lefkothea signalled ignorance and silence.

The mourners jumped with alarm from the sudden sounds and lights of explosions taking place in the corner of the room where the television screen had suddenly come to life. The room was transformed into a theatre of war, orchestrated by Tryphon who, remote control in hand, seemed to be operating the tanks crawling like gigantic cockroaches on rubble. And the mourners were alarmed again when the war abruptly changed faces and places and actors and languages creating a pandemonium of violence. Tryphon enjoyed being the animated dictator of the world for a few more minutes, before Sophia turned the television off. The relatives got up one by one. Tomorrow another day of lament – they needed to preserve their strength.

The family stayed on to keep vigil over the body that was lying elsewhere. While Tryphon sat back watching an old Hitchcock film, the sisters prepared for the night: mattresses were put on the floor, blankets were found, mother's embroidered sheets were unfolded. Father stayed in his place, too dejected to stir. Alexis walked restlessly around the apartment – his mother, like a plant to the sun, perennially tending towards him.

The sisterly triangle was broken, suspected plots were suspended, and grieving hearts were exhausted. Kaliopi and Eleni sat back together in temporary alliance. They were after all sisters, they grieved for their mother, they grieved for their father. They might, in the intimacy of the night, remember their mother, her good days and sulky days, her affectionate moments – not many. Her daughters admired and envied the pleasure and pride she took in her embroideries: years of her life spent bent down over her needle and thread transforming cloth into a work of art. She had put into them a sensuous passion and imagination which she had kept secret from daughters, perhaps from her husband. That was her way. Serious, austere, laconic.

"Of course, you were born so late, Mother was old and tired by then." Kaliopi had ambushed the enemy, but she was willing to give something, or somebody, away: "You were Father's girl. Whereas I was totally Mother's girl. I look like her, I've got her body, like her I'm good at cooking and housework. When she was unhappy with Father she came to me."

Eleni stood up and walked away from that alliance which made her the loser. She surprised Sophia and her son in the kitchen. Alexis was bent over a steaming bowl of giant prawns swimming in their juice. His mother stood in front of the cooker, preparing to ladle more. The smell and sight of the delicacy was irresistible, comfort floated tangible and delicious before her. Eleni accepted readily the bowl of prawns tentatively offered her, the warm fresh flavour of the Aegean sea reached down to her empty heart.

At the far end of the living room, in a low voice, Tryphon was explaining something to Koulis; they stopped when Eleni came into the room. Tryphon got up with self satisfied slowness and walked, belly first, out of the room. Eleni knew they were discussing the inheritance. She must confront them and ask about the will.

Father came into the room in a fury of business, and stopped all activities and conversations. He searched with noisy suspicion for his briefcase, it had been lying old and floppy behind the sofa. He made sure it was locked, then searched his pockets, and finally produced a handkerchief on which he blew his nose.

Eleni led her father to a bed in the spare room. Holding the briefcase tightly in his good hand, he looked in bewilderment around the strange room. "I want to go home to my bed."

Eleni said, unconvinced, the family should stay together. Her father gave her a searching look. He did not ask why: he just looked round the room with new suspicion, demanded a chair which he made sure was placed very near his bed. Then he asked for some water. When Eleni brought him the water, he was searching his pockets.

"Did you lose something, Father?"

"No, no." The searching became frantic. "My keys – I lost the keys to my flat. And the keys to the shop, and the building, and the warehouse."

Eleni offered to help him look, he refused. He searched the pockets of his trousers, and then of his jacket; he tried his brief-case, turning his back to Eleni so that she could not see what was in it. He asked for some water, to send her out of the room: she reminded him that a glass of water was right next to him.

With relief, a small triumph, he produced a heavy bunch of keys.

"Father, why so many keys? What are they for? You don't need to carry all these keys around. They're so heavy."

He gave her a look signifying "Mind your own business". To confirm his independence and security he had a sip of water. He secured the bunch of keys in the pocket of his jacket, then he proceeded to take his teeth out and place them in the glass – particles of food floated in the water. And her father was transformed into a little old man. She helped him with his pyjamas, and he accepted her attentions like an obedient satisfied child. When she rested the cover on him, he held her hand in his, strongly. He had tears in his eyes.

"Your poor mother."

"My poor father!" Eleni kissed him on the forehead.

Snoring reverberated through the apartment. Through the half-opened door the bedroom was flooded by an unearthly storm of light and noise from the miniature TV set thrown into perma-nent tantrum. Tryphon had abandoned body and soul to the exuberant sleep of the young and the thoughtless. In the living room Koulis, in well-pressed pyjamas, was attending meticulously to his final preparations for bed. He took a sip of his warm milk, mumbling to himself, loudly enough for everyone to hear, that it was not sweet enough – someone was stingy with the honey.

Sophia and Kaliopi were discussing the funeral. Kaliopi was inspecting the bills, Sophia was calculating what each one's contribution would be. Eleni sat near by.

"The funeral will be the day after tomorrow. It cannot be any earlier. To-morrow you will settle this, I hope." Sophia was business-like. "Also we should discuss Father. He shouldn't live on his own." Kaliopi nodded, Eleni was unprepared. "Also we have to secure the property. He may sell it, give it away, there are impostors around, there are shrewd women, he may even want to re-marry."

Eleni noticed they made no mention of a will. The two had already discussed things and taken decisions.

"He should entrust the handling of his affairs to us, to one of us." Kaliopi was Sophia's loyal lieutenant. They had made the division.

"Which one?" Eleni regretted her question. She felt the threat in the words take hold of her.

"Which one do you think?" Sophia was in her stride. "I happen to be a lawyer. I live here. What could you do, in England? What have you ever done for him?"

Kaliopi was nervous. She remained silent.

"I am not discussing anything tonight, not tonight."

"We'll have to settle things as soon as possible before you go back. You could leave us a power of attorney."

"No. We'll settle things before I go."

Sophia and Kaliopi looked at each other. "Let's discuss things tomorrow." Kaliopi offered a compromise; Sophia said nothing.

Eleni walked to the other end of the room, and sat back on the couch. Surrounded by conspiracy. She calculated: there were four of them, two lawyers, a businessman, and Kaliopi was amenable but shrewd, not to be trusted. And she was one, and alone. Father was only an old man, a forgetful old man.

But she must have her portion of the inheritance; she must

know what the inheritance is, what is left of her parents' estate. She must claim her dowry. She must find the will. Could it be in Tryphon's office? No, she must speak to a lawyer. She must remember who her father's lawyers were. She must go through her father's papers in his flat. The world was again closing in on her. The world made up of two, three, five people, her family. The permanent, slowly, imperceptibly ageing faces; the permanent ageing household; their moral verdict on her own life; their unquestionable power.

The rest of her life, abroad – her true life – seemed now distant, abroad.

In her voiceless dialogue with the room, she might find fragments of mother, home, her lost questionable life. She might find illusions, half-truths, temporary consolations. Like the music. The music she tried to produce on that inert silent mass of the piano. What vain hope made her desire it now so desperately! Or what jealousy made her prefer to see it dead in a rubbish tip, rather than be an ornament in her sister's home. The carpet, that mother used to lay in the front room on her name day, hid in its subtle patterns the spirit of a well prepared, warm, bright festivity. Could it, if she rolled it up and carried it away – could it magically carry her back to those moments? What did she seek, with such futile persistence, through its worn pile? Perhaps her mother's own dedication to those things: the silver, the glass, the furniture, the cloths, the household, the home which had enclosed her in its muffled comfort all her life. Her mother's life gone, its furniture still kept her secret and ambiguous scent, vindictively enticing her children still sniffing for her love.

She looked around the flat at Sophia's possessions. Old large icons of the Holy Mother, that had belonged to churches or chapels, covered the walls irreverently. A wise investment. On the desk a seemingly leather-bound volume of Shakespeare's works proved on inspection to be a cigarette case. And on the wall, the stolen pastoral scenes embossed on silver led to no Arcadia.

*

The sisters held their separate vigil through the night. Sophia finished her yoga exercises, then placed her head low and her feet high, applied ear-plugs and eye-mask, had a sedative pill, and tried to rest. It was important that she did not let this experience undermine her. It was important that she did not let her father undermine her life and health – as her husband had. It was important that she organised her father's affairs so that he could not – absolutely could not – run risks. It was important to organise Alexis' life, to help him take the right decisions, to take them for him if she must. The worry that Alexis would one day squander the property that she had, through such sacrifices and shrewdness, amassed, was gathering into a fury, that exploded: as her husband's snoring suddenly reached a crescendo of uncontrolled exuberant abandonment.

She pushed with all her rage his plump uncooperative body till it rolled on its side. The snoring changed pitch and tenor. She hit him. He was startled, his eyes were momentarily those of a bewildered child suddenly attacked by a satanic mother. Then they shut again, and the snoring resumed with quiet secure regularity.

Her sisters' voices from the living room grated on her nerves. Loud and gay, and on such an occasion. She could not make out what they were saying, except for the odd useless word.

Doors opened, lights switched on, someone pulled the toilet chain, once, twice, without success. She recognised her father's cough, which meant he wanted attention. She tried to relax the muscles of her face, she massaged her forehead with her fingertips in light arching movements. She pressed on her temples, then released the pressure, then repeated it. Her jaw had tightened again, her teeth were grinding, she forced them to relax. The noise from the living room was getting animated; the blue phosphorescent light from her husband's Japanese radio-alarm-clock bombarded her deliberately with deadly rays. She got up with maximum disturbance, walked round the bed, and pulled the plug, killing all light and sound. She fell back satisfied.

Eleni's laugh from the living room, short, not too loud but loud enough, stung her back to alertness. The heartlessness, the irresponsibility, all her life. The immaturity! Just pack and go. No questions asked, no answers given, she appears out of the blue, and vanishes. She has become a foreigner. She tried her breathing exercises. "I envy her freedom," she admitted to herself. With the rhythmical control of her deep slow breathing, pushing out the diaphragm and side ribs then letting go, letting go, she fell, against her will, into the secure rhythm of her husband's snoring.

A vigil of a kind continued in the living room. Koulis, in his expensive baby-blue pyjamas and black eye-mask, was asleep at one end of the room. Kaliopi and Eleni, still awake, lay stretched on the couch at the other end, absorbed in family gossip. Kaliopi's face was transported by the sensation of her stories. Eleni, weary and defenceless, was yet again drawn into her sister's fantasies. She knew, since she was a defenceless child, that half of her sister's stories were exaggeration and distortion, yet Kaliopi was so vehement that you had to believe her. Her whispers hissed with conspiracy.

"He sees other women. He likes women, he always did. Mother suspected something."

Eleni couldn't believe that her father could long for anything other than new and old fortunes.

"After her first stroke, mother kept saying – 'At our age! Such things at our age!'" Kaliopi was captivated by her words. "I asked her what she meant, what 'things' at their age, but she wouldn't say."

Father, as if he knew, appeared at the door, startled, dishevelled, barefoot, holding together his pyjama trousers. His hair was wild, his eyes frightened. His daughters hurried to him, made him sit down.

He looked round the room, then confided that he had lost his wallet. He looked accusingly towards the door that led to Sophia's bedroom. "I had it last night, now it is not there. It has disappeared."

Kaliopi scolded him, Eleni believed him – once she was within the family walls she was prey to their fantasies and suspicions.

"The wallet is here." Kaliopi assumed authority. "Are you saying one of us has stolen it? Your own children? We'll search, and I am sure we will find it."

Eleni wanted to contribute. "Did you search your pockets? Your briefcase?"

They looked behind and under the furniture, they brought in his clothes and briefcase, searched his pockets, emptied the brief-case on the floor. A feast of possessions spread out irreverently on the expensive carpet: ragged pieces of paper, out of date prom-issory notes, old receipts, faded dirty samples of material, a dirty handkerchief, a pair of disposable razor-blades, a pair of reading glasses, paper-wrapped candy, old bus-tickets, a torn page of newspaper, a pair of new socks, crumpled pieces of blue carbon paper that had smudged onto everything. His life had poured out and lay before their eyes. The battered briefcase sat up out of habit, supported by the bulging emptiness and by the sheer memory of its life-long accumulated contents. It gaped in injured wonder.

The wallet was not there; they pushed their hands into the upholstery of the couch, grazing the skin, down into its empty belly – nothing. They searched the bathroom, the kitchen. They looked around and under their father's bed.

Eleni's hand went under his pillow – and grasped the wallet. She looked at him – his eyes, the eyes of a child, were wide open in cheerful wonder. Kaliopi scolded him tenderly – "Dad!" He gave a big naughty smile and signalled to them to keep quiet.

They tiptoed back into the living room: the daughters, relieved and concerned, gave maternal admonitions to their father, who was now searching through the contents of the wallet. He accepted their scolding high-spiritedly, flirtatiously, wondering at the wise fate or good lady-luck that helped him find his wallet.

Holding the wallet close to his chest he went back to his room: in a few minutes he came out again and went into the bathroom. The tug at the chain was vigorous, the flushing half-hearted. Noises came from Sophia's bedroom, her voice was raised, Tryphon's snoring stopped. The two in the living room went quiet.

"Is there something wrong, father?" Sophia called wearily.

"No, no my child."

"He cannot look after his affairs." Kaliopi tolerated no objections. "We must get a power of attorney. And we had better hurry before he presents us with a new 'mother'."

A figure she could not see rested a heavy hand on her, holding her paralysed, in pain. She could only see the shadow, unsure whether it was a man or a woman. She tried to move but she could not, and to speak and she could not. She tried to move her mouth, her tongue, there was no movement and no voice. And no hope of help.

She struggled for a long time, it seemed a life-long time, to find a voice and move her lips and form a word. A word of a kind, a vestige of a word, a possibility of a word perhaps was uttered – any other person present might have heard something, a squeal, a noise, rather than a word. But, like a wordless infant, she knew she had finally managed to utter her first word, which to her mouth if not her ears was in her mother tongue. The sound was broken, and with hard effort she pushed into the break, and into further breaks and splinters of a prolonged dis-integrating inhuman sound. It brought no answer and no help, and no movement from the figure above her. Then with the extreme effort of the deaf and dumb she struggled to make another sound and form other words. "Who are you?" she asked the shadow above her, in a foreign, a step-mother tongue. And the shadow still did not answer. As she asked, she somehow knew that the shadow was a woman, and was a man. There was still no answer: but her own words, in whatever language, had freed her tongue and voice, and now freed her limbs and body, and slowly, with the hard effort and courage of the long paralysed, she turned her head towards the shadow. And there was no shadow. Yet the heavy invisible hand clasping her chest was still there. But there was no shadow, no figure, no mother to help and stranger to harm, and no hand clasping her heart, only a disembodied presence that, with the opening of her eyes to the sunlight in the room, fled. Leaving behind the pain – and absence.

3

SEPARATING LINES

Her black clothes absorbed and kept the sun's warmth. The air smelled of sea: the sky was blue, immaculate, and the sun could resurrect the dead. Its light raised each object and event, and gave them a significant shape and spirit.

Pleasure is a simple thing: it stood at a distance from her, complete, tangible, separate. She thought of a deserted street between garden railings, a place without blocks of flats, without cars, a few pedestrians, at noon, when the sun in the spring is high and hot, the grown-ups at their siesta and herself playing hopscotch. She remembers drawing on the pavement with the chalk she pocketed at school strong clear lines, making more or less equal parallelograms. Finding a smooth, flat stone. Keeping her balance while pushing the stone with simple rhythmical acrobatics over the drawn patterns. Then leaning against the wall in full sun waiting for her turn, watching the friend do her own dance. No desires and regrets other than waiting for her turn to negotiate the sun-washed symmetry. Patterns and movements in the sunlight is one kind, a rare kind, of happiness.

In summer, you live behind separating lines: between the blinding light and the deep dark shadow, where you stand, cool and intact, and watch the world ready to go up in flames. At other seasons you live for the unexpected voices hidden in the dapple.

She inspected those seasonal pleasures which at that moment belonged to another world. In her own universe on this April morning the sun had a brittle brilliance of spring. This light, this air, this morning was no time for a funeral: her steps were taking her to the cemetery, but her wishes returned to faces and voices of half-remembered lovers. In this sunlight without regret or embarrassment she wished she could look at a loved face, and be looked at, and desired. She wished she could walk with a lover, hand in hand or in each other's arms.

The city of the dead was free from the encumbrances of life. A symmetrical marble city, that was devouring the countryside. In the eye of God, or through an airplane porthole, it must have looked like the endless marble stage of an amphitheatre made of hills and mountains. The tombstones, of pure white Thasos marble, so many regular clean patterns gleaming in the sun, with no trace of long shadows. Sunlight and breeze travelling freely. The trees were young and low, and the flowers short-lived. The gate splendid, as of a fateful palace. And the unending black-dressed chorus — fresh flowers in their hands — traversed the tragic stage, or stood, or knelt, in hushed lament.

At the gate she was besieged by children thrusting candles and bunches of flowers into her hands. She bought what she could hold. Red carnations — because she liked the scent, and thought they had something to do with flesh. She walked through neat paths, lost in the quiet labyrinth looking for her mother, and her father.

She shuddered as she entered the concrete, windowless, refrigerated room, that contained her mother. Her father was already there, sitting on the cement bench along the wall, gathered, cold, frost-grey, his hands folded together, his face pensive. At the centre of the room on a concrete pedestal, the coffin — her mother resting snug among the cut roses. Her face still swollen from the steroids, her hands resting on her chest — her rings and wedding ring were missing. Her forehead was hard and icy to her daughter's lips.

Eleni rested the flowers at her mother's feet, and stood next to her till the cold reached her centre. She snuggled next to her father, both of them shivering in death's icy lap. She embraced him and pulled him out into the sunshine. They stood arm in arm in the warm sun, shivering guardian angels to a kingdom of frozen shadow.

The hum of the city's life was distant, constant. But near at hand the world lay in sun-washed silence. The solitary women would stop at their own plot of land as if arriving home, and undertake slowly the daily rituals of death, moving with the quiet air of housework. They threw yesterday's flowers onto a mountain of discarded flowers, mopped the marble pedestal, arranged the flowers in fresh water and the candles in their stand. They dusted and re-arranged the photograph of the deceased, weeded the grave, watered the shrubbery, then sat and talked to the dead in quiet intimate whispers. They might pause to gaze at other mourners, comparing losses and sorrows. They might inquire of their neighbours about the newcomers: did they die of age, illness, accident? And they would show pity for the young untimely death.

The priest made his rounds about mid-morning, a good hour for visitors. He chanted a quick liturgy, swallowing words and melodies, accepted his fee, and hurried to the next client.

Eleni and her father sat on a bench in the sun, lost in their private remedies. They took short journeys, together and alone, into the icy room where mother was lying. Eleni arranged the red carnations, contemplated the face, searching in it for her mother's face, kissed once more the forehead which felt like cold rubber. She recognised the hands, mobile with needle and thread, creating mysterious patterns of rhythm and colour. She raised her own hand to her cheek as if expecting now a long overdue caress. There must be a beauty that a mother's caress imprints on a daughter's face, Eleni imagined, as she bent and kissed her mother's crossed hands.

She went back and sat with her father, who was searching his pockets, the nearby shrubbery, the horizon. He walked back into the room, where he stayed for a long time. Eleni sat alone on a bench, without jealousy, allowing them, the perennial couple of her life, to have their last private solitary moments.

Alone, she was comforted by the warmth from the sun, and fragile fragments of memories. The warm sunlit silence of home – a corner in a living room where the afternoon sun reached at an appointed, brief, time. The nicely drawn red lipstick on her mother's lips, revealing a foreign woman from a forbidden fiction lurking behind her mother's face. Covering herself with spider-web fabrics to be transformed, and to be endlessly transported into the lands of love – the ecstasy of self-love. A transitory desire filled her head, a passion for a body, anonymous bodies, the love of her youth. Almost a hold on happiness: which brought back with renewed life the loss, the remorse.

Sophia and Kaliopi arrived together in expensive funereal elegance. They held large bunches of dahlias and gladioli – "She loved dahlias and gladioli," Kaliopi remarked, before she entered, with queen-like formality, death's room. Sophia interrogated father, why he left alone, what time he had come? She inspected his shirt, and shoes, rearranged his black tie; she told Eleni to keep an eye open for the hearse, before she moved with small high-heeled steps into the icy darkness where their mother lay, preserved.

Sophia came out first, pale and shivering. Kaliopi followed her, she had been crying. And Eleni, recognising their private grief, wished it might be possible to mourn their mother together. She revisited her mother, and observed again her naked hands – where were her rings and bracelets? Her loss concentrated on those small, tangible, missing things; and on that empty-handed need to hold onto proofs of life or love.

The cold square concrete emptiness of the room embraced her with maternal possession. She stood at the entrance, where the sun almost reached, doubtful whether to stay and abandon herself to death's deep sorrow, or walk away from that cold stone heart that drew her in and in the same cold breath expelled her. Like a vanishing dying breath the faint memory of a moment: of someone leaving a room never intending to re-enter: leaving behind her no scent, no trace, but only the certainty of absence, and the knowledge of an early, unrecollected flaw.

The sound of crunching gravel brought a large rectangle of black in front of her eyes. The coffin was carried out, lived briefly in the sunshine, and passed into the hearse. The family members followed, loosely together.

In the cemetery chapel the aged faces of relatives and friends floated in the incensed air, ghostly witnesses of a vanishing life. Faces that once had been delicate, spirited or flirtatious, or ruddy with the Macedonian mountain air; that had confided and conspired and competed with the woman lying dead, stared out through the layers of flesh, wealth and time. They gazed with curiosity and in judgement at the surviving Gregoriou family standing in hierarchy of age. Staring back, Eleni guessed at each separate sentiment those half-hidden faces felt for her mother, timidly making her mother real to her. A woman with friends and enemies, loyal or treacherous or comforting; a woman who had been a young girl, bride, daughter, who had a life of her own. A ray of sorrow for that woman whom her daughter hardly knew.

She turned to her father for consolation. He was restless, examining with busy suspicion those sudden ghosts from the past. Dubious friends, unwanted witnesses to his loss. There's well-padded, well-fed Evripides, shedding crocodile tears. He had made his fortune out of Gregoriou's destruction. When they arrived refugees from Turkey, Gregoriou managed to get the donkey, and the merchandise and customers all over Macedonia. Evripides had to make do with the remnants – just not quick enough, not good enough with words. And now he struts around in his cashmere coat – the big capitalist. Of course his wife is still a peasant. For all the jewellery and the fur-coats, she probably still crouches down to piss. Kind hearted, but a peasant. Of course he had the luck to have sons rather than daughters, fat-thighed sons, mind you, but sons nevertheless.

And the others. Lefteris, Sotiris – they were his assistants, his salesmen, now thrusting out belly and double chin. He had fed them, taught them a thing or two, and now they are the shop-keepers and he, an old man who lost everything.

He lost her. She was difficult and glum but always by his side, keeping the shop with him, together, selling and buying together, making money and losing it together. She provided him with clean clothes and ironed shirts, with a warm home and nicely cooked food; she scolded him and advised him, and entertained his guests and clients, and found his papers and reading glasses for him; and remembered deadlines for payment, and brought him down to earth when he dreamt of starting new shops. What would he do now! His daughters ... His sons in law – they took his daughters and their dowries and now they treat him like the poor relative.

Sophia touched his arm and told him to calm down, did he want to sit down? Did he need some fresh air? Kaliopi came and stood on his other side, and sweetly asked him if he was all right. He glanced at the attentive bodyguard on each side. He said nothing, but looked at them as if he had never seen them before. And when all those people approached him in a slow orderly line, he looked as if he had never seen them in his life before, and accepted quietly and politely their extended hands.

During the slow procession to the interment, his mind travelled back. He had tears for the wife he lost, and the youth he lost, and the home and country and family he lost. It was the will of God that he was saved from the *katastrophe*. Because God was always on his side, helping him buy a donkey, and a shop, and another shop. He had given him a quick merchant's mind, and He had given him a good wife. But then he started taking everything away. Poor Anastasia!

The open coffin rested on boards across the grave. The family concentrated on the face propped on a pillow – the flowers around it dishevelled – they wiped a smudge of earth from the forehead. The contours of the body visible through the white sheet, already a little soiled. The priest took a handful of earth from the mound at the foot of the dug grave and threw it on the body. The family, in order of seniority, threw their offering of earth, trying to avoid the face. The grave diggers replaced the lid and efficiently lowered the coffin, then the shovelfuls of earth came down in haste. Eleni felt the earth fill her own mouth, trickle under her eyelids, shovelfuls of it settled onto her belly. Father and daughters embraced each other for protection, and cried for her and for themselves.

The rituals of the living led them away from the grave into the reception room. A large rectangular room, in beige-brown colours, unfurnished except for the wooden chairs lined against the walls. Two large long tables stood laden with tiny liqueur glasses, and large bowls of boiled wheat. The lights were switched on, a waiter came in carrying half a dozen bottles of brandy – a whisper, a sigh of life, in the room. The guests sat with stiff, corseted self-respect, their expressions sad, sombre. But eyes were concentrating on the food and drink – with sudden hunger and thirst they grew uneasy, wanting to get to the table before others.

The brandy and the sugared wheat were passed round, condolences were given, victuals consumed, and tongues set free. Tryphon reminisced about a court case where he had left the judge speechless. Koulis looked away with a sardonic expression. Sophia prodded her sisters to get up and pass the brandy round, Eleni had to answer questions about life in England, the weather, the rain, the recession. Father was neither eating nor drinking, his shut mouth played with his false teeth while his eyes surveyed the gathering with scepticism.

"How did you manage to put on all that weight, Kaliopi?" Cousin Mary's voice echoed in the room. She was a big, broad-hipped woman, whose presence naturally filled all space. In embarrassment her nose gave its habitual crinkly twitch under her thick glasses. "Why don't you look at yourself in the mirror! Look at that ass!" Kaliopi's whispering voice palpitated with hurt. Cousin Apostolos' wife recommended a new diet, and a very good gym. Cousin Mary said she kept starting every month – her laughter was briefly restrained, then returned to its belly-deep gusto. The aunts exchanged looks and comments. Mary enjoyed this gathering of so many relatives, cousins she hadn't seen for years, full of news and gossip. "How everyone has aged!" – she turned to Eleni and peered at her face looking for signs.

Worries about age, weight and health brought the women together and soon carried them into the pleasures of food. Recipes were exchanged, disagreed about, improved. Time was passing, and life made its demands.

The family sat round the table and with different noises and in different rhythms they sipped the egg and lemon soup.

"It was mother's favourite." Sophia at the head of the table ladled out the appropriate food for thought. The family, as if watched, sipped respectfully, murmuring between sips reminiscences and encomia.

Their stomachs full and comforted, they confronted each other. Father crossed himself with tired resignation. He got up and looked for his coat and briefcase. Eleni decided she should go home with him.

"There are a few things to discuss," Sophia announced with suppressed, accumulated energy.

Father looked alarmed and angry, he grabbed his coat but remained in his seat. Eleni was numbed by a deep melancholy. Kaliopi shook her head in agreement with Sophia, Koulis walked to the television for the evening news. The fruit was in the middle of the table, but only Tryphon noticed. He started peeling an orange with slow deliberation.

Sophia put her reading glasses on, Father looked at her with worried contempt. He grabbed his briefcase.

"I am tired, my child." He was conciliatory. "Can't it wait till tomorrow? When we are all rested."

"Where are you going to be tomorrow! Eleni will be flying off, you will disappear on who knows what marketing expedition. Things must be settled, while we are all here." Old and young in the room shrank to classroom age under Sophia's gaze.

Father observed her with unease, and some fear. He had feared his eldest daughter as she progressively accumulated legal shrewdness, and money from her various speculations, and power over husband, child and even her own elderly parents. She was a good business woman, tireless, still young, shrewd. It crossed his mind she took after him. He observed her with untrusting envious fear. He thought he should talk to a lawyer. She was a lawyer, her husband was a lawyer, and he was an old, failing, failed man. He must find a lawyer he could trust. No discussions, no business, no documents, no agreements and disagreements, until he found a lawyer. Not that he trusted lawyers. They cheat and they rob you.

Money, he would have to find money for a lawyer. If Anastasia was with him, she would know the solution. She would scold her daughter, put her in her place, put all of them in their place. She knew how to keep the family, and the world, in its place.

"I am discussing nothing. I am going home." He got up. "Eleni my child, will you come home with me?" He wanted an ally, and so did Eleni. She saw with silent resignation their lives and fates weaving together. She got up.

Kaliopi tried to find a compromise. "Perhaps tomorrow, when we are all rested." Her husband agreed.

Tryphon gave Sophia support. "Tomorrow, I will be busy. There isn't much to discuss anyway. I can explain the situation to you. All you need to do is agree and sign, and the people at the office will do the rest".

At the sound of the word sign, Father's face sharpened, Eleni held onto her handbag.

"I have papers and receipts for the money I spent during

mother's illness." Sophia started producing them. "And of course there is the question of the flat, the property, father's life. Has mother left a will?"

Eleni reached for her father's hand. Father's life, mother's will. This death was engendering calculations and dilemmas; its sorrow was spawning figures and intrigues, of material profit and material loss. She should talk to a lawyer.

"What happened to mother's jewellery?" Kaliopi looked at Sophia, Eleni was alert.

Eleni looked at the other things in the room, the piano, the china, the rugs, that had found a new home in Sophia's flat: she kept quiet, perhaps from cowardice. Father, only half understanding, gazed at his daughters, one after the other, in bewilderment, as if at strangers.

"Tomorrow evening," Sophia threatened. Eleni shook her head non-committally, Father was pressing for the lift with a life-or-death urgency.

4

THE POWER OF THREADS

Her father unlocked once, twice, the double-locked flat. She went to her room and found the door locked. She walked round the flat and saw pieces of what used to be her furniture. Her desk in her parents' bedroom, her bookcase and sofa-bed in the living room. Teak – the latest fashion when they bought it for her.

The flat had her mother's smell – sweet, sharp, yeasty. An old jacket hung at the entrance, her shoes neatly waited in the corner. The air was stale in the kitchen. She opened the balcony door, a sack of potatoes stored in the wire cupboard were covered with bright green sprouts, a tea towel hung on the line. She threw away hard dried bread, and a moulding yoghurt carton.

The curtains, richly embroidered, were heavy with immobility and time. The damask armchairs offered empty laps, the black carved furniture – all volume and weight – was a dark family citadel of schemes and alliances. A monument of grandiosity and hard labour. It had carried ostentatious feasts, and bruised with its carved curvatures young limbs, it had devoured the space and the air of the home. Now dusty and dishevelled, it sat morose in the middle of the room, immobile and unavoidable. The piano was absent.

She found sheets and blankets and made up a bed. "Why do you keep that room locked?" She meant 'my' room.

"Ah – I keep my merchandise in there. Fabrics from the shop. You know, old stock. It's my business room. My shop." He was getting annoyed. "Well, good night."

"Would you like a cup of mountain tea?"

"No, I'll have some water."

She brought him a glass. She wanted to share her loneliness with him, but he didn't want her, or her loneliness, or her comfort.

He went into the bedroom. Through the open door she heard him take off his shoes. Barefoot steps around the room, then a soft mumbling. She recognised the hasty sound of his prayer. He came out of his room and checked that his store-room was locked, then sat on his bed. She heard the soft sound of his false teeth on the side table.

"Eleni, a glass of water," he ordered. She went in and handed him the glass from the bedside table. She avoided looking at the false teeth. He had a few sips then he placed his teeth in the water.

"Good night, dad. Shall I switch the light off?"

"Yes, my child. Good night, now."

She walked quietly round the flat – touching and smelling and breathing dust. A row of pots with shrivelled carcasses of plants stood along the balcony railings. Summer and winter the balcony was her mother's luxuriant garden, which she tended as if it were her only child. The dead flowers brought into focus a melancholy without end – and the homelessness of the place. Quietly she went to the kitchen and got some water, as if she could revive the plants. Her father gave a cough, which meant she should be quiet. She sat on her sofa-bed, holding the jug of water, looking around her at the dark opacity.

She plugged her ears with earphones, but could not bear the beauty and symmetry of music. Through the night the savage sound of motorcycle engines harrowed the emptiness and abandonment in the flat and perversely gave her comfort. Through the night she was besieged, by the flowers she had not watered enough, by the locked room, by her father next door coughing, switching the light on and off, walking barefoot about the room, to the bathroom, to the kitchen and back, never finding peace, never finding his wife.

She lay awake, a willing prey to nightmares she snatched from the air. An aged child materialised out of the dark, crouching naked in a corner hiding her eyes from the world. She came and sat on Eleni's chest: it was herself. Or her mother. The weight permanent, and unbearable. Shouldn't it be mothers that carry children?

Her mother's head leaned sideways on the pillow, the face relaxed its hold on whatever it confronted, the eyes closed. And as they closed they took the light from her daughter and threw the room into darkness. Eleni let herself sink into the dark that her mother had produced with the simple movement of her eyelid. She lay unseen by the eye she had all her life believed to be all-seeing. In an ancient dark the child's minute finger slowly pointed to the closed eye, touching it, trying to lift the eyelid, to lift a loneliness not yet conceived, a melancholy that is heavier when one does not yet know the word for it.

The desolate city, the scattered household, concentrated into the black thought of a mole: the birthmark under her mother's breast. The intimate, hidden beauty-mark; the traitor within. The small precise comely blackness, a millimetre on the white skin, storing death. How small is one deadly cell lying dormant for ages, till it decides to strike. The cruelty of minute things, like the murderousness of chosen, measured and numbered words. The wrong move, the fatal turn, the unfortunate coincidence of lives. The particular edge of iron, or meaning, tearing precisely into the live tissue. If she could only unravel her life back to the moment before and before and before. Before the errors and fatal coincidences. Back to the moments of young selfish pleasure, and self-love. And back to the trust that mothers can change the contents of words and the destinations of the stars.

The morning sun rescued her. It came into the room without obstruction or subtlety or inhibition. It is only good, the spring sun. Bright, clear, warm. None of the scorching and devastation of the summer, when mind and body stop. Even the dust covering everything in the room became a light transparent iridescence rising with each slight movement, the light catching each dust-mote suspended in the air, every stitch of her mother's embroidered cloths, all the different grades of her sienna reds. Even the mistakes – Eleni followed the course of the thread, dwelling on its slight deviations, or shortcomings, wondering what had caused the missed stitch, or the extra stitch, the hardly noticeable asymmetry. She fabricated causes for her error – who, what had taken her attention?

From the quietness of the flat Eleni gathered that her father was already out. She felt the old freedom of being alone, silent, un-watched. She stepped out on the balcony and watched the housewives beating their rugs over their balcony railings. The rug started at each beat, formed a wave – startled – a question mark, then fell.

She watered the dead flowers. There was no instant life, she walked back into the flat. She tried the locked room: locked. She looked round her parents' bedroom. The furniture was old, no sign of vanity or indulgence, or temporal beauty. Newspapers on the floor, her mother's bed covered with a blanket, old newspapers lying on it. Her father's pyjamas on his unmade bed, women's magazines, out of date, resting on the large old-fashioned radio. A heap of business files on a chair and another on her father's bedside table. On top of it, samples of fabrics. The glass of water was still there. She picked it up without looking at the cloudy contents, and took it to the kitchen. She walked round the flat gathering the dust on her bare feet, leaving her footprints on the floor. The large movie-star photographs of her sisters on the wall followed her with sultry, soft, passionate smiles. Their eyes had no hardness in them. There was a photograph of her, smaller, taken on a deserted beach. Her lips looked full, you couldn't tell how bruised and swollen they were, on that day, from so many secret kisses.

"We'll go home, one of these days" – the last thing she promised her mother when she first went into hospital. She knew she was lying.

She used to dream she crossed barbed wire from one country to another. And strolled through continents. Going home – was it ever such a simple thing?

The phone rang, she picked it up and instantly moved from Greek to English, her face and voice straining to travel the distance. Another life and history rushed into the flat demanding their clear ample space. And other loves and loyalties reclaimed her. A man's intimate voice, from a world foreign but immediately her own, embraced her back to womanhood. "My love – yes, yes. I'll tell you later. Tell me how you are." Her husband – she listened and smiled, absorbed. And then a young girl's voice, so like her own voice in timbre ... How could that voice, her own daughter's, be at home in another language? "Yes, I 'll come back as soon as I can. I will, I promise. Yes we will, we'll do that when I come back. I miss you too." Her daughter appropriated her totally: from every other part she ever played – daughter, lover, wife – in any language or country. How she confounded differences of native and foreign!

Eleni sat down cradling the phone, happily at home in her English language and life, her chosen life. She listened. "Look after each other. I love you too, I love you both." With her eyes shut she reached them, and came back. She put the phone down and remained sitting, holding onto her words.

And yet there is a tear in her, right through her – as the lingering echoes of her words become foreign in this dust-hushed familiar room, where she moves as in a puzzling territory where the minute, innumerable, intimate pieces don't quite fit.

The phone rang again, before she had time to recover. The familiar language and accent. Sophia's voice stretching out wires of control. "Listen, we have to find mother's jewellery. Try the desk drawers, or the sideboard, under mother's embroideries. Who knows whom he might bring to the flat! They used to have a day-cleaner, she might have a key. Also Aunt Lefki may have a key . Father may have hidden it. You have to find it. And the bank book. We should know what he's got left in the bank. How's Dad? Gone again! This can't go on."

Eleni put the receiver down. She walked back to her unmade bed, heavy with old coagulated rage – familiar, homebred. She went back to the telephone and dialled Sophia's number. Engaged. She waited, stubbornly she waited, till finally she put it down, in tears for small and trivial hated things

She walked from room to room. Her mother's slippers in the middle of the floor, one turned over. She pushed them under the bed with her foot, then in an afterthought took off her shoes and put the slippers on, looking for a residual warmth. She went to her mother's wardrobe and put both hands between her clothes, almost embracing them. Her hands travelled from dress to dress – fine light materials, small prints, subdued blues and greens favouring her eyes. She felt for a second her mother's body inside the printed cotton lawn dress. She picked up her mother's dress-ing gown from the bed and put it on. She inspected herself in the mirror. Mauves, yellows, browns: chrysanthemums – with the odour, not of death but distantly of stale things in life. She sniffed in the tanginess of sweat, the nauseating sweetness of fabric con-ditioner, a hint of olive oil?

Her image became small and young so that the dressing gown, vast on her, trailed on the floor. She saw her tiny image trying dress after dress, climbing up on high heel shoes, parading in front of the mirror.

She watched another reflection of herself, at the threshold of memory, opening and shutting the scissors, learning with fascination that she could transform things, that out of one piece she could make two or three and of a different shape, and refashion the world. If she managed a long straight cut in the middle, she could change a dress into a coat, a nightie into a dressing gown. If she could only manage a straight cut right through the middle.

She was not willing, was incapable of understanding, why that woman towered in savage fury over her, waving the transformed garments, calling them rags. Her humiliation and confusion flowered into purple hand-shaped flowers on her cheeks and thighs.

In revenge, later, she cut the photograph of her mother and herself through the middle, separating the two paper figures for ever. Their hand-hold was cut with precision and justice right in the middle, their separated hands for ever extended towards something not there. She kept her own minute figure and cast out the other half to be swallowed in the lifelong accumulated household clutter. Now, years too late, she tried a drawer, and another, looking for the other half.

She wandered through the disorder of this questionable, vanishing home, touching dust, breathing, even tasting dust. With each step and movement millions of motes were raised in the air to form feathery snatches of lives. These minute particles of matter floating in the air had not so long ago been breathed by her mother. Might they not be something close to spirit, visible and almost tangible? A faint hope, a resurrection? Might her finger spell in the soft layer the hieroglyphics that obliterated death?

Amongst a life's hoarded household she searched, for things missing, or hidden, for valuables long abandoned. For the jewellery, that had travelled from mother to daughter. That must bequeath who knows what good fortune, and potency, and beauty. The ring that had never left her mother's finger was now missing. Disappeared, like her life. Like her soul, and all it had left behind was a narrow band of sunless thin skin. Her hand was already fingering the air wanting this magic circle that could restore – lives, loves homes. She must have it and even more importantly her sisters must not have it. She searched with rough appetite, with hasty desperation, like a thief or usurper: while her soul lay entangled in the heap of domestic clutter and the family's inherited bric-a-brac. Till she paused, fatigued and disappointed, alert, suspicious.

Her eyes caught the marks on the floor left by the piano, the dark shapes on the wall left by the embossed silver plates. The Persian rugs had gone, and all the crystal glasses from the cabinet. Who knows how much more was now decorating her sisters' homes? Her grief could concentrate, and fit snugly those unnatural empty spaces, and grow into greed.

As she walked from room to room, the house remained locked. Inert matter, deaf and dumb. The heart of the home had gone – and the principles that held the family together. All she could do now and all she wanted to do was to take whatever she could. Grab – whatever she liked, or always wanted, or whatever had some meaning for her, or might one day reveal its meaning that so far escaped her. She would stuff her suitcases with these tokens of superior, invaluable wealth and beauty. Whatever was left. The embroideries, the other rugs, the stretches of woven devotion and art. She wished to steal. Whatever her mother still owed her. She needed to settle the old debts – yet feared the unforgiving eye.

She approached once again the locked room that used to be hers. Her lost self waited on the other side of the unrelenting door, which shut out from her, and shut in, her appropriated youth, its well-locked secrecy, its tormented intimacy. Perversely, her past life – out of reach – was growing in the forbidden dark staleness into an all-consuming plot.

Perhaps he was hiding money in there, shares, deeds to property, valuable merchandise. Surely, that's where the jewellery is. She looked everywhere for the key to the room. She searched desk drawers, bed-side drawers, coat pockets, a battered suitcase under his bed, the top shelves of their wardrobe where her mother kept her gloves and handbags. When she was little, she had found amongst them a box that contained what looked like balloons: she showed them secretly to her sister Kaliopi, who in tearing whispers of hurt and ignorance condemned her, the box, their parents, the world. A malignant mystery had enveloped the room. Kaliopi pushed the box back deep into its dark space, the sisters walked away in a cloud of suspicion and shame. Eleni never again approached that place, and her parents' violated intimacy stayed hidden in the box – a yellow box advertising Cuban cigars.

Eleni's fingers hesitated, trembled, feeling their way. There was no box on the shelf. She felt a beaded evening handbag, which her mother had not held for years. She brought it near her face and held it, in sorrow for the passing of things. The bag was heavy. She undid the delicate braid around the beaded button, pulled out a lawn handkerchief with a smear of lipstick – such a small ordinary detail from a moment of life. She brought it to her lips. Her fingers crept further into the heavy bag – and instantly knew, this was her mother's jewellery.

She tipped bracelets, chains, crosses in her lap. She covered them with her hands, holding them, possessing them, hiding them from others' eyes. It was all gold. Then hesitated, as if she handled sacred relics, the devil's tools. Then lifted with care a chain to her neck, passed bracelets round her wrists, then her eyes locked on the ring that had never left her mother's finger. Had she taken it off before she went into hospital? Did she know? A perfect sparkling circle: the central jewel, the even periphery of the smaller stones. She put it round her finger, it was too large, she tried another finger – just right. Just right.

She gathered the jewellery into the beaded bag, then opened doors and windows. The light and breeze, playing on the curtains, gave the place and herself movement and grace. She dressed, in black, looked at her image in the mirror, and gave another look at the ring round her finger. Rich, satisfied, like a thief in the night, she slipped out.

5

UNCERTAIN RESURRECTIONS

Like fat women in mourning, plastic garbage bags leaned against each other in mutual support. Outside the fast-food restaurants, the colonies of bags formed gigantic black shiny creatures, lying inertly, humped and stupid, as stray cats picked at their entrails and scattered them on the pavement. Pedestrians kicked indifferently at the empty plastic boxes and beer-cans.

The melancholy of what used to be her home extended its tentacles after her as she hurried down the street. Yet again, as in her familiar nightmare, she was wandering, looking for home in a city which for her had no home.

She came to Ippodromiou Square where a crowd of students were organising a vast street party or political rally – a young man urged them to join the striking garbage collectors. Precarious benches on the pavements carried at reduced prices black and white paperbacks with long political titles, while bearded young men and dark-eyed girls in army-surplus anoraks argued with intensity.

The larger part of the square was occupied by a gigantic grave containing the excavated remains of the Roman Hippodrome – small groups were sitting sunning themselves on its marble edge. She sat for a while envying them their carefree spirit and passion. Amongst the ancient stones below, a plastic bag made vain attempts to lift and fly.

As she strolled along streets which she half recognised, the heaps of garbage became bigger, the boutiques more extravagant. Car hire offices, funeral parlours, estate agents, a cinema advertising erotic films, locked-up night-clubs waiting for the night to blossom into electric cacophony. Cars, motorcycles, pedestrians, in unceasing movement, while tall concrete apartment buildings overlooked with stolid indifference the panicked mankind at a permanent noisy standstill.

Through the shop-window displays she saw the well-to-do Thessaloniki she knew – of expensive boutiques featuring Italian and French fashion: of imported Jacuzzis luxuriating in astonished shop windows, and modern furniture, collapsing into comfort, solitary and irrelevant.

But that other Thessaloniki, the perennial maternal lap for refugees from wars and persecutions, had gone into hiding – or was it only a creature of memories distorted by forgotten fears and unadmitted wishes? The city of dark doorways and back streets, hiding places for hasty last kisses: of deserted alleys along the city walls protecting lovers from the wind and the city's curious eyes. The city of cardboard shanty-towns crawling out into the shallow valleys of the surrounding hills, put together hastily and permanently. Of dilapidated solitary walls, bullet-ridden doors, roofs sinking into themselves from the weight of time and war. It was a damaged city – which had been for her a playground within a perennial, static sunshine. And also a dark labyrinth of lovers' hiding places.

The ghost of that city, raised by early misplaced terrors and locked away loves, was now the staring face of her nostalgia. It had pursued her, in the irresistible, incontrovertible reality of dreams and nightmares, all her life: and now that she pursued it, it vanished into cafe-bars and fast-food restaurants. She meandered in the haphazard, immobile expanse of concreted landscape, tracing the fine borderline between freedom and forlornness.

She entered shady narrow streets which led uphill to the old city. The tall buildings grew light-hearted as they climbed towards the sun and air – their terraces transformed into gardens, and white sheets, flags of peace and happiness, flapped in the breeze. Empty square holes revealed antiquities waiting, unloved and unattended, for the archaeologists and city planners to agree on their fate: persistent, inconvenient windows to ancient histories always interfering with the present.

In the upper old city, in the shadow of the city walls, clusters of old squat Turkish houses, hamams, mosques, and Byzantine churches were forgotten in their dilapidated neighbourliness. And higher up, stretches of the ancient wall that had withstood so many invaders were succumbing to the wisteria in bloom.

A short alley, which she did not recognise, brought her to a small Byzantine church. In the midst of a hectic consumption of images, food, politics, ideas: a work of art, self-contained, beautiful in its quiet symmetry, was folding itself inwards as it was overlooked from above by ugly backsides of tall apartment buildings. Balconies, loaded with household junk, hung like fate over its perfectly curved domes. She paused at the entrance to listen to the music of the Greek Orthodox liturgy: it carried her to a candle-lit Easter spring happiness of order and cleanliness, new white clothes and shoes, family rituals, and the undiluted unquestioned self-pleasure of youth. She walked into its secluded yard where the air smelled of orange blossom and sat under the forgotten orange trees surrounded by the scent.

She got up with determination and walked to the nearest telephone box. She dialled, turned away and buried her face into the regular ring. She spoke for a time, feeding the phone with coins and feeding her spirit with sounds vaguely familiar, vaguely loved. She reappeared after a long time, her face red – perhaps from the hot close air of the phone box, perhaps from anxiety, excitement – her eyes narrowed by the contemplation of schemes.

As she walked back towards the waterfront, she was repeating an almost forgotten panicked journey she used to make, from the bus stop to the bench in the park by the sea. She would walk, at a normal pace first, in case someone saw her; when she was between the trees she would run, her school-bag wrenching her shoulder. Nikolas was always there, waiting. Although still a school boy, he wore a trilby – straight out of Hollywood films. They would sit on the bench, behind the shrubs, protected from spiteful eyes by the falling twilight and the massive stone body of the White Tower. They held each other as tightly as humanly possible, and, imagining the whole world was galloping after them, at the point of sin, squeezed even tighter into each other with innumerable, desperate, panicked kisses. For more secrecy they slipped through the labyrinthine lanes between gigantic square stones waiting to become a new quay-side. The two would stand woven together, to protect each other from the cold, or from the gangs of children, or the policemen who kept vigil over the moral order of the city. In the depth of the winter, when coats and hugs and love were not enough to keep the cold wind out, they climbed into an old disused lighter abandoned in the harbour and hid deep in its wet rusty entrails.

The thrill of simply being together, boy and girl, separated from the outside world by a wall, even if that wall were a tangle of wires and steel plates: of being enclosed in a room, alone, even if that room were made of iron. They floated in furtive forbidden pleasure, as love and desire grew in that damp and dark iron island surrounded and gently buffeted by a wintry sea. Their hiding place was an island, and it was also a universe; hours were seasons, seasons were eternity. With endless life ahead of them, time and youth stood still. He undid the two top buttons of her school uniform one autumn evening – and another evening near the end of the winter, he slipped his hand under her skirt. They lived, during those twilight evenings, on the precarious edge of the devouring excitement of their single, singular acts of desire. A kiss would be contemplated, relived, multiplied, magnified till the next kiss; a caress changed the balance of the universe.

Now the fish are dying in the harbour. There are no lighters, and the stone blocks have become a long promenade for families and children, and for free and unafraid lovers. She supposed she was sitting on the same bench. And she supposed, she was quite certain, that she had come here in order to conjure up presences of total, cavernous, unadulterated feelings. To spell words in her mother tongue – *eros, amartia, agnotis:* love, sin, chastity – that had an absolute clarity. And to replay actions – of running to a lover, walking away from the lover, promising for ever, contemplating the word 'forever' – which under the maternal shadows rose with stark, monumental meaning. In the clear-cut frontal sounds of her native Greek, those desires appeared even now in bright, life-or-death simplicity, without play of irony or ambivalence, or illusion of reflection.

She had come to this bench to tell herself that she wanted to see again that boy, the lover of her youth, almost of her childhood. To tell herself that underneath, under the sorrow, the pity and the fear, she had all the time been considering how and when she would recover him. Recover with him the stark contrasts, the clear definition of all-consuming light and deep black shadow. There was something, quite inaccessible, that her native light might still reveal to her. The perennial body of Mount Olympus stood still and silent across the sea: its outline was set aflame by the sun setting behind it, but its heart remained dark.

As its lights played with the twilight, the city recovered its dangerous excitement. It became once again the temporary refuge of young lovers who did not know yet how temporary the infinity of the moment could be.

As she waited for the time of their meeting, she conjured different and unsatisfactory visions. On the phone his voice had hung bodiless and timeless; the unexpected, remotely familiar timbre, the direct intimacy, made her now wish uncontrollably to see that body resurrected. Underneath the expected remarks and questions, and during the brief intervals of silence or hesitation, she heard his unaltered presence, their exclusive mutual attention.

"Agapi mou". It was his voice, the tone tentative.

She turned. And returned, "Agapi mou".

His body was thicker, his hair probably a little thinner, he had a small beard, not grey. He called her 'my love', and he would be her love. She looked at him with squinting eyes until the two figures were superimposed and made one. He wore a suit, a tie, he smelled of aftershave, he stood comfortable and dignified, he could be a young father. The young lover with the trilby, with the lean body and the serious face: he was almost visible, intangible, almost present. She willed that boy who was in his youth, or in spite of his youth, the source of absolutes, the beginning and end of all love, to come to her and love her again. He emerged, fragile, staring at her with hard devotion, through the softer playful features of this upstanding, good-looking man.

Only then it occurred to her what Nikolas' hard stare may have meant. Was it devotion, or a searching for his own image of her? She must have changed, of course – she ran her fingers over her face to feel the passage of time. Magically to erase it.

They walked for a while, but then sat opposite each other, across a table, in order to watch each other's face. They searched. Their eyes, like blind men, felt each other inch by inch, turned away when caught, smiled with pleasure and embarrassment, and unease, but especially with pleasure. They talked about their lives, explained themselves, confided, confessed. They remembered – did they forgive?

Her lover of the past played ghostly games through the stranger opposite, but in this man's presence her native soil stopped slipping away under her feet. As she talked, her native language found its normal depth and dimension, and her hands retrieved their old gesticulations.

He told her he was a doctor now, which she knew. Quite successful, a senior surgeon at the State Hospital. He sat upright, his chest expanded, his face looked full – he enjoyed his success. She forgave him – on their island it was so easy to forgive. He reminded her that she had persuaded him to become a doctor, like the character in Cronin's novel. "*The Citadel*, I think." He owed his career to her, his life. Had she become a teacher, as they had planned? Indeed – she remembered with astonishment – they did live by the novel: planned their lives according to a novelist's plot, formed careers according to fictional characters. But then there were other novels, and other lives.

She told him she did research and she translated – it meant she read a lot of novels. What did that mean to him, she wondered. He was married, he told her, with two children – which she already knew, from old school friends. She tried to hide a smile. He talked to her about his wife. She was totally dedicated to him, he said, answered all of his wishes – no, she did not merely answer them, she guessed them. Not only guessed them, she foresaw them, knew them to be his wishes before he did.

"So, you are totally in her power." How could she loosen the grip on him of this other woman. The total grip of self-effacement. Or was this love? A love she couldn't feel?

He looked at her surprised.

"If she decides your very wishes, she must have great power over you." How could she – only with words, with mere words – break whatever bond was between those two. Whatever love. She was overcome by an avaricious, innocent certainty that he was hers and for her – whatever other loves and loyalties existed and whatever treacheries were involved. In her eyes, and in the eyes of whatever spirits dwell in that blue sky, this was the truth, however unreal. Or else?

"It must be excruciatingly boring." She only now realised what she had then been too young to know: a quiet silent play of power was always tangled up with their love games. It was more an unspoken assumption: of his power and her powerlessness, which like generations of women she would learn to transform into subterranean power. She had been then too young to realise it, could not articulate it – did not own the words – so she just walked away. Is that why she walked away? Even now she did not know why she left. But right now it did not matter.

He looked at her hands resting on the table, pulled them gently towards him, and gazed at them silently. She looked at her hands, the wedding ring on her right. Her mother's ring on the other hand. A plain gold bracelet. She looked at her own hands, and at the circles of gold that encircled and bound her life. She looked at him to see perhaps an answer in his eyes to a question she had not asked, she perhaps did not even know. He covered her hands with his, and let them stay there, as if following a new strange ceremony.

"You are my only love, you always were my only love." He cut the tangled knot, and looked at her expecting something. She stayed still, hands body face. Her eyes moved and rested on his – whatever they said he accepted. For this moment and this place it was enough, it was everything.

So, the passions of the past, the separation, the many hurts, again and again, were left behind, dissolved within the sweet nostalgia of the restaurant music. What remained was the half-recognition of the fragility and transience that was hidden in their love – not yet grown up – that made it all the more haunting.

They ate and drank, enjoyed doing together what adult couples do. She even smoked with him although she had stopped. He asked questions, too many, she selected her answers. Not out of coyness, but because whatever happened in another language and land seemed to be a story and a world apart. It involved other actors, with different tastes, rules and accents. That other self of hers, abroad, looked at her here and now with bewilderment, and protectiveness, while this indigenous self stared back at her life beyond the frontier with yearning and some disbelief. She felt the tearing within her. Right now her perennial homeland was reducing her to fragile unruly youth. She kept her eyes shut to all the betrayals that she was busily weaving.

She was certain he would, as of old, provide the refuge, and escape. He said the expected things, which he meant: he was sorry for her mother's death, and for her father's old age, for all the persecutions. And as he talked it crossed their minds, without being articulated, that now that the old despots were gone, and defeated, he and she, the newly emergent man and woman, might want to love each other not only in fear and adversity.

They talked about other things, but his voice filled the room with good sounds, even if the meanings escaped right and left, like half-understood, hardly remembered, motherly sounds. As she had looked at him, he said, her eyes had narrowed, half hiding half revealing. He knew that look, he said, and she narrowed them even more trying to hide what she knew she could not and did not want to hide.

6

STOLEN GOOD

Before she rang the bell Eleni slipped her mother's ring off her finger and hid it in the zipped pocket of her handbag.

Sophia lay in a pitch-dark bedroom, with her feet up on two pillows.

"Mrs Sophia has one of her headaches," the maid said to Eleni, without compassion. She was getting ready to go.

With visible displeasure Sophia got up, opened and shut drawers and finally produced some money. After complicated calculations of days and hours, money owed and money advanced, they came to an agreement: the maid put the money into her handbag and said a sullen good-bye. Eleni, still with her coat on and her handbag on her shoulder, was looking at the sea through the balcony door. The sun already reddened the sky as it slowly hid behind Mount Olympus.

"Did you find the jewellery?" Sophia sounded aggravated, tired.

"I –" she stumbled, "No." She moved to an armchair and sat down holding her handbag into her lap. She changed the subject. "Where is Kaliopi?"

"You tell me where Kaliopi is." Sophia sat and let her head rest back: she shut her eyes. "She is shopping for antiques! She rang me two hours ago, from some junk shop, saying she was on her way. I'm still waiting."

Eleni sat up preparing what she would say or do about the jewellery, trying not to think about the ring in her bag,

Sophia returned to Eleni – "Where were you? I rang and rang, there was no answer."

"I was out."

"Where is Dad?"

"I don't know. He had gone by the time I woke up."

"This can't go on." Sophia rearranged herself more comfortably on the chesterfield.

Eleni noticed the black caftan wrapping her sister's small body, nestling, self-protectively and invitingly, on the divan. Eleni recalled her persuading Mother to give her the sofa.

"We have to discuss what we do with father. And we'll have to find the jewellery. Did you look well?"

"I'll look again tomorrow." Eleni tried to decide about the jewellery, where she should hide it, the suitcase was too obvious – what should she do with it? But she knew she would keep it, she could not let her sisters touch it.

"Would you like some coffee? I should have asked Efterpi to make it before she left."

Eleni refused the coffee: she didn't offer to make it, wouldn't move from the armchair. "How is your headache?"

Sophia, surprisingly, was prepared to talk about her life. Her frustrations with her husband, her worries about Alexis, her discovery of yoga and meditation and winter swimming. Eleni recalled their conversations about books: exciting, amiable, sisterly. When Sophia was a university student – and Eleni still a child – she would let Eleni read her copies of foreign novels. How good or accurate the translations were – who cared! They were the only books in the house, where furniture took all the space and air, and Eleni read and reread them. Till they were woven into the fabric of life, their plots imposing order and symmetry and a beauty of reason on the careless arbitrariness of her world.

She had invested her beautiful elder sister with the enthralment of 'literature' – of the great European Literature. Because it was Sophia who had after all bought the books and would therefore possess them for ever. But secretly Eleni felt that she herself had a deeper possession of those northern plots because she was the interloper, the thief. That they reached her in translation only lent an aura of captivating unnatural remoteness to the mother tongue.

Later on Eleni would repay the debt by telling her sister of new and different novels she was reading. But by then Sophia, a wife and a young mother, a lawyer, a hostess, had little time for books. Eleni tried to keep hold of her – her dark sensual face appearing through texts. But then Eleni left, in pursuit of the originals.

Now Sophia's face was smaller and older, the dark hair was hennaed, and love seemed to have abandoned her. Eleni wondered what patterns of bird-flight her thoughts followed in her sessions of meditation. What treasure did she seek in the cold winter sea? She wondered also about herself: what valuable secrets did she seek in the pages of a newly acquired book, or in their mother's jewellery hidden in her suitcase, or in the ring hiding in her handbag. What was the value, what the price of those things? She wondered at their violent faith. And the avarice that like a greedy religion was taking hold of them.

Kaliopi arrived late, full of excuses. As the other two were busy with complaints and counter complaints, Eleni, falling instinctively into the role of the youngest, offered to make them coffee. She tucked her handbag between the cushions, like a cherished child, and got up.

When she was alone in the kitchen she half-knew she was following someone else's gestures and steps. Her sisters' voices from the living room sounded neither quarrelsome nor conspiratorial. They reached her with an indistinct animated music of pleasure. And for herself, she tried, with some reverence, to recreate the small daily ritual that had been a property of their mother. With attention she measured out the water, the spoons of sugar and coffee, concentrated on the liquid coming slowly to the boil, pulling it away from the heat three times, making sure that it rose without breaking the crust of coffee oils. Then pouring into each cup a little at a time, with care and justice, so that they all had their share of "the cream". The cups were small and held a small quantity of coffee, but the sipping could be slow and lasting; and the family strife would pause for those few moments of pleasure and tranquillity.

As she came into the room, carrying the tray, she found them crouched over a splendid cloth spread out on the floor. They were disagreeing about its origin and date, Kaliopi thought it was a bedspread, Sophia said it was an altar cloth. They examined the exquisite elegant arabesques of gold and silver threads on a deep turquoise blue, and all three together followed this other woman's patient thread of imagination. Like children learning to spell, or daughters groping for their hearts.

They drank the coffee in silence. The sipping was only a punctuation to a stretch of contemplation – of the beauty spread at their feet, and because this was an art and pleasure that had belonged to their mother, her ghost was hovering within that air-pocket of sympathy and peace, demanding of her daughters a few shared moments of remembrance and grief.

Sophia finally said she thought Kaliopi had paid too much. She brought two cushion cases she had bought at the same shop, real finds, they compared their acquisitions and bargains. Eleni felt their father was also present in this room, his shop and trade, his recognition of things fine and beautiful, was right there, spread on the floor, and his daughters shared the appreciation of valuable hand-made things, and also the passion for bargaining and trading, and grasping – for tokens, tangible proofs of love.

The embroidered cloth was folded and put away, and the sisters confronted each other. Sophia put on her glasses, spread documents, receipts, bills on the table. Kaliopi seemed acquainted with them, she looked at Eleni's face for reaction. "Where is Father?"

"No one knows. He's disappeared again, he's been missing since morning." Sophia took off her glasses and looked at her sisters. "This is getting serious. We'll have to discuss it and take proper decisions." Her eyes rested on Eleni. "But first we have to deal with other matters.

"The Jewellery. We have to find the Jewellery." Kaliopi was excited. Eleni stayed still.

"What jewellery is there, by the way?" Kaliopi continued restless, suspicious.

"Everything except what you have taken, Kaliopi." Sophia was prepared.

"What did she take?" Eleni was losing her complaisance.

"The cross and chain I have taken, I declare it now, and I am not returning them." Kaliopi announced her coup with military determination. "They were mine, Mother gave them to me when I had Andreas, and later I lent them back to her."

"Lent them! As if Mother didn't have her own cross and chain!" Eleni wanted to thrust forward, but she remained sitting.

"At least I waited till she died. You, Sophia, took the other cross and chain from her neck while she lay dying in hospital."

Eleni had not remembered the crosses, or the chains. Now the exact shape of the cross with the fine engraving, and the old twisted dark golden chain around her mother's neck, her neck sweaty from cooking, were alive before her. And with them the sinister image of their mother's body that lay unable to resist or forbid, or bequeath. And the image of Kaliopi sneaking behind Father's back, not to be left behind by the older and cleverer sister, and stealing the other cross. And the picture of herself stealing the whole box, and from it the highest prize, the ring. Her shame at these images was equal to her rage at the other two for having stolen so much else. In the cheating between them when they were children there was in the end a judge, arbitrary, unjust, but at least, in name, a judge. For these acts, there was no jury or judge, other than their own conscience and decorum – no eye watching from above.

"You just have to return them, now, just as you will return the rugs and the crystal, and the silver, and the piano, and who knows what else that you have stolen from Father's flat." If they do return everything, Eleni calculated, then I will release the jewellery.

"Never. What I took was mine. Mother had promised me. Let Sophia return what she has taken. And she has taken much, much more."

"I took the piano as payment for the bills I paid. Because I know I will never see any money from you, or Father."

"And the rug, the orange prayer rug?"

"Mother gave it to me, in exchange for a loan I had given her."

"Shylock!" Kaliopi was triumphant.

Eleni felt secure while they fought with each other. "You should both return everything." But there was weakness in her voice. She was a thief – but they were clever thieves.

"You cannot talk. You left, you abandoned home and family, washed your hands of parents, illnesses and responsibilities. First pay back the money and time and emotional strain I spent on our parents, pay it all back, and then speak." Sophia pushed a stack of papers at her sisters' faces. "Bills, bills, bills – that's what I have been paying to doctors and hospitals."

"Paid? Bills?" Kaliopi stood up. "Let us see."

"Mother's eye test, and another test, and father's new glasses, and the dentist ..."

"Who did a bad job." Kaliopi added.

"Nevertheless he cost money." Sophia peered into the pieces of paper before her, her eyes shining with the pleasure of recognition. "And antibiotics for his bronchitis, and for mother's flu, and the X-rays of her leg when she had the fall, let alone the brain scan."

The bodies of their parents lay before them anatomised, and they, their children, snatched at pieces, morsels of what?

"You both took and took from our home, much more than you ever gave. I have taken nothing." Her mind was pawing that warm shiny jewellery, that still kept Mother's warmth. "Before we

63

discuss anything you should return the crosses and the chains and whatever else you have taken." The jewellery was already her own property, legitimised by her possession, her lie for it, her desire.

"I should tell you, by the way, I am washing my hands of father." Sophia took her glasses off and waited to see the response to her words. They both looked at Eleni, and Eleni was predictable.

"What do you mean wash your hands of him. Write him off as a father? Pretend you are not his daughter?"

"That's exactly what I mean. I mean since you are his daughter, his favourite daughter, come back and look after him."

"It is true, Eleni," Kaliopi readily agreed, "You've gone and left all the burdens on us." But instantly she turned with new animus towards Sophia. "But it is not true, not true at all to say you've had all the responsibility. We've been sharing the responsibility – equally."

"Not quite! Not quite, Kaliopi, since you live a few hundred miles away, and I live right here, all my life right here, where all the responsibilities are, all the burdens, all the diseases. Where I confront every day death and old age."

"They visited me more than they visited you! I paid for their flights and they came to stay with me for weeks: because they liked staying with me. And because they did not like to stay with you. They did not like you – or your husband."

"But when they needed somebody in the middle of the night, they came to me, not to you in Athens, nor to her in England!" Time was static, their mother's death no longer registered. What registered was the fear of death and of old age.

There was a deal between them, Eleni was calculating, but she did not know what the deal was. Kaliopi would give her support, but only at a price, and Sophia, she knew, would not give an inch. She would like to know what they wanted from her. Her nerves, faster than her thoughts, were tracing the way this vicious triangle worked.

"The point is that I have nothing to do with our father, unless he is put into care, officially and legally," Sophia announced.

It was not her they were threatening, it was Father, and the threat was ugly. How could she go to him for help? Pity, for the old man that was her father, was a still centre in the morass of fear and self-preservation.

"Over my dead body."

"Then you come back and look after him. Whenever he disappears, you go and look for him all over town. You come and clean the filth in his apartment. You stop him from who knows what crazy deal, from selling his property for nothing, or giving it away, or signing who knows what and to whom. You come and protect him from the impostors that are already sniffing around him!"

"Let alone that he may want to remarry – the first harlot who decides to gobble up his fortune." Kaliopi's imagination instantly leapt into flourishes of sensation and scandal. Eleni knew it, yet always believed her, and was still touched by the angels and devils – Kaliopi's familiars – prowling in the corners of their room, real and tangible, and ferocious in their punishments.

"He is an old man. He loses things, he forgets, he is lost without Mother. But he is our father. He was always forgetful, he had Mother remember for him – he is very lonely." She was not putting a case, she was pleading for pity.

"That's what we are saying. Of course he is our father, that's why we want to protect him. Because he cannot look after himself and he cannot look after his affairs. He could commit tragic mistakes." Sophia uttered her words with slow emphatic sweet reasonableness, her eyes piercing the air.

"I agree. He should be put into care." Kaliopi was quick and unguarded. "He might not even know the difference. It would only mean that his signature would be invalid, that any dealings, bank accounts, business transactions would be invalid. But why would he need those things? You said yourself, he is an old man!"

"He will die. If he cannot do his business he will die." Eleni thought this journey was not only for her mother's, but for her father's death.

"He will die if he is let loose to do as he likes and go where he likes."

"Do you know that for months now, perhaps a year, he would just get up and go. Where? To Thasos! For business! He would go one day carrying all those suitcases, come back the following day, spending hours, days in buses and boats. He would come back rejuvenated, while our mother, stuck between four walls, swallowed her loneliness and desperation." There was vengefulness deep and personal, in Sophia's voice.

"That's why she got cancer." Kaliopi gave her diagnosis with an authority that reduced all three to silence.

"He will be run down by a bus, you know." Sophia's confidence was quiet, seductive. "He will die simply from exhaustion. Think of his own good."

"Let him be killed by a bus. Or sell his property. Or give it away. Or get married if he wants a wife. It's his life. And his death." Eleni's words flew, while she slowly realised that, for whatever they wanted to do, they needed her signature. Without her, and her signature, they could do nothing. She had a card to play.

But now she must go. She took her handbag and walked to the door. She murmured a good-bye and pulled the door behind her gently. She didn't wait for the elevator but ran down the flights of stairs. She would care for her mother's jewellery, as a good man cares for a secret virtuous act. It was a consecrated tree of priceless fruit which she would tend and water. For now she would do penance. She would look after her father, make him a home, take her mother fresh flowers, make her a home.

And talk to a lawyer. Rehearsing her resolutions gave her strength. She opened her handbag, and with miserly secretiveness her fingers found the ring: a circle of pure, perfect light. She put it round her finger, and, enclosed within herself as if she were her own ghost, went out into the sunlight.

7

ONE THIRD OF PARADISE

He neglected to wipe from his eyes the thin liquid of age and sorrow – nor did it dry in the wind. But he did smooth his hair – thin, silvery – and he did make sure his tie was in place and his jacket buttoned. Remaining touches of an almost forgotten vanity and decorum.

He stood over the new grave, where nothing yet grew, undecided whether to stay or go. He looked distractedly at the fresh earth of the grave, while mumbling a quiet argument with himself, or with his wife, now out of reach. He might be confiding, or complaining, or planning. He held his battered briefcase tightly, seeming to be in a hurry to go, yet not sure where he might go. He walked back and forth, then took one of the paths that led to more and more graves, as if looking for someone. Then he came back. His face was transparent to the quick passing thoughts that made his muscles move, his lips form inaudible words, his eyes light up with anger.

Spasmodically he hurried to the entrance of the cemetery where he was surrounded by girls and women selling candles. He bought a few from a woman and a few more from a girl, his eyes attending elsewhere. He walked away without waiting for change, and re-entered the cemetery.

He was given matches for his candles by a woman at a

neighbouring grave, and that gesture and the few words they exchanged helped him collect his thoughts, and attend to his solitary duties of grief. He stood still, his hands together – the good hugging the disabled – his head lowered, his eyes closed in an effort of prayer. His eyes were dancing beneath tender lids. He crossed himself with the decisiveness of a bargain concluded. On his way back, he wandered through the graveyard, as if making, indifferently, an inventory of who was dead and who alive.

The bus journey was restful. The timber and reclamation yards were full of movement, building and demolition, change. His face came alive with possibilities, his eyes measured and planned. It was good he was taken from sight to sight before he had time to dwell on anything. Ideas and plans passed through his eyes quickly, just long enough to excite his imagination and awaken furtive desires. While the bus moved he sat back. No peace, no security showed on his face, only a brief fragile rest.

He jumped up at the right stop and leapt from the bus with young agility. He was in the middle of the market, his briefcase secure in his grasp: he had purpose and determination. He walked with intimacy along the shady back-streets of warehouses and dark wholesale shops. The smells of spices and herbs, tobacco, freshly ground coffee, cloth dyes, tanned leather, grilled meat, were familiar and rejuvenating. He found his way through the alleys, zig-zagging round carts overflowing with oranges, or tables exhibiting plastic kitchen utensils. He hardly noticed the three-wheeled vehicles half-mounting the pavement, or the coils of rope, or small forests of potted trees blocking his way. He gave only quick glances at shops selling fabrics or girls' dowries.

He disappeared into a dark entrance. It smelt of damp, the elevator was too slow in coming, he hurried up the dark stairs blindly and securely. After three flights, hardly out of breath, he rang the bell with the confidence and impatience of a landlord.

The man behind the desk, emanating stale greyness, got up, in curious cautious excitement. He had a civil servant's eyes, deadened by life-long indifference, a sycophant's stoop, a chronic compromiser's tilt of the head. The air was tired with old cigarette smoke. Stacks of paper on tables and desks gathered dust, documents overflowed from bleached wrinkled folders, a large typewriter was covered by an opaque plastic cover.

"Ah, Mr Gregoris!" The absent-minded affability turned in time into the sad demeanour of condolence. "A saintly woman, Kyr Gregori! My deepest condolences! Such sad news! Coffee?" He ordered two coffees on the phone, his back straightening slightly with the brief power of technology, his head thrust forward with the knowledge of who's boss. He lit a cigarette with style, slammed the cigarette pack and lighter on the desk with bravado, took a deep inhalation, and sat up with fragile dignity. Outside the grimy window – the only one allowing in natural light – a piece of tissue paper floated elegantly down the light-well.

He shook his head towards his client with tentative commiseration. "This life – it's hard, it's cruel, Kyr Gregori. Such a good woman, such a good wife! Tireless, Kyr Gregori, always at your side, always a good soldier!" In his eyes there was a small light of inquisitive expectation, and caution. He looked at his papers on the desk, then again at his client, waiting.

"You look well, Kyr Gregori. As young as ever."

"I am young," the old man asserted with sudden light-hearted frivolity. "I flew up the stairs. I'd like to see you climb up." The boasting raised his spirits. He put his briefcase on his knees, preparing for business.

"We've all aged, Kyr Gregori! How the years have gone by!" He touched tenderly the thin long strands of hair travelling from one side of his head to the other, covering carefully his bald scalp. "It seems like yesterday I was an assistant to Mouratithis. You were then our best client, Kyr Gregori. You kept that office going."

"That rascal, that impostor, that dirt of the earth." Gregoris rearranged his false teeth that had suddenly moved out of place. He shook his head threateningly. "He was paid by the other side, you know, Andoni. You were young then, you didn't know, but he was on Tsaousoglou's pay-roll. He had his come-uppance, mind you." The lawyer shook his head in agreement, or doubt, or disagreement, or commiseration, or embarrassment, or vague nostalgia.

Gregoris' old eyes shone with malice and titillation. "Found dead in his car, in the middle of the fields! He stopped for a rest, they said, because he felt the heart attack coming. Coming, my foot! With his trousers half down, his shirt undone, a man his age going with whores, of course he had it coming – or rather not coming!" He laughed harshly, his imagination revelled in the obscene indignity of his enemy's death. "He had the heart attack because … because he couldn't get it up. That's why he went with whores!" His voice rose, his face reddened with the excitement of prurience.

The lawyer shook his head with agreement, and disapproval, and embarrassment. "A sad ending. And he left a young family." Then a forced change of tone. "Anyway, you were a great busi-nessman, Kyr Gregori." He landed on new enemies. "These cow-boys now, they are not worth a penny. All music and neon lights, blue-jeans, hippy stuff, rubbish, Kyr Gregori, rubbish. You touch cloth now, its cold, slimy. Synthetic stuff, plastic!"

"I had enemies, Andoni." He shook he head with sad recol-lection. Then with a new flow of recognition. "Never trust the locals, Andoni! The Macedonians – they are not that clever. Slow, thick, Albanian heads!" He tapped his head lightly. "With the Jews, the Armenians, the Karamanlis, the Pontians, with us, you know where you are: we are sly, we are shrewd, we are good merchants. I take my hat off to them. But the locals, they are dan-gerous. You know why? Because they are envious people. Small hearts, withered souls. Envious, and treacherous."

The lawyer shook his head. "Well, not all of them, Kyr Gregori. You married a Macedonian, after all."

"She was an exception." He became serious, and collected. "Anastasia was clever, very able. They didn't let her finish school – her mother. A great pity – but with me she learned the business."

The lawyer agreed wholeheartedly. "She ran the shop, Kyr Gregori, when you were away. She ran it single-handedly. She did the sums in her head." Relieved that they were in agreement, the lawyer picked up the phone again, and shouted down the line with new energy. "What happened to the coffee – has it got bones?" He slammed the phone down, and turned to the client who had opened his briefcase and was peering at his documents.

"Since I was a little boy, Kyr Gregori, I remember you struggling. Always struggling. With shops, with lawyers, with new schemes! Tell me Kyr Gregori, have you ever had a holiday in your life? When will you have some rest? Now that Kyra Anastasia has left us, may she be forgiven, you must sit back and let your daughters look after you. Sit back, enjoy your grandchildren, take a trip to an island, enjoy your old age."

Kyr Gregoris shook his head disdainfully. "Holidays! Those things are for the playboys, the lazy and the stupid. I have work to do, Andoni. I have business to attend to, plans. Big plans, important responsibilities, Andoni."

The lawyer looked doubtful, and interested. He looked his client up and down, measuring him, deciding whether he had something good up his sleeve. You never know with those old eagles. They take time to die.

"What responsibilities, Kyr Gregori, at your age! Tell me, between ourselves, how old are you? I was fresh from the university when you came to Mouratithis' office and you were then, well, a successful, a very successful, middle-aged businessman, in your prime. I'll be a grandfather next month, and I'm thinking of packing it in, and you are telling me about plans and responsibilities!"

"You retire, if you like. As for me, I refuse even to draw my pension. Why draw it? So that they make me stop work? No thank you very much."

The lawyer was struck with genuine puzzled wonder. He shook his head, weighing his recognition of this different breed of man. "You mean you are not on a pension yet, Kyr Gregori? At your age? That is a mistake."

The old man waved him off. He returned to his documents.

"Our hair's greyed waiting for this coffee!" The lawyer was relieved to see Nikodemos, from the cafeteria, arrive with the coffees.

Nikodemos, a wizened sharp-eyed youth, was economical with words. He put a bill with a long line of numbers on the desk.

The lawyer looked in his pockets for change, then said breezily "Tell your dad I'll settle on my way out." He hoped old Kyr Gregoris was too preoccupied with his documents to notice.

Nikodemos banged the door as he left. The lawyer's eyes dilated with anger, then concentrated on the black thick liquid.

The two men took long noisy sips. A good sound of agreement.

"Blessed be her memory."

"May her sins be forgiven. Andoni, I want you to handle a very important case. A large investment. It will make some people in this market, some playboys — let us not mention names — who strut around with the leather jackets and tight trousers, and call themselves businessmen, choke on their spittle."

Andonis leaned forward: a smile of apprehension, and avarice. "What are you cooking, old Kyr Gregori? Let us see."

Gregoris held tight his documents. He took his glasses off, and looked at the other man with significance. He only now noticed how the young "odd jobs" Andonis had aged: he was bent, he had shrunk. Gregoris sighed with resignation. Old Andonis was not a genius of a lawyer, but there was no one else. Lawyers had devoured his fortune, they were all scavengers; at least this one was a bit naive, perhaps honest. "I bought, years ago, some land — for a piece of bread. Prime position. The best view on the island. You know Thasos? The best, the greenest island." Gregoris, the old tradesman, waited to see what impression he had made on the lawyer. "That island, Andoni, is … paradise!"

"I take my family to Thasos, every summer. A beautiful island, Kyr Gregori. The best in the Aegean. They have a few barren rocks in the south, and they think they have something. I've been to all these touristy places, Rhodes, and Kos, and Hydra, and the rest. Rocks, barren rocks. Indecent, shameless, obscene, with the women going around with their – with your sympathy – breasts hanging out, and bare bums, shameful, shameful things. The beauty is here in the north, our Thasos, our Halkithiki! What beauty, what greenness! For the family. And as for Turkey …" He stopped short.

Gregoris was impatient to continue, but paused, then said suddenly, "Turkey is beautiful, Andoni, beautiful." He paused again. "And Thasos is beautiful, almost as beautiful. It reminds me of the old land."

"I know about the beauties of those lands. My mother was from your part of the world. You come from Panormos, in the north, is that right? She came from Rethestos, not far from you. She was no more than thirteen when they left. But she never stopped telling me."

"I was … not even fifteen. Alone of the whole family. Barefoot and hungry. But with my hard work, I created. I created a whole fortune." Gregoris' eyes were red, rheumy. He looked a little old man.

"We have suffered!" the lawyer concluded. He sipped the dregs of his coffee, traces of black mud clung on his lips. "We refugees have suffered, eh, Kyr Gregori!"

"I found my brother, two years younger than me, years later. The only one from my family. The rest – the knife." He made a sudden brutal movement across his throat. "The youngest, Achilleas, was only eight. He may still be alive, who knows!"

The lawyer shook his head. "And then our own people here finished us off. I grew up in a corrugated-iron shed, Kyr Gregori. My mother worked in the tobacco factories all her life, she died from tuberculosis."

"I am going to build a hotel on that land, Andoni." Gregoris would not let the past, his own or other people's misfortunes, stop him. "A hotel, not bird-shit like the ones near Moudania. I'll build a hotel that will have the mountain, and the bay, at its feet. A skyscraper of a hotel!" He leaned forward, wanting to grab and hold the other man's imagination. He wanted Andonis to share his faith, his unshaken certainty. He tapped his closed fingers on the desk for effect, calling his money-making genie to come back to life, to youth; calling – a dying Anthony losing his Alexandria – on the god and his troupe not to abandon him, not now. His eyes were burning with desire and desperation.

"Do you have the capital?"

"Capital!" The old man gave a small explosion of contempt. His eyes became hard with irony. Whoever was not with him was against him. "With such land, such gold, who needs capital! Other people will come with the capital. I put down the land, he puts down the capital, we own the hotel half and half." He laughed with hard triumph at the ease and simplicity, the beautiful geometry of his wishes. He looked at the other man's cautious face with suspicion.

"How big is the land, Kyr Gregori?"

"It's big. Big enough."

"Where is it?"

"It's the best spot. It has a view of the whole bay. It's paradise, I tell you."

The lawyer was thoughtful, Gregoris was getting irritated. "That island will be developed. Hotels, skyscrapers from end to end. It will get Germans, Italians, all of them. It will be Florida, it will be the Riviera." He had never been to those places, he had never been out of Greece, but he knew, he knew what he was talking about.

"The land is in your name." There was only a tiny question in the lawyer's words.

"Of course it is. It's my land."

The lawyer was still sceptical.

"We bought it together – with Anastasia. I decided to give her one third – she was my wife, she had worked hard by my side, she suffered with me, why not? And we gave one third to Eleni. She has nothing – not like her sisters who own, what don't they own! Anyway, the land is mine, I gave them each a piece out of my good will. I was always a caring father, and a good husband. But now – I have my plans."

"Have you talked to your son-in-law about this, Kyr Gregori?"

"Leave him out of it." The old man leaned forward and banged the desk, his teeth out of place from the outburst of hate, his eyes steady and tyrannical on the younger man.

"He is one of the top lawyers, Kyr Gregori."

"I am talking to you. Do you understand me, or not? I said leave him out of it."

"According to what you tell me, the land is not all yours, Kyr Gregori. One third is yours. The other third, you say, belongs to your youngest daughter. And Kyra Anastasia's third will belong now to all the beneficiaries: your three daughters and yourself. Did she leave a will?"

"What will? What was hers was mine. I had given it to her. Whatever she had, I gave to her! A will!" He looked at the lawyer with contemptuous pity.

"According to the law you now have only one fourth of that third."

The old man half stood from his seat. He shoved his papers into his briefcase, which he embraced tightly.

"You have contracts, I suppose?"

"Of course we have contracts!" He spat out his contempt. "The land belongs to me. Legally. With signatures, and stamps, and everything." His face was ravenous. He searched in the lawyer's face for a crumb of encouragement, hope.

"Perhaps your daughters will let you have their part. It's small anyway. And they have enough. Your son in law, Kyr Gregori, can do anything he likes. He knows people, he has the means. You should talk to him."

The old man stood up. "Leave him out of it, I said." He shut his briefcase, ready to go. But he paused. "Are you interested, yes or no? Will you find me a developer – somebody with capital, willing to multiply it." He paused, waiting. "You will be paid well. A percentage of the profits."

"I am a lawyer, Kyr Gregori, I'm not an agent." But he could not bring himself to say no. "Still, we'll see. Let's untangle the inheritance first. You say she didn't leave a will."

"Andoni," Gregoris sat down again. "I don't trust my daughters." He looked at the other man openly, with young, bewildered eyes in an aged, wrinkled face. He beat his chest and slowly spelt it out: "I don't trust my daughters, or their husbands." He kept his eyes on the other man, driving the meaning and passion of his words hard into his understanding. "I don't trust them. Do you understand me?" He beat his chest again, his face, gathered into the anguish of a life, cried without tears, turning to the room, as if the room were full of witnesses, and turning to the ceiling looking for a god standing up for old men.

The other man cleared his throat. He was a humble lawyer. He needed clients, he did not need enemies. "Clear things up with your daughters, and we will talk again, Kyr Gregori."

Gregoris was immersed in his agony. He had given the lawyer up, he would make other plans. "There is nothing to clear up, and I don't need to speak to any daughters. The case is crystal clear, and one day you will see – such a palace! We'll stand on the top of the mountain. Think about it, Andoni." He stopped his vision, and walked towards the door; then turned back. "I haven't told you the whole story, you see." He waited. "I own much more on that island than you think. I could even provide the capital myself!" He laughed with cracked triumph as he searched the other man's face.

"So, come back, Kyr Gregori, for further discussions. Who knows, something may come of it." There might be something for him in all this, who knows! "Perhaps we should go to Thasos together sometime!"

"I'll show you the most beautiful island on earth. I'll take you to paradise."

"And, again, my true condolences for Kyra Anastasia! A saintly woman!"

"May her soul rest!" His words were lost in the dark stairwell.

8

TENDER EUCHARISTS

She lay on a double bed covered with a red satin spread, in a room which found instant body and colour as her eyes travelled round its walls looking for a window. There was none, yet the place was bathed in a low secretive light. One by one she noticed the few ornaments: a doll in a taffeta dress sitting on a lacy cushion, an ancient silver samovar, a brass mortar shell used as a vase with red organdie roses standing in it, a china boy with a dog posing on a table. The objects seemed without dimension – props in a stage set ready to crumble once it achieved its purpose. Nor did she know what its purpose was.

The room she had not seen before, yet the samovar and the china ornaments, the satin quilt, the taffeta doll, they all belonged to a family home lost in a colourless past. She knew, with the arbitrary knowledge of a dream – snatches of fear and wish – that this was a brothel and she, lying on the bed, was waiting with excitement, and without a trace of shame, for the clients to come. They never came.

Her attention was on the old woman in a dark corner of the room bent over a copper coal-burner preparing – the dreamer knew – magic potions and potent aphrodisiacs. The woman approached her with handfuls of the food of love – white and light like milk, or like foam, or like candy floss, or like an old woman's snow-white hair, or like light snow-flakes, or popcorn, or polystyrene. Handfuls of it, which the woman stuffed into Eleni's mouth, while Eleni lay in bed accepting like a pampered baby the old mother's food that fed her desire: and left her with the taste of ash in her mouth.

The clients never came, nor did they matter. The woman and the illusory food mattered. And Eleni, unwilling to move out of the dream, stayed with her: while the old woman appeared now like a witch and now like one of the Fates bending over her crib, and finally settled into her mother's suddenly aged dying body and face. A dying mother, yet still feeding her, in great abundance yet never to satisfaction, with handfuls and armfuls of that mysterious food of desire, or love, or womanhood, or death. It was a feast transubstantiated, its power that of the Eucharist, its flavour of the moment, now candy-floss now ashes.

For an indistinct time she stayed wrapped in the dream's seductive satiny pleasure. Its reds bled into the hues of the world. Its flavour in her mouth a vanishing insubstantial sweet airiness that concentrated into tangible desire: for a lover. But the bent old woman with the airy white hair prowled at the edges.

The apartment was quiet, she was alone, and the day through the curtains had already reached a full sunny warmth. The close air of the dream, permeated by her mother's blessing, had invaded the wakeful world of the apartment, and slowly concentrated on the man who did not appear. She allowed herself to murmur the name of the man who, she knew, would become her lover. By uttering his name she was allowing him back into the asymmetrical plot of her life – already vitiated by breaks and betrayals.

She rang Nikolas – he was already at work – and arranged to meet him. Until the meeting, she killed time. She stood in front of the mirror examining her face, her body, her heart. Fleetingly her conscience.

They drove out to Vyzantion. Her red satiny dream would be sculpted evanescently into the air, or superimposed on the landscape – its organdie flowers for a brief explosion of time would bloom into reality, and vanish. She remembered Vyzantion – an endless stretch of countryside to the east of the city, of fields and woods and expanding refugee villages, plain whitewashed dwellings hidden under roses and honeysuckle. She used to visit relatives of her father's, refugees from Anatolia who never made it to the expensive apartment blocks of the city. She remembered staying with great aunt Eleni, watering the vegetable garden while the adults sat under the olive tree reminiscing. She remembered the scent of mint as she brushed against it, and groups of boys and girls dancing under the trees to Stathis' accordion.

The Vyzantion of the kitchen gardens and birds and dancing had vanished. Bulldozers of monstrous size and greed had razed her own fragments of history to the ground, to make way for a modern European Greece. The earth was dug up, asphalted: and broken uprooted families no longer tended vineyards and orchards to feed and appease their nostalgia. Nikolas, at home in this heartless suburb, parked his car in an empty avenue of new tall buildings, the balconies empty, the sidewalks still without trees, the plots in the middle of the avenue well-dug but bare. 'For Sale' signs lined the pavement.

They walked in the deserted artificial city, for the moment at least in love. Away from the curious eyes of their home town, he slipped his arm round her shoulders, she slipped hers round his waist. The embrace confirmed her possession and dispossession of his familiar, changed body. The movement, in the rhythm of the walk, was the same, and loved. They walked, and the city stretched endlessly, the anonymous uninhabited buildings, the empty balconies, the treeless avenues. A few cars, a few pedestrians in a hurry, a café, a grocery shop. The beginnings of a community. And themselves, attentive only to each other, in the wrong place and time.

She missed the real Vyzantion with its kitchen gardens and roses and accordion music. He said the new Vyzantion was becoming the most expensive suburb of Thessaloniki. She complained she didn't recognize any longer her own hometown, he said this was progress.

She wanted them to make love, and, she knew, so did he. They knew from the quietness of their voices and their bodies – listening to each other's wishes.

"I own a flat here." His words hung in the air.

She looked – surprised. Yet did not ask "Why did you bring me here?"

"Would you like to see it?"

"Yes." There was a plot they were both following.

"Why didn't you tell me?"

"Because you don't like it here. And ... I don't know what will happen to it – or to my marriage."

She did not want to know either. She did not, perhaps, want to know the present 'him': dealing with his marriage, seeing his patients, arguing politics with his friends, living a life that excluded and ignored her. She did not want these realities to interfere with what he right now meant to her: she only knew that he touched something vital in her.

The flat smelled of fresh paint, wood polish. When he switched on the lights the place looked immaculate. The dining room furniture carried prosperity, and abstemiousness; the suite offered soft feathery embraces, un-crumpled; the bottles in the bar were unopened; the bed untouched. The polished mirrors reflected angles of a fully-furnished uninhabited life.

She wondered what he wanted from this place. What he wanted from her in this place. Might it be a copy of their own marriage that never was? Or was it a model for any and every marriage lined up along the treeless flowerless streets of Vyzantion? Was this the end result of love – down to the merest domestic detail? Or was it the shell that remained after the souls had merrily flown away?

She moved through the constricting orderly world of kitchen to dining room to living room to bedroom to children's bedroom to living room again – a world concealing: cancelled feelings? At least discarded schemes. She had adulterous thoughts and adulterous desires – and a wish to crease, stain, inhabit.

Mostly she was guided by the need to come out of her exile and repossess: images, rooms, phrases of love. She handled kitchen gadgets, left her fingerprints on the polished wood, allowed her body to sink. He followed her, or led her, taking her by the hand or touching her arm, her back. She thought – he was trying perhaps to connect her with the place, and to accommodate her presence within its well-defined emptiness. Did she go with the furniture? Did the decor suit her? How did she differ from his wife? Or, how had she changed through the years? Or, who is she anyway?

To cut all these ambiguities, questions that did not need urgent answers, she wanted them to make love. In this place: which seemed like a well-appointed grave, or just another room, love's room. It mattered as much or as little as the other rooms they had made love in. Did they remember them all? Corners amongst iron clutter, clearings amongst trees, borrowed flats of friends or acquaintances, his boyish room, his parents' bedroom. The red satiny room of her dream slowly descended and settled in this foreign tastefully decorated flat of Vyzantion.

A message read only by them passed between them. Whatever tender thoughts or wistful desires they had for each other through the years of distance contracted into a simple, undiverted, monopolising desire. They lay on the show-room bed and made love.

9

MERCENARY HEARTS

The telephone ring drilled its way through the thin air of peace in the apartment. It tore the flimsy fabric of sleep blending into day-dream, desire, sorrow, and slowly brought Eleni into wakefulness. Her father, in his pyjamas, had picked up the phone – she strained to hear. His answers were dry, negative. From the annoyed repetition of 'my child' she gathered it was one of her sisters. He quickly lost patience, and shouted down the phone he wanted to be left alone to deal with his affairs. And hung up.

The telephone rang again, Eleni was there first, Sophia at the other end was giving orders and directions. Father should, absolutely must, retire. He must start getting his pension – it's wasted money, money owed him. They must start now gathering the necessary documents. Eleni must look for his insurance contributions, tax statements, any papers she could find. They themselves would do the paper work, then he must be persuaded to sign. He is old, and like other old men he should retire and let others more capable deal with his affairs.

Eleni agreed. Oppressed by Sophia's tirade she agreed, with displeasure. She sat back on her bed, encumbered by the heaps of dusty papers forgotten or hidden in drawers, cupboards, locked rooms – waiting to be read and decoded. She envisaged the thankless task of putting her father's life in order, behind his back.

She could argue or plead with him – but with no conviction. She worked her mother's ring on her finger, finally pulled it off and hid it with the rest of the jewellery.

Father and daughter had their morning coffee on the balcony, their feet resting between mother's dead plants, which would not come back to life for all Eleni's watering.

Such moments, in that balcony, were the fresh and peaceful moments of her parents' marriage. He would tell his wife his plans, she would advise, and caution. He belittled his competitors, she smilingly listened. She warned him, while he came up with even grander designs. Eleni used to sit to one side, unnoticed, sunning herself in those moments of good marriage. Cheerful words, and shaky hyperboles flowing from high spirits and large-heartedness, were to her signs of a general, possible love.

Her father was restless. He inspected the world around them with dissatisfaction, watched her with a sharp calculating eye. He stood up and went back and forth, preoccupied, looking for things. When he thought she was not looking he unlocked his room – that used to be her room – and disappeared into it. He reappeared after a while.

"Things are missing."

"What things?"

"Furniture, rugs. People come here and take things." He stared at the empty floor-space where the piano used to be.

Did he not remember giving those things to Sophia, and Kaliopi? Did they just come in and take them when he was away? Do they have a key to the flat? She kept quiet, not to anger him, and not to find out what he meant, how confused and bewildered he was.

She recognised the growing suspicion that would swoop down on anyone in his power. She tried to guess his silent calculations in his circlings around her, the furtive glances in her direction. He suspected her, clearly. But of what? Had he missed, or found, the jewellery? Did he also want something from her? What?

*

In the bus Father looked straight ahead, rubbing and exercising his damaged hand – his mind exercised by his private schemes. She was mustering the courage to mention his retirement, he suddenly turned to her.

"You know that piece of land I gave you, Eleni –" He looked for the right words. "It's a good piece of land, very good."

"It is, dad. Really nice."

A long silence. He exercised his bad hand. She put her arm around him, momentarily rested her head on his shoulder.

"Dad, don't you think its time you had some rest?" She did not mention the word retirement.

"Rest!" His contemptuous astonishment scorched all words. "What do you take me for? A layabout?"

She stopped, because she knew that talk of age would come to a dead end of joking, or lying. No one knew his age: like other refugees, when he arrived in Greece he gave whatever age suited him. Since then he would hide his years in playful enigmas.

He stopped, because he did not like the topic.

They got off the bus at the old market. The district still kept some of its ancient order. They walked along the narrow street of the coppersmiths, and Eleni made them stop to investigate the rows of brass and copper items set out on the pavement, gleaming in the sun: tall cylindrical coffee grinders; pestles and mortars; finely engraved trays. They conjured the pounding and grinding and slow loving labour of food, and love itself.

The copper-traders' ancient church, the Virgin of the Coppersmiths, stood alone and lost in a large square, in the middle of the dirty deafening traffic: an untouched, tangible vision of grace. Behind it, another black congregation of garbage – stray dogs tearing the garbage bags and spreading their filthy innards with riotous belligerence.

They went deeper into the old market, a colony of low domes and arches, remains of a Byzantine, Balkan, oriental city, humming with its trade, pleasures and appetites. Its ancient, derelict facades were hidden by the wares of fabric shops – that had passed unchanged from father to son. They were selling household linen, curtains, wall hangings, rugs: entire trousseaus – material promises of young fruitfulness and wealth. The city, which would parade itself as a European, Western city, had for centuries drawn its life from this oriental bazaar at its centre, a sprawling pantheistic temple to household gods, domestic values, opulence, and art. Women went in and out of the shops, excited, demanding. And the shopkeepers, like comfortable inhabitants of an invaded country, politely obliged.

After so many years, and so many thousands of miles from her childhood, Eleni knew that fabrics – stretched, draped, folded, stored – protected her from fear and war. The thick kilims hanging across her grandmother's window kept out the sight of parades of soldiers – its earth-coloured geometry a temporary fiction, a fabrication of meanings as enticing as the real free landscapes that were out of bounds. Its dense weave never betrayed to the enemy the tremulous light in the room, nor the family comforts and daily violences it cocooned.

Her father, merchant of fabrics, walked ahead of her, distracted, negligent, half-appreciating the merchandise. She followed, enticed into the web of pattern and colour, and searching for the weave of ultimate pleasure and meaning. They were at home – at heart erratic itinerants, nomadic dwellers in desert tents, woven, wavering, transitory homes.

They traversed together the geography of the place, ancient and intimate, leading them to an entanglement of remembered unshared pleasures and sorrows. So she knew now why they found themselves taking this journey through the markets. She had thought they stayed together through the long day because they wanted something from each other. They did, but it was not only for unspoken bargains and palpable profit they had come here.

"Let's go and eat."

He wove her arm round his with relief – their appetite was a bond. And for now, other feelings would be left to lie, awake, at the bottom of some sea.

The old iron gate of the food arcade pulled them into a carnival of tastes and smells, a singing panegyric of food, nature's banquet. Perhaps it was an illusion, the drops of water balancing on the lettuce might not be dew drops, but sprinklings of tap water; the abundance, part of the hyperbole.

Father and daughter crossed the magic mirror halls of appetite, and meandered along its alleys of enticement. Barrels of anchovies smelling of sea sweetness; barrels of olives, from Kalamata, Halkithiki and Thasos. They tasted the full fat cheeses, from Olympus and Metsovo; they tasted raw fish eggs of Messolonghi, raisins of Corinth. They bought halva from Komotini, and *loukoumia* from Xanthi.

Headless carcasses of baby lambs hung in neat rows; anonymous limbs; blinded heads; garlands of sausages. Heaps of birds, their plumage sticking to the blood-stained floor, made foul hieroglyphics of death – food and death. People inspected and bargained, their faces consumed by passion. The passion of consumption, and communion? The passion for salvation of body and spirit? The passion of obsession and dread of death?

Eleni followed, trying to avoid the bucketfuls of water sluiced on the stone floors. Jumping over rivers carrying fragments of animals and fish, they smelled their way to the soup restaurant.

The Armenian's shop was steamy, noisy. Mr Agopian in his white apron stood behind large vats of liquid with parts of animals floating in them – a calf's head, eyes dulled and ready to pour out, naked teeth, hollowed cheeks disintegrating with each gentle movement of the boiling liquid; delicate white tangles of intestines; indiscriminate innards, inert flab of belly, ox bones whose rope-thick marrow slipped out and melted in the mouth. With his gigantic spoon he made them swirl and collide and gently and deliciously fall to pieces. Vinegar, garlic and red pepper were waiting on the table. The tables were full, the clients mostly men, Macedonian traders or smallholders on a business trip to the capital. The waiters knew her father, they welcomed him – with respectful restraint when they noticed the black sleeve band. Agopian, a large, large-headed man, with black wavy hair and a boxer's squashed-in face, came and sat with them, with a natural tired-limbed ease. Father accepted his condolences, was proud to introduce his daughter. Agopian ordered the waiter to give "the best, only the best, to Mr Gregori and his daughter." They exchanged remarks well rehearsed by both of them for many years.

"How's business?"

"Eh, glory be to God! It could be worse. We pray we have our good health. Without our health, what do we want business and money for!"

They shook their heads. The familiar words of wisdom, which carried no argument or disagreement, and the draught retsina that appeared on the table, with the owner's compliments, and the smell of cooked meat, all in unison, were good for the mood and appetite. The conversation turned to business and money.

Another carafe of retsina arrived, glasses were filled, wishes exchanged. "This one is on me," Father insisted. "As I was saying, my brother Timoleon ended up in America. But it was wasted on him. He remained a tailor! But his children are doing well, proper Americans, with the dollars and the crewcuts." Father took his jacket off. "I was learning English to go to America, you know. Ah, I had great passion for America. But my Eleni went to America, and England! My Eleni went everywhere! A refugee, like her father."

"We are all refugees in this place. I am Armenian, my neighbour is a Karamanli. And between us, Gregori, once a refugee, always a refugee!"

The sheer mention of the other Greeks of a lost Greece, and lost lands, put Father into a mood of nostalgia and appetite. He started laying his plans for the hotel on Thasos.

"I thought you had retired, Mr Gregori!"

"A true businessman never retires!"

"But why start such projects now? Your daughters are grown up, married. Now you can enjoy your grandchildren!"

"He is right, Dad. Listen to your friend. Friends much younger than you have already retired and they take it easy, enjoy their life."

Father looked at her and then at him with bewilderment and compassion, and a little contempt. He continued with the description of the hotel. There was also this ferry boat. He had shares in it, he would buy more.

The soup arrived, Agopian presided with dignity over the brusque casual serving. "Nostimo," his customers acknowledged; and having graciously accepted their satisfaction, the host got up and slowly proceeded to the next customer.

She sipped the soup, brooding on the intimate illusory pleasure in each spoonful. Brooding on the pleasures she had inherited from her father. The taste for strong flavours, Turkish words and sounds, spices, strong, un-Greek accents. Both of them, uprooted, from flavour to ancient flavour smelled and tasted their way home. They felt blindly their eastward far-reaching roots. This was the flavour of home, and homecoming, she judged: the flavour of "nostos" – "returning home" – and of nostalgia, of aching for home. And "Nostimo" – "delicious like home". She allowed herself to relish her contemplation of words.

She listened to his eating noises: the self absorbed, absentminded satisfaction.

"What hotels and ferry-boats are you talking about, Dad? We said, you will retire and live on your pension, and enjoy yourself." She didn't believe her words made a difference, but she did her duty. "You'll take trips to Thasos, come to England, stay with Kaliopi at her new villa, visit Sophia."

"I don't need any pension, thank you very much." His contempt was uncontrolled. "Nor do I need your sisters' villas."

"How old are you?" Her voice was raised.

"I am still young. I have years of work ahead of me." His voice became intimate, conspiratorial. "I tell you, I'll give you part of this hotel. You can advertise it in England. Send us groups of tourists, and you'll keep your cut." He waited, looked around, then at her, rubbed his chin with indecision – a red blotch on his forehead, since his youth a sign of unease and excitement.

"Will you sign your part of the Thasos land to me? Will you? If you sign over your part of the land to me ... Sign it and you will see."

So that is what he wanted from her. What he had been scheming all day, for days, since her mother's death. A lonely, old, forlorn, selfish man, an avaricious heartless man, her father.

"If you promise to take your pension. Then we shall see." She had a bitter bargain on her hands.

Something was agreed, they both felt they had secured something from each other. For the time being. For the time being they should be pleased.

Their heads thrust forward, a thread of equality in bartering passed through their eyes. Only, her voice trembled a little, in fear for both of them. A movement of bewilderment in her eyes.

So in temporary agreement, they ate and drank in the noisy smelly lap of the market place.

10

FORGETTING

"It must be difficult for you, Kyrie Gregori, without Kyria Anastasia. Difficult, and painful!"

Father sat up in unease. He nodded politely. He had told her he didn't need to see a doctor. He was very well in his health, and no doctor would bring her back.

"You see, Michali, my father can be a little forgetful! We were wondering if you could prescribe some pills to help −" Sophia was reticent yet insistent.

"I don't need any pills, thank you very much." He got up, to go. "We shouldn't take any more of your time." Politely, decisively.

"There's no hurry, Kyrie Gregori! Sit down! Let's have some coffee! We are family friends after all!"

Gregoris remembered him, vaguely. He looked a good young man, bookish behind those glasses, and with all those books on the walls. Well-heeled, judging from his office − brand new and on the waterfront. He wondered what his income was. They were not family friends, though. He hesitated, then sat down out of nervous politeness. He sat upright, his knee moving rhythmically, ready to jump up.

"Michalis is a friend, an old friend of Tryphon. While we are here, why don't you tell him of any complaints, symptoms, anything − he is our friend."

Sophia was sweet and patient, Father became distrustful. That he was Tryphon's friend made things worse. He looked at her, searchingly, then at the doctor. Not bad looking – he wondered if they were having an affair. She was still good looking, and she – well, she did ask for it when she was young. That low-cut dress which he tore in two. And when he had to lock her up in the evenings to stop her from meeting that bum, Tryphon. All three of them asked for it; all girls in this day and age ask for it. It's not our fault if we are … led astray. We are men. What business had she to visit this doctor without her husband – he imagined his hands coming up her skirts, playing doctor – his head felt hot with moral rage. Tryphon's friend! He knew what he thought of Tryphon's friends.

The doctor was asking her about Tryphon, and his health, had he stopped smoking? "He should, and he should take more exercise, walk to the office, cycle even." Then he turned to her father. "And how is your heart, Kyrie Gregori?"

"It's the heart of a young man. Better than yours."

"That is very good news, very good news."

"I never smoked in my life. Never drank, not heavily, eh, a glass of retsina with an old compatriot – that is good for the heart and for the spirits. I never gambled, never looked at women, unless they … insisted." He was pleased with himself, he wanted to continue. The doctor smiled, Sophia looked austere and embarrassed.

"Let's have your blood pressure?"

Grigoris tightened his fist.

"Good, very good, Kyrie Grigori. I wish I was as strong and youthful as you are. You sleep well?"

"Not well, but without my wife, all our lives together, what do you expect!"

The doctor nodded in serious agreement, Sophia was getting tense.

"And … how are you managing by yourself, Kyrie Gregori? It must be difficult."

"It is difficult, but I am managing, thank you."

"Your memory is – good?"

Father paused – searched the other man's face, looked at his daughter. "As good as it could be. After all the sufferings I have been through, the losses and persecutions, destruction upon destruction, what do you expect? As good as it wants to be. Who wants to remember, anyway."

"Well, you are quite forgetful these days, Dad!"

"With all my burdens, and responsibilities, with all the things I have to worry about – it is only one mind!" He held his head with both hands.

The doctor noticed his shut fingers. "What is wrong with your hand, Kyrie Gregori?"

He was glad to change the topic. "It has been shutting, with time." He extended his arm and closed hand to him. "Years now, but I never had the time to see a doctor about it, so many duties, so many responsibilities."

"You should have seen a doctor, Kyrie Gregori." The doctor looked at Sophia.

"We told him."

"It may still be not too late. It's a simple operation, you know. You should look into it, Sophia. Why not?"

Sophia nodded.

Father liked him better. He almost trusted him. It was his hand that had been worrying him, but however much he exercised it, it would just close on him.

"Well, Sophia will make arrangements about your hand. You have good insurance, Kyrie Gregori, and probably a good pension."

Sophia gave a deep sigh.

Father tensed. "I don't draw a pension, I have no intention of retiring."

"Kyrie Gregori, why not make your life easier? Why not rest, enjoy yourself?"

"Because I like working."

"But you have worked all your life!"

"That's why I can't stop working now." He got up to go.

"The coffee is coming, Kyrie Gregori. Please sit down."

He sat down, looked at his daughter. "I've got things to do," he murmured.

Sophia looked at the doctor, the doctor looked back, Father could not tell what this secret communication was. He looked at her clothes, her legs, her breasts – she looked respectable enough now, but you never know with them.

The secretary brought the coffee. Young and pretty, Father noticed. He looked at the doctor, then at her.

"Your father is very well, Sophia." The doctor smiled seriously to her.

"That's very good." She was not satisfied. "Physically, he is in excellent condition. If he didn't keep disappearing, and forgetting, he could make our life much easier, eh, dad?"

"What do you mean disappearing? Do I need to ask for permission before I go to my business? Give you a written account of my movements?"

"They are worried about you, Kyrie Gregori, you are their father. In case something happened to you."

"They can worry about their families, their husbands." He stressed "husbands" with malice.

Sophia's voice was daughterly. "But if something happened to you, we, I, would have the responsibility. When you forget, what am I supposed to do? Let you get lost and end up under a bus?"

"Are you really forgetful, Kyrie Gregori? I could give you pills to help, you know."

"I don't know what she is talking about."

"What did you have for breakfast, let's see if you remember, Kyrie Gregori." The doctor tried to be playful.

Father looked alarmed. "I drank my milk, I always drink my milk."

"Very good, very good. And what did you have for lunch?"

Father's eyes stared at a vacuum. There was silence. They waited. To catch him.

After a long silence, Sophia's voice reverberated with hushed victory. "We had stuffed tomatoes."

Father looked at her with bewilderment, and hatred.

"Who is prime minister, Kyrie Gregori?" The doctor's voice was cloyingly sweet and reassuring, and was growing distant and lost to Gregoris losing himself into a long dark tunnel of fear.

11

COINCIDENCES

"What did you say to your father?"

"That I am staying with an old school-friend."

"Did he believe you?"

"I don't know."

The room – next to his office – had no character. No pictures, no books. A double bed, a shut wardrobe, two side tables. An ordinary lampshade hung from the ceiling.

"He believes no one." The smell of his body – an earthy fecundity of fresh tobacco leaves – had not changed. His silences, timely, never inert; his voice – rooted, self-satisfied. His total absorption in her. She let her body slowly climb and half-lie on top of him, conquering with her body a momentous landmark.

"I believe you."

"And I you."

She sniffed blindly the skin of his neck, his shoulder, the fine folds at the joint of his arm, slowly inhabiting him, re-colonising the half-familiar contours, wondering. "I may not believe you, but you are here."

Her voice articulating words in her native Greek sounded foreign, nauseously familiar, a forgotten accent suspended over his skin together with her breath.

She applied her weight on him pressing on his chest and stomach and belly, pressing on his flesh, soft and pliable, seeking to know and love underneath it his obscure anatomy. She played with the soft hairs that formed a herringbone pattern down his belly, wondering if she loved him. Feeling his midriff and guessing at his diaphragm – the seat of our soul, as their common ancestors had believed.

He kissed her mouth and made her recall the foreign, bitter flavour of 'another', seductively intimate and forbidden. His arms round her body, their limbs weaving together, her head and body, limp, hanging on him, her native land had spread its tentacles and fiery tongues round her and held her. And she had given in.

She explored the land which had shown her good and evil starkly and unforgivingly in black and white. With its innumerable Byzantine icons it confronted her. With the ascetic bodies, and the hermits' burning eyes, condemning, it damned. With the perennial parental faces forbidding, it forbade love. She was once again caught in the world where there was nothing outside the dark shadow and the sunlit fields, the Elysian Plains, and Hades. And she had made her choice.

Their love-making slowly took her to an exhilarated liberating sigh of long loss. She wondered where his soul, at that moment of ultimate solitude, was. Her mind flew hither and thither, her body told her that in those moments of total self-enclosed pleasure they perhaps were together.

The time between this meeting and those persecuted assignations of their youth in the iron entrails of the harbour hung above them like a chandelier shrouded in linen for an indefinite period of mourning. For her a time of perpetual exile: for him, she imagined, an obscure rooted stillness. She did not ask him, she only asked questions about his wife, his children, the furniture of his home.

She remembered dreaming of walking from one country to another; crossing over the barbed-wire frontier, with a small, simple effort. Or simply crawling underneath. In the silence of open lands, without passport controls, or a noise of air-plane engines, she crossed into the homeland, drifted in from the exotic deserts of New Mexico or the cornfields of Kansas, or the spongy Fens. As easily as crossing the threshold of an English cottage after a walk on the windy North Sea coasts. With the ease of desire she travelled vast distances on this man's body, which stayed obscure, yet was possessed by her, and ready to be transformed to what she desired. A foreign body probably, with an unfathomable intimacy in its centre.

She preferred that he didn't speak in case he proved her wrong. And so that he did not break the perfect quietness of solitude she felt with him. But he spoke, of them, of himself, a lot about himself, then of her, he wanted to know why, why she had left. Why she gave no signs and sent no messages. Why she had to go so far away, what she did, whom she had loved, especially, pressingly, whom she had loved.

As he spoke she heard the familiar intonations, the confident possessiveness, the self-possession, the knowledge of his wishes and demands, and guessed now, years later, why she had blindly and thoughtlessly left. Would he now, she was wondering, start guessing why he had let her go?

During the long afternoon there were silences, and there were explanations, and many questions, and love. Her mother's dead body had receded from her and her own body was again alive and loving. Her father's old age had found its natural place in time, and was releasing its grip around her still young body and still desirable face. The household furniture and golden jewellery and bric-a-brac had temporarily lost their animate will, were dispersed, and had found their allotted place.

At six o'clock he had to get up and dress, and see his patients next door. She stayed alone, a naked woman alone in someone's bed, like a prostitute waiting for her clients who never came. She racked her mind to know who the old woman was, feeding her with popcorn or candy floss or polystyrene – all the time knowing it was her mother.

And who was he? Who was the man next door seeing women clients, touching them, healing them? What was she to him? He to her?

She held on to her own, young, exclusive possession, trembling that she might lose her definition of him: fugitive perhaps, made up by nostalgia, and memory – real or false. She trembled that, with it, she might lose part of her own self, a vital self, fearless and careless in taking and being taken. A fugue self that breathed its nourishment from the native landscape, the air and light, the native loves and sorrows – and he was in it and part of it. She carried the candle with attentiveness, keeping its tremulous whispering flame of memories and nostalgia alive. Memory, her memory, might in the end be her true homeland.

She heard voices, women's voices who came to him to be cured, his voice dutifully asking and promising. With the knowledge that perhaps he was healing someone, next door, she lay waiting. She lit a cigarette – although she had long ago stopped smoking – because she thought it was fitting.

Between patients he made them cups of coffee, exchanged harmless words, contemplated light-spiritedly how it would have been had they got married. They dreaded the bell ringing.

Alone, she imagined them, or remembered them, walking in the old city, along bullet-ridden walls and war-torn houses. The black-clad women sitting outside their doors watching them, without envy or disapproval, or much feeling. Some of them came closer, others came out and spread their blankets on the uneven ground and sat, as if at a May-day picnic, and watched them. She and he stood there kissing each other and giggling, not minding the black-clad women circling around them like well-fed ravens. She made a policeman appear out of nowhere and approach. She didn't know what he had wanted to do. She made him smile, at the lovers. And then turn to the women and ask why they did not leave the lovers alone, did they not see they were lovers? So the women one by one dispersed like black fears, and obscure guilts, till they were only black specks in the air, as if there had been a fire, and they were specks of ash being blown into nothing.

The lovers, free, said something, they both said it at the same time, the same words, the same meaning and intention and aim. It was an ordinary thing, like "Isn't this like a film? Or "Isn't it like a dream?" Or "Do you like films?" Or "Do you like Tarkovsky?" A very ordinary coincidence, but a perfect matching of words and moods and meanings; an agreement in tastes, in the frivolity of youth. A small miracle.

"This must be love?" she questioned, seriously wondering at the rare good fortune of the moment.

Yes, this is love, she gave the answer to her question and the conclusion to the story. Outside this room, and outside this city, she had another love – loves, lasting loves. She had her husband and her daughter to whom she will return, and she will return different, changed by other loves and losses and by the here and now and home. And changed by her betrayals.

Betrayal was woven in her life, of those she had left behind, of a mother dying and a father ageing. Of daughter and husband now, asking and waiting.

She remains however here, naked on this bed, visible through the cloud of smoke – which like her past life gathered around her and cocooned her. She remains, still, in this room and in this love, young, unfinished. And healing.

She heard the telephone ringing, the elevator coming and going and women coming and going, the bell ringing, the door opening and closing. She imagined her lover examining women's bodies, then putting the envelope with the money into his drawer, thanking them discreetly. On other occasions he would check the sum after they had gone, but not now, because he came straight to her – more important than money – with words and small gestures of love.

COINCIDENCES

When it all stopped and the front door was locked and the telephone unplugged, he came back to her and they stayed together till dark. The room lost its ordinariness, and in its irresistible dark symmetry their bodies were removed from time and distance, and other lives were hardly audible.

12

THE SOUND OF A KEY

The city outside was gripped by its daily traffic of trade, appetite and survival. Appetite took the ectoplasmic form of wisps and wreaths of barbecue smoke suspended outside shish kebab stalls. And round the corner the mountains of garbage were fraying at the edges exposing the half-digested secrets of the city.

She looked at her face in the mirror of the elevator, reflecting back at her the pale bewilderment of guilt and lies. A ghost of the pleasures of the night was swiftly vanishing. She concentrated her mind on daughterly dutiful thoughts, rehearsed explanations as she rang the bell, timidly. There was no answer, so she slipped her key in the lock and turned – but the key didn't turn.

Only then she registered the damaged wood round the lock – a new lock. She looked at the number of the flat, the familiar door. She rang the bell again, gave a kick at the door.

The door of another flat opened slowly, Eleni felt someone had been spying on her. A pale-faced woman emerged timidly.

"Your things are here."

"What things?"

"He threw out your things. Your bag, and books, and clothes."

The woman was embarrassed, took a step back as Eleni's face directed at her all the shock and indignation meant for her father. "I collected them after he left, because, who knows …"

"Thank you." The words turned back in her throat. He's found the jewellery. He searched her bag, found her mother's jewellery, threw her out. Or found out where she was.

She pushed at the door, simply needing to feel its dumb strength resisting her; seeking to feed her defeat, and feel her punishment. She pushed – at all locked doors, simply to see herself, in a perverse triumph of guilt. She raised her fists at the perennial tyrant, that all-powerful being who changed faces and languages. Was it a mother, a father, a god, or a careless fate who tossed her out as if she were a broken doll? Her father's face appeared – and disappeared. It left behind a large adult shape, indistinct, fluid, faceless, hidden in the shadow. And the sound of the key locking, locking in and locking out, in and out.

The neighbouring door creaked timidly, she knew she was watched but paid no attention. She remained outside the locked door, knowing now the ending to her recurring dream which made her walk endlessly the endless streets of this city looking for a home. The home did not exist. And her spirit found peace, and a home, in joining at that moment the ghosts of the real, homeless refugees that had paraded through the history of this city.

Tears of pity and self-pity cleared her mind. She could stay with her sister, or at a hotel. She could go back to her lover, or she could leave. Again. Go home. Give up this city and a vanishing home – and go home.

The next-door neighbour opened the door – which had not been completely shut – and let her in. A heap of her possessions were in a corner of the entrance hall. She put her clothes and books into her travelling bag; her hands puzzled, comforted, touched the jewellery box, solid and heavy, her secret treasure and sin. From that stolen Pandora's box new questions flew free: why then did he lock her out of the home? Did he know, did he not know, what did he know?

"Your mother talked of you often," the woman said quietly. "I feel as if I know you."

The mention of her mother, doing ordinary things like talking with her neighbour, or talking about herself, brought home to her, as suddenly as if she had just woken up, her mother's death, and life. And immeasurable regret for all the unrecognised instances of feeling. Her grief had the infant's simple logic: "If she talked about me, perhaps she loved me, then how could she have died!" And the infant's insupportable guilt: "How could I have let her die!"

The sight, sound, knowledge of her mother talking about her gripped her mind with the stillborn possibility of a love. Why had such a normal thing not crossed her mind? Why had she not searched those small secret folds in the life of that other woman, so intimate to her?

"She missed you, you know."

Eleni knelt over her bag, huddled over this new bereavement. She zipped her bag with one forceful swing of her arm. Was this pale woman a ghostly embodiment of regret?

She looked up at the woman, suddenly remembering, years ago, on a short visit from England, the younger woman in the next-door balcony greeting them and watching with curiosity. Surrounded then by the securities of home, she had scarcely attended to the solitary figure spending her hours on the balcony watching the traffic, and following the small family incidents on other balconies, waiting. Her hair was now a compact reddish brown, evidently dyed, in neat tired waves. The cardigan and skirt and indoor slippers made her look as if she had stopped waiting.

Eleni got up and faced this woman who knew things about her mother that she did not know. "Were you friends?"

"We had our afternoon coffee together, whenever your father was away travelling."

Eleni searched the woman's face, looking for those long leisurely coffee breaks that lasted perhaps all afternoon, gossiping, confessing. Her mother's life, irrespective of her.

"Would you like some coffee?"

"Yes, please." Repeating that scene might bring something of her mother and of herself back to life.

She led Eleni into a living room crowded with heavy furniture, loaded with bowls of family photographs, artificial flowers, albums, porcelain creatures. The balcony doors were shut and curtained, the traffic-hum from the street was faint through the dusty glass. There was a smell of stale food and time.

"I tried to calm him down, but he got worse."

"Where did he go? Did he say anything?" She tried to sound calm and matter of fact.

"He had a suitcase. He used to go to Thasos, all the time. He said he had business there. Sometimes they went together. He would get angry with your mother and the poor woman took it all quietly. She used to talk to me."

Eleni did not want to hear more. She thanked the woman, whose name she did not even know. She did not want to know her name, preferring to believe she had been sent by her mother. A messenger, to say things unsaid, to alter actions. Perhaps she was one of the Fates whom her mother had frightened away on the night of her birth. And she perhaps came back to take up a thread and continue a weave, perhaps conclude a story.

"Your mother always said she would find a good husband for me." She smiled bitterly.

Eleni smiled back, regretful, envious. "Thank you for the coffee, and for taking in my things." She kissed her on the cheek. "Forgive me, but what is your name?"

"Frossini. Your mother called me Frosso."

"Good-bye, Frosso. And thank you, again."

In the street, she went into a phone-box and stayed for a while. In the phone box she was mouthing foreign words. Through the glass, as in a dream, no sound escaped. The expressions on her face were strong, multiple, quick: native images of native lives. Familiar stories. The tension in her face, the stretching out of features, was from the effort to cover distances, and cross bridges. How do you translate private sorrows and home-bred outrage?

Yet her face became calm. It smiled with a depth that her

relatives and parents might never have seen. The smile played in her eyes as they moved round the telephone box yet was directed at inner, intimate images, which played on her face, making small wrinkles round her eyes and at the top of her nose, making her lips move in small tender kisses. She gave many rounded, light – maternal – kisses into the telephone before she hung up.

There was still a happiness on her face as she lifted her bag and walked down Vassilissis Sophias Avenue. Her mother's sister, Aunt Lefkothea, was her immediate refuge: she would find in her at least a temporary substitute.

13

A VIEW OF THE COMMERCIAL FAIR

Aunt Lefkothea's uncorseted body surrounded her. Her eyes dwelt briefly on the travelling bag, then on Eleni's face. "What's the matter? Did you quarrel?" Eleni heard the whispers of conspiracy between mother and child, and burst into tears.

"He locked me out of the flat! Locked me out of my own home." In this maternal lap, tears that had been gathering for days, flowed. "He changed the lock, and locked me out!"

"Ah ..." she drew out the vowel in meditative disapproval. "Kyrie Eleison, bless the man!" She crossed herself. "He was always like that, Lenaki mou! From the day they were married."

"My mother just dead, and he locks me out!" All the orphans' cries, lived through books of her childhood, were now breaking her own heart.

"What is the matter, Lefki?" Her uncle's voice from the front room. "Who is it?"

Aunt Lefki took the bag from Eleni's shoulder. "You will stay here – just like at home, and don't pay any attention to him, or anyone else. Come, wash your face, and say hello to your uncle and cousins."

The three "boys" of the family, large, well-fed men, sat round the table while Aunt Lefki was busy making a place for Eleni.

"Oh, what a surprise!" Her uncle, in his silk-like pyjamas, sat at the head of the table like a potentate. He pushed the heavy chair back and in round-bellied dignity waited for his niece to approach and bend down to kiss him on both cheeks.

Her two cousins got up, wiping their mouths, though the grease of their mother's rich cooking left a residual shine on their lips. They had their father's self-regarding fleshy handsomeness. Their long eye-lashes, inherited from him, curtained large blue eyes that, caught unawares, begged, demanded love, care, attention. Easily that look could be transformed into a heavy-lidded measuring up of a small simplified universe.

They exchanged pleasantries, without losing interest in the food their mother had stacked in front of them, and offered their views with unquestionable authority. Their parents listened with quiet pride.

"Your father always had a quick temper, Eleni." Uncle gave his diagnosis with tired superiority. "It's the Asia Minor mind – full of quirks. In a couple of days he'll have forgotten everything, and so will you. Come, sit here next to me and have some of your aunt's 'yemista'. It's so delicious, my wife – I'll have some more."

She immediately filled his plate as he watched her and her food with love and pride. "The best wife, the best cook - as good as your mother, Eleni, may her soul be forgiven." He stabbed his stuffed tomato with his fork and the spiced rice spread on his plate: "May we be given life and prosperity!"

Aunt Lefki took the compliments in her stride. She filled her sons' plates without even asking, and they did not complain; she gave Eleni another stuffed tomato for all her objections. Her own half-eaten tomato was getting cold on her plate. She checked the table to make sure nothing was missing: the stuffed tomatoes, salads, cheese, taramosalata, melidzanosalata.

"And the beer waiting in the fridge?" Uncle looked up at the eternal mother, eternally on her feet, with playful reprimand.

Eleni got up, but her aunt brusquely pushed her down

and, slapping both cheeks in playful self punishment, ran out of the room.

"Sit down. Your aunt is fed by feeding her boys."

Eleni asked her elder cousin about his family.

"Oh they're very well, very well."

"Vassilia has a job now," Aunt Lefki volunteered. "She teaches at primary school, and doesn't come home till four or five. Awkward time. So her mother keeps the child, and my boy comes to his own mother for his lunch, and siesta."

Eleni turned towards the younger one, divorced and to be remarried.

He was more talkative than his brother. "Mimi is preparing for the wedding. So I let *mama* look after me." There was perhaps a hint of irony in his self-satisfied chuckle.

"They are going to have a wedding... that will be the envy of Thessaloniki." The father sat back with paternal pride."

"You've done well, eh, rascal!" Aunt Lefki slapped her son's full thigh with congratulatory exuberance. She turned back to Eleni. "A hundred and more guests! At St Sophia's!"

"The girl's father" – her uncle bent close over the table confidentially – "He doesn't know what he has. Property, shares, and all for his one and only daughter. A good girl, however."

"Ah," the groom-to-be dismissed them with self-pleasure. "We love each other. That's the important thing." His face radiated worldly wisdom.

"Of course you love each other," the parents volunteered in one voice.

"Without love, all the riches in the world are worthless." His mother added, for good measure.

The younger son winked at his brother, his face broadening into an open-ended meaningful happy smile.

The elder brother slowly moved to the sofa where he sat back, in boa-like stillness, digesting.

"Love is the foundation of the home." Uncle's father had been a minister of the church, and uncle still sang as a chanter at

Candlemas Church every Sunday. He delivered sermons at the first opportunity. "Ask your aunt if she knows another woman luckier than her!"

Aunt Lefki agreed with every word as she hurried with her lukewarm stuffed tomato, before she got up to make preparations for her dear men, "her spoiled sons", for their siesta.

Eleni lay down obediently on the sofa in the living room. The blanket her aunt lightly placed on her turned her – with the magic of a whimsical god-mother – into one of her children. Her body resting in the warm, food-smelling comfort of the room, her mind, restless, pursuing her unjust father. And always rebounding from that locked door – always scattering in repeated futile questions. Did he find the jewellery? But then why did he not take it? Did he find out? Did he follow her – as he used to? He must have followed her to the building, and recognized Nikolas' name. Whatever he knew – how, how could he lock her out! Their alliance in tatters. His pension – he never meant to take it anyway. Their bartering – the land he wanted from her? Her mind went back to the locked door, and moved away from it, retreating into the sweet refuge, staged by day-dream sleep, of last night's loving.

She must have slept. She sat up startled by the room that surrounded her. Her eyes ran from wall to wall, and a post-card Greece jumped at her through the hot claustrophobia of the sleepy afternoon. Her uncle's paintings – lurid thick-bodied copies of copies of the beauties of Greece – covered the wall space. Bright paint instantly flattened everything it touched: the windmills of Mykonos, the Parthenon, the White Tower of Thessaloniki. The air was smothered by the brand-new, freshly painted corpse of a country.

This was her uncle's fabricated homeland, a postcard Greece. She threw off the blanket and got up – the room around her became small. This could be her own, vanished home. Being locked out of it was not different from being locked in it. The walls burdened with pattern and colour approached her. The heavy curtains hiding memories in their folds; the slumberous rugs; the needlework that had followed Macedonian patterns circulating amongst the housewives of Thessaloniki for decades. The homes and families of this city were bound to each other with the same threads and patterns, fashions and appetites. She knew them, and had long ago freed herself from their delicate knots. She had already fled from this city of the high-rise blocks – out of it, to the windy alleys of the upper town, and to the shanty neighbourhoods of the refugees. She had long ago flown away, to find refuge in her own fabricated city of nostalgia and fiction.

She walked out on the balcony and let her eyes travel over the Trade Fair sprawled below her, and to the hills and mountains beyond. Her uncle appeared in his crease-free pyjamas, plump and fresh with sleep. He occupied his place on the balcony, where the sun was still warm and welcome. Aunt Lefki appeared, tired and cheerful, with the coffee tray. The sons arrived heavy with siesta, and joined in the chorus of sipping and sighing with appreciation.

Uncle encouraged Eleni to appreciate the beauties of the Commercial Fair. Weren't they fortunate to have a whole city of modern buildings at their feet? The Fair, Eleni vaguely recollected, was built where the "Thousand Trees" used to be, a small pine forest that gave refuge, summer and winter, to secret unlawful lovers. The area now was a vast jumble of different, abandoned film sets, sorrowful in their forgotten pretence of glamour: a wilderness of concrete, glass and plaster taking weird architectural forms without rhyme or reason. The city, it seemed, had lost its mind, memory, and purpose. Its buildings – unconnected, temporary, vacant – followed each its own lawlessness of style, size, location or use. Every year the place would suddenly wake at the end of summer to an alarm of blazing neon lights and frantic last minute renovations: to the arrival of truckfuls of exhibits, jumbo-loads of foreign representatives, busloads of visitors from Macedonia and Thrace, and the city's own, commercially-minded, progressive, gregarious, spectacle-and-food-and-fun-loving citizens. For a few weeks the place was a playground of consumption, a vertigo of curiosity, excitement and hope of profit – which with the first autumnal rains were silently extinguished, abandoned until the following year to the pleasure of the elements. Dimension and life gone, what remained was a gigantic out of date advertisement, of itself – its conviction and seductiveness, the paint and the cardboard posters, battered by the northern *vardari* wind. The odd pedestrian wandering along the aimless avenues punctuated the desolation.

But Uncle, the artist, the believer, saw in the corpse at his feet a paradise of noise, movement and electricity, a figment of eternal life. He absorbed in his permanent armchair-stasis the energy that made the world turn.

As long as Eleni remembered, Uncle had lived in his armchair, since in early middle-age he was made redundant at the Commercial Bank. In honeymoon pyjamas, pampered, scented and immaculate, he took, for the rest of his long life, to the armchair, out on the balcony, where he dedicated himself to the pleasures of art.

He ordered the tray to be taken away and the painter's tools to be brought. In that mellow afternoon, his bodily needs temporarily satisfied, his spirit, or his views and visions, had moved him to art. The folding table was placed in front of the artist, the pencils, the paints, the glass of water, the white paper, the tracing paper, the postcard – of a Greek landscape: and the artist composed himself for the daily purpose of his life.

Eleni watched with what precision, care and patience he prepared to copy from the postcards an infinite variety of subjects. He explained to his one spectator the secrets of his art. First, the care in tracing, the choice of colours, "Ah, Lefki, I'll need some more water!" Many of his paintings, he explained, had a national subject matter or message, a flag, an Evzone; some were of brand-new immaculate Greek villages in reds, whites and greens. They were all framed and hung on the walls of the room, of the entire house. "This one is for you", he promised Eleni.

The sons politely took their leave. Aunt Lefki took them to the door and came back quietly – a permanent patient smile on her face – not to interrupt her husband's serious exposition of his duty to reproduce the beauties of Greece. From art he passed to tourism and patriotism: he, coming from Tinos, an island that housed in its cathedral the famous miraculous icon; and that had produced not only artists but also fighters in the 1821 Revolution, great politicians, and famous ship-owners – coming from such an important island, and having a degree of talent himself, and moreover being the son of a priest, he felt it his duty to contribute to the enhancement of the nation.

As day abandoned them, the artist added his finishing touches. The day's work done, his soul at ease, it was time for something – something tasty to tempt the flesh.

Just in time the door-bell rang, a lady in black from the flat above: "Oh, what pleasure, what a surprise!" But he kept his place and peace as his wife took the visitor for a quick tour to show her the latest works. The guest was led to the balcony, where she sat in flourishes of compliment and expectation of the hostess's inimitable fruit preserve.

The loaded tray arrived, the words of appreciation were offered with cloyed syrupy enthusiasm; the bell rang again, it was another lady in black, from the lower floor. The melancholy of the sunset must have sent the women, both of them widows, out of their homes, in search of company and comfort. More cherry preserve, and cold water and thick coffee. More noises of admiration and appreciation, and condolences to Eleni. Then a pause, a melancholy silence – before the latest disasters to mutual acquaintances were related, then the well known tragedies of all mankind; then sighs of compassion and acceptance, then sighs of relief that "at least it's not happening to us". The artist in his shiny pyjamas, the lover of light and colour, looked gloomily at the widows, surrounding him like ravens and taking away his view.

The sun set, and the hour of sadness passed. Aunt Lefki switched on the lights, and the outside world was suddenly black. They came into the electrically lit room, and started in a different mood on different topics. Eleni – her mind far away – hung on the others' presence like an unclaimed coat. She asked questions and answered questions, and cast words to hook on meanings.

14

RECESS

She held her cup of coffee in both hands, looking into his eyes for she didn't know what revelations and solutions. They were quiet brown eyes. The animation was not in his eyes, more in the quick, noisy way he drank his coffee. He was a little heavier than he used to be, in the face, around the stomach. His movements somewhat slower, more deliberate. His lips were full: she recalled from the past a vestige of attraction and recoil before the provocative accumulation of flesh. This moment her eyes were registering the sensual beauty of his face.

She too had gained some weight – she knew the precise places, and hid them. So they had that in common. And much more, that she couldn't define. Perhaps a mutual undistracted absorption in each other; the unquestioned certainty that a secret destiny had always meant them for each other. That they themselves had side-stepped that secret destination did not weaken their bond. They moved in a capricious universe.

She looked round the office for photographs of his wife. There were none. There was a photograph of a young boy. A delicate face – his son, but there were none of his daughter. She returned to him. Respectably dressed, his tie expensive but conventional, his telephone manner confident. Some parts she liked, not all – but he was irresistibly more than the sum of his parts.

She wondered what he thought of her, but she had no doubt that he was hers.

"He locked me out."

"Why? Where are you staying?"

"At my aunt's. I think he knows about us, he must have seen us. When I got home the lock had been changed, my things were thrown out."

He was visibly upset and sympathetic, a little puzzled. He stretched his arms to her, in love, but didn't say "Come and live with me."

Nor would she – nor did she want to put his love to the test. But she noticed. Would she want to move in with him? "No" was the answer: but in a no man's land, where all other claims and loves were in recess, then yes.

"We could meet in a hotel in Switzerland, or lake Como! Other places in Europe where I go to conferences. We could stay there – indefinitely." He spoke with devotion, meaning his words.

She was not sure. About his wishes, and about the exotic geography – why abroad? Because she supposed they could escape their lives? What fantasy and which novel was behind this? She would like to say "yes". This coincidence in their wishes and desires mattered, and made her love him.

"He did it to punish me." Like a child wrestling with frightful absolutes she reasoned: I have transgressed, and was punished, and cast out. And the next step was to be cast out with him, and follow him to any hotel on a mountain or lake. And prepare to transgress again with renewed passion, and a little desperation.

They did not need a remote hotel. Because together they already were in a house of fictions they had built and inhabited – the dramas of the past, the domestic tragedies, the small-town romance. A glass-house world enclosing and fostering those exotic flesh-eating flowers of their youth.

They went next door, and closed the door behind them. They held each other with a lifelong want of each other. They made love, and loved with body and heart. And all the time listening for the sound of a key, listening for punishment prowling in dark corridors. Hiding from father's eye could make her squirm within its barbed confines. Yet, her body was now in maternal hands, loved and tended, and the eyes that followed hers were those of her childhood's loyal lover. His history belonged to him, but at this moment he was all for her – and that was all that mattered.

They made love. It assuaged her fears – they tried to think together what she should do.

"It must be old age. And the loss." He tried to be realistic.

"Yes, yes", but she was still certain that her father knew. He must have followed her to this flat, as he used to follow her and spy on her.

Her lover didn't contradict her – it didn't matter. Disagreements and arguments were of no significance since there was no tomorrow. This love was – not unreal, perhaps all too real, yet not anchored in yesterdays or tomorrows. Not anchored in anything other than lives lived in rare, solitary dreams and memories, unexpected memories. For that reason this interlude was hooked into their flesh more painfully than any other reality. Tomorrow, or the day after tomorrow, she would go back to the northern mists she had arrived from, that embraced other lives and loves, and slowly, not together, they would get a little older.

She was thankful to him. She gave an encompassing glance at the unmade bed, the plain room – a wistful glance at him, not as if for the last time, but as if for one of the last times. Then an embrace to last for a lifetime, and she walked down the stairs. There was a silence from the elevator descending.

15

HOUSE HOLDS

Sophia rang her at Aunt Lefki's. She had been ringing Father's flat, there was no answer. She had no idea what had happened to Dad, but no, she was not surprised. "I told you he is not in his right mind. You have to come here to discuss what we do with him." Eleni agreed to a meeting: it was difficult to fix a time, Sophia had her winter swimming and a sauna and yoga, Kaliopi was driving around the villages looking for antiques.

"Tonight then?"

"Tonight," Eleni agreed. What did her sisters know? And what did they want? What did they intend to do with him? In her anger she didn't call him Father.

On her way to Sophia's, dark thoughts cut her eyes like fine strands of cobweb on country paths. She tried to remember landscapes that had given her happiness. Olive groves, the silvery playfulness of their leaves, the intricately tormented trunks. And sunlight: that sacred sunlight that consecrates the world in clear, defined shapes and ineffable harmonies of colour and meaning.

She thought of the beauties of the world, but what her eyes saw were the black bags of garbage accumulating on the pavements, smelling of decomposition. Why did no one mention the garbage taking over the city? Was she inventing the miasma she saw hovering over their heads?

Sophia was recovering from a migraine. In her kimono she looked petite and oriental – but there was no ingratiating smile on her face. She sat back on the sofa, in a posture of agile sensuousness, leaning her head back with her eyes shut, as if stretching up to an invisible lover standing behind her. But there were no love embraces – no visible ones. Sophia pressed her temples on both sides. She released the pressure but kept her eyes shut. She pressed again for several seconds, then let go. The maid stood at the entrance of the living room, and asked Eleni if she wanted coffee. Eleni said "Yes", Sophia said "Tea", the maid turned back without looking at her ailing mistress. Sophia called after her to hurry with the washing up, she received back a tired nondescript sound.

"She will be the death of me," she moaned and continued her ritual massage. "Did you find any documents?" Her voice showed she expected a No; her eyes remained shut.

"What documents?" Eleni's voice sharpened, to pierce the other's blindness.

"The documents. For his pension. How can we get his pension without his birth certificate, and his ID card, and voting book. I told you, how many times do I need to tell you." Her eyes opened slowly, wearily the words clung onto sighs of desperation.

"How could I get the documents when I am locked out of the apartment!" Eleni shot at her.

"Now you know." There was victory and resignation in Sophia's voice. "Now you know how … old he is. So you had better go and find a place for him. I've had enough. I've had enough of diseases and deaths. I need to look after myself."

Eleni's anger was multiple and wordless. So many enemies, so many aims. Her mother tongue, or any tongue, was letting her down. The cause of her life-long impotence was visible, tangible, lying prostrate before her, lithe, sensuous, feline, pretending to be half dead, but preparing to leap up and pounce. Eleni sat up: Would she for once face up to her sister, or pack and go? The journey to the airport stretched before her seductively: the flight booking was in her handbag, all she needed to do was leave. As she had done before – stealing away in the dark, like a thief in the night.

She stayed sitting – arrested by the thought of her mother's will, her jewellery, her own inheritance. She wondered whether her sister knew what she knew. Was her sister giving up? Was she well? Something was eating her and her life. She herself was younger, stronger, independent. If she stayed, she might this time win.

She stayed: out of ugly inventive fascination with the sight of her sister coiling like a snake, preparing – to suddenly dart her poison, or vanish under the shrubs, go to sleep, or die.

Kaliopi arrived late full of business and exasperation. She collapsed on the chesterfield, Sophia's eyes calculated the damage. "You are about an hour late," she announced in dry exasperation.

"I had to wait for the architect, we waited for ages." No one quite believed Kaliopi, not even herself. Nevertheless she went on with the explanations, while Sophia's eyes inspected the roll of paper.

"Have you got the plans?"

Kaliopi was in no hurry.

Sophia sat up, folded her kimono around her and stretched out towards the plans. "Let me see." Kaliopi with automatic obedience started unrolling the plans.

They were the planned alterations for the old monastic farm Kaliopi and her husband were buying. A true find. A unique investment. They had borrowed money, bargained, but now this ancient home of prayer and contemplation belonged to them. To do as they liked – with enough money they could turn it into a villa, a Macedonian *archondikon*, a *palazzo*. It was only a matter of money, and their own incalculable wishes.

Sophia, revived, tensed her body with aim. She had put in a bid for it, but she was not quick enough, and they didn't have so much cash available, the villa in Marmara was devouring their capital.

They sat near each other studying the plans. They had a good eye for bargains and investments, they were quick. Eleni could see what brought them together – a shared avarice, for money, property, things.

Eleni stayed apart, but knew she was with them, one of them. She could not compete, but shared this passion of acquisition. It could unite them in love, but only brought war. Perhaps the cause was a common loss. Perhaps their greed was for a more remote, mystical unnamed prey.

"What are these arches?" Sophia was uncoiling.

"They are arches. We are not going to live in monks' cells. We are knocking down walls and replacing them with arches!" Kaliopi repaid contempt with contempt.

"You mean you are turning a monastery into a Mykonos villa? Are you so ignorant? Are there no planning regulations? Is this man an architect?" Sophia sat back in quiet convalescent readiness.

"We told him to include arches. We wanted large spaces, open plan. Full of air and light."

"Then you should have built an island villa. Cheaper, easier. Instead of demolishing a medieval monastery. It's probably a listed building anyway, and most likely you cannot touch it!"

That was a blow to Kaliopi. "And who is going to know? Who is coming to check what walls we knock down, and what arches we raise." But her new home already felt insecure and she could not rest in peace under her as yet un-erected arches.

Determined to have the last word she produced from her bag a jumble of utensils, candlesticks, engraved plates, an incense burner, a pestle and mortar. They were black and dirty, but Kaliopi rubbed them with rage and faith, until the brass and silver shone pure and bright. Pieces from who knows what broken household or church, destined to make up little by little Kaliopi's new home.

Eleni was moved by her sister's labour – she briefly loved her. Their war, like all wars – she speculated with sorrow for all three – was for a manufactured home, a place of beauty, goodness and peace that did not exist, and for which they sacrificed any peace, beauty and goodness they ever had.

"So he locked you out." Kaliopi dumped on Eleni whatever attack came her way from Sophia: this was the family law and ritual.

Eleni indicated almost a yes with her silence, perhaps a no, perhaps nothing. She did not want to admit, to her sisters' ultimate triumph, that her life-long ally had turned against her. Or that he was indeed going senile – which would prove them right all along. Either way, this turn of events was their victory, and she would not articulate the words that confirmed it. In any case she was not going to get sympathy from them, nor did she want it, nor would she stand to gain anything from an alliance with them.

Eleni admitted to herself that she feared her older sisters. She feared them especially when they were together. Because they had already occupied their ground long before she arrived, and the arrival of a newcomer brought them together into a precarious alliance. In all three an infernal futile anger was simmering, rooted perhaps in the forgotten or half forgotten past. All three were caught in a triangle, that stretched its lines and angles to them at whatever distance. But now the remnant of home and family kept them pinned in one place locked in a vicious geometry. Until, when home and family finally went, the three sides might drift apart in peace and forgetfulness.

"I've taken him to a doctor already – a well known psychiatrist – there is no doubt –" Sophia tossed this information at them with superior brevity.

"And who gave you the right to act on your own?" Kaliopi would pay her back.

"There is no doubt of what?" Eleni insisted.

"You had disappeared to your monastery, I was not going to wait for you for ever."

"What is there no doubt of?" Eleni repeated.

"That he is senile, and that he should be put into a home."

"Who is this doctor? What is his name?"

"Apostolou, Michalis Apostolou.

"Ah, Tryphon's old school friend."

Kaliopi did not seem to approve, but she stayed silent. Eleni wondered if she could draw her to her side.

"Yes, Tryphon's school friend. And one of the best psychiatrists in Thessaloniki."

Eleni's vengeance against her father melted. Only plain pity – for an old man, in ignorance, at a loss, being asked by a stranger irrelevant questions. Not knowing whether this was a friendly casual visit, a visit that might heal him. Or was it a trap? An old man talked to as if he were a child, an imbecile. She imagined the doctor's voice, loud, artificially pleasant. She imagined her sister's voice, impatient, hard. Yet Sophia's voice had in her youth been stopped and muffled by that same old man. And she had been humiliated by this same man, their father, when he shouted at her, then no more than a girl of seventeen - "You think he wants you for your beauty? He wants you for your dowry!"

But what tyranny merited this! Eleni knew, they all knew, the pain he could inflict. Her own mind was bruised by his sudden violence, appearing and vanishing for no reason, or for reasons mysterious and obscure. Her own voice had been made hoarse and choked in its sound, words swallowing words – till she spat out mother tongue and father tongue. But no father, even a tyrant, merited this. And from a daughter.

"So your friend proved your father senile? How long did it take him?" Eleni's voice cracked, the crack an abyss of anger. And where was her voice now, and the string of words to wrap round her sister's delicate neck?

"Show us this doctor's report, then." Kaliopi still took no side.

"There is no report. He wants to see him again."

So perhaps Sophia was bluffing. Perhaps Dad had answered the questions and passed the test. Perhaps it is not so easy to lock people up, after all. Or is it? It had been so easy for their father to lock them up in a room. He took down the icons, made them kiss them and vow to tell the truth: swear to the Virgin that they were virgins. His power had shaped the world for her, for all three of them, and had decided the order of things. Their father had the key, and he turned it to lock the world in or out.

"In any case I even found a home for him. A nice home." Sophia was tired, defeated by her own successes.

"An old people's home." Eleni wanted this confirmed. Her voice was quiet. "We get our father out of his home, in order to have him locked up in a 'home'."

In confirmation, a long dark silence settled in the room reverberating with guilt and sorrow.

16

THE SOLACE OF PATTERNS

The word "home" entangled her, as always, in strong cutting strands. It was perhaps the plain orderliness which the word "home" promised, and betrayed, that created such disorder. She walked round a town that used to be home, confronting at each turn her father locking her out of home yet now losing his own home.

The word, she had learned at school, extended far back to Aeschylus' large and terrible word 'oikos' – encompassing the blood-stained house of Atrides, whose curse stretched backwards to wars and unnatural sacrifices, and forward to the Furies.

She walked without aim or destination along the waterfront, and sat at a café, a familiar place, that had been there as long as she remembered. It had a spacious, high-ceilinged room in a simple neo-classical style. The decoration plain, the proportions good, the tall windows allowing plenty of light. It can be such a seductive disease, nostalgia! Its symptoms a way of life.

Sipping her coffee in the silent square room, she stopped. Stopped the scheming and suspecting, the coming and going back and forth. She allowed herself to retreat, to assemble – between sips – the secretive, ancient geometry that was her refuge. The regular squareness of this room, and any other room, held for her an original meaning of home: straight-lined, orderly, peaceful. Its lines parallel, its angles equal, no room for war. It was the shape that she carried with her. No divine circles or eternal triangles. Perhaps it lived in dreams, or childhood memories, in thoughts that exist in patterns. For some people they may exist in colours. Perhaps it was the shape of a bare ceiling coming into its own life in the infant's slowly registering eyes.

In idle sorrow, she imagined an infant lying, without reason or words, in a family room or parents' bedroom, staring for a short eternity at a ceiling: empty, orderly, probably white, registering her hunger, satisfaction, discomfort – the infinite field of slowly meaningful noises and sights. The quiet square shape absorbed, reflected, became home to the world.

In a child's picture, the simple square might multiply and become a room, of white walls, and blue or green windows and a door. The pencil might place it – a complete house – on a mountain or by the sea, under a blue sky and a Greek sun. Adding no voices, and no sounds. Or, it might stay a symmetrical courtyard, the wisteria out of bounds, the air, eluding figure and colour, heavy with scent – a transformation into brief happiness.

Equally the pencil might take out the windows and make it a room for the dead. She saw her mother in the simple square room of the cemetery, tiled sky blue from floor to ceiling. Airless, dead, it repelled her. But the room had a glass door and she contemplated herself with her mother escaping out to the sun and to the real blue where together they might – and that is where the contemplation stopped.

"All the homes you and Dad had lost, I had lost too."

Rags of a dream were suspended around her, leaving in their passage only vapours, scattering, dissolving, becoming wreaths of image and meaning. Her mother, sitting at the table with the white tablecloth draped on it – and no food. Waiting for her daughters to come, to sit at the table with her, to serve and be served. But no daughters came.

The dream had a story, so Eleni put the fragments together,

and sat down with her mother, who took out of her bag – not food – but accounts. Mountains of paper, an army of numbers, which she tried to justify laboriously to her mother, who sat indifferent. A daughter showing to the speechless Mother that she can count, and give an account. Showing the blind Mother she can read, and spell, and write. A daughter spreading her stolen treasures on the table – a dazzle of jewellery rolled out before her mother's closed eyes. She embraced her mother's knees, suddenly shrinking down, and asked to be forgiven, for everything and anything – for being alive: and her mother neither smiled nor frowned. She only sat unmoved, alone, at a table empty of food – her face made of stone.

Eleni turned away from the dream and concentrated on her coffee cup. The old café and the world outside appeared in its old familiarity: the bay, the flotsam, Mount Olympus in the distance, the dirty walls of the White Tower. A group of tourists came into the café, and sat at a nearby table examining – in a foreign language, which was English – maps of this, her own, foreign city. Eleni, the small coffee cup in her fingers, was held still on her fake velvet armchair by an absence – total, irrevocable.

The sea was taking over. Its mists arrived, eclipsing the city and its inhabitants and buildings, until they were only watery forms floating in and out of shape according to the whims of the sea. The landscape was of water and mist playing with each other, invading and becoming each other, swallowing the world and people – longed-for people – within their grey translucent element. Eleni called, but the only sound she heard was a distant fog-horn.

17

CALL ME ANTIGONE

The posters were of minimalist art, an artistic photograph of a flood in India, a women's chorus of Bacchae in Epidaurus, an African woman with a baby on her back, out-of-date announcements of law-school demonstrations, old newspaper photographs of a general strike.

The secretary apologized for the lawyer's delay. She had a good look at Eleni. "Do you live in London?"

"Cambridge. Not far away."

"I would like to come to a language school to improve my English."

Eleni told her the little she knew about language schools, the girl resumed her slow typing. Eleni leafed through old copies of the communist newspaper, *Rizospastis,* read titles on the spines of law books on the shelves, glanced at the photograph, on the lawyer's desk, of a man's large, wet-eyed face smiling to the world. She very much wanted to dust the large meaty leaves of the ficus plant and let them breath.

The lawyer came in with controlled fury, offering her abrupt excuses in a decided, low-pitched voice. She was short and stocky, her hair cut in a boyish style. She shook hands with Eleni man to man, sat behind her desk, all business, asked the assistant whether she had finished the document, turned to Eleni. "Call me Antigone," she announced. She had seen Eleni before, a familiar face, perhaps at the Party, strikes, demonstrations? She asked Eleni what she did.

The telephone rang. She gave a series of justifications, then strategies, then clarifications, then she rattled a volley of No's and hung up. She explained to Eleni she was trying to organize a lawyers' strike. In a monologue that guessed and misguessed in advance any possible response, including or discarding it, raising her voice at any semblance of utterance from Eleni's mouth – she explained the lawyers' petitions, the government's evasions, the intrigues within the committee, manned by men of course, except for her.

"They accuse me of being power driven! The phallocrats! Anyway, you said you teach, you translate – excellent, you should meet my husband. He is a poet!"

"I'd very much like to. About my father…"

"You must have seen his books in shop-windows. But not enough of them. He doesn't get enough exposure. There are networks – you know us Greeks. It's all a matter of knowing the right people. All the riff-raff are translated into English, and French, and he is gathering dust in the three local book shops. Although he has talent. True feeling. Passion.

"He gets frustrated, exasperated with reviewers and publishers. I am suing his previous publisher – because they had as good as given us their word they would do that series of stories. They said they had expected stories, short stories, not fairy-tales. They don't know how to read, the illiterates. Now we print them at our own expense, I've got copies here. Of course it costs money. It's true that friends and relatives buy them, and we recoup something.

" No, no, I am giving them to you. All I want is for you to read them and tell me frankly what you think. It is great poetry. Every time he hears of someone getting translated or winning a prize he takes to his bed. He is a sensitive man,

Eleni – it is Eleni, isn't it, you don't mind if I call you by your first name. You have to meet him. You literary people understand each other."

Eleni took the three copies she was offered with gratitude, promising she would read them and tell her frankly... She suddenly felt tired, it was almost noon. She wondered whether she was being charged by the hour.

Eleni started telling her about the case, her father, her sisters, uncertain as to what she wanted from a lawyer, whether it was a lawyer she wanted. The lawyer took notes, negotiated a yawn which finally broke forth, but not without distorting her face in her efforts to hold it back. Eleni raised her voice, leaned forward: in spite of appearances, she thought, this woman was right for her case. She had authority, was already exercising power over her. The voice, like a mother's voice, thundered order into the world. The mother tongue laying down the law, silencing the squabbles, squashing rebellions. "Who are these daughters who dare, over my dead body, to bargain for the soul and body of their father!" These were the words that Eleni wanted that woman opposite her to utter. She wanted her to articulate the principles of nature: to dictate the rules of a good life and a decorous death. She expected her to defend the home, house, family. How does one translate the word 'oikos', Eleni the translator mused.

"They want to put my father in a home."

Eleni expected moral horror, she got routine matter-of-factness.

"They cannot. They need your signature. Probably those of other relatives. The reports not only of one doctor, but of many, it will take them years. How old is your father?"

"I don't know, no one knows. He won't tell us his age."

The lawyer looked puzzled.

"He is over retirement age – but he won't retire."

The lawyer suddenly looked fatigued, and bored with the complications. "He will have to retire. The state owes him a pension – and businessmen get a good pension, better than others, who do proper work. He should know his rights." There was no room for disagreement.

"He still plans to do business. He owns a piece of land and wants to build a hotel."

The lawyer looked contemptuous, resigned. "Entrepreneurs have ruined our country. Where is this land?"

"On Thasos. I own part of it, he had given it to me when he bought it, and now he wants it back."

"Out of the question. At his age – the old should sign over to the young rather than vice versa. He wouldn't do this to you if you were a son, would he?"

Eleni nodded with vehement agreement. At last someone was on her side – another woman, a woman with power and a sense of justice.

"He has disappeared!" She vaguely hoped this force of nature might find her father for her. "He locked me out of the flat and went. He vanished."

The lawyer was oppressed by the human complications. "Is he … getting old? Senile?"

"No, no he was always like that." Eleni hastened to dispel the doubts that were quickly dismantling her case.

The lawyer examined the few documents Eleni had brought with her, death certificates, nearest relatives to the deceased. "Is your sister married to the lawyer Koumandaros?"

"Yes."

The lawyer came back to life. "Yes, yes, I'll be glad to get this case. We'll show them." She folded the papers. "Don't worry, they haven't got a case."

Eleni was relieved. The woman was interested in the case, never mind the confusion of motives and reasons.

"Your brother-in-law is trying to stop the strike. He is not interested in rights, or right and wrong. Because he charges what he likes, he does what he likes." The woman was preparing for war. "Don't worry, we have got our networks."

The Motherland was pulling Eleni deeper into her cavernous lap.

The lawyer gave Eleni a piece of paper with a list of the documents she wanted. "Contact all your relatives, get their signature certifying your father is of sane mind." She paused. "A sum of, let's say, 300 euros will be needed for preliminary enquiries. Thank you."

She pushed the money into her large handbag, like a trivial detail put out of the way, then leaned towards Eleni with significance. Her voice changed tenor, it became conspiratorial, protective. "I'd like you to meet my husband. Tomorrow when we close, around three? We'll go for an *ouzaki*." She hesitated. "When you meet him, say you have heard of him, say you know his poetry."

"Of course."

18

ORDERING THE UNIVERSE

She waited outside the door of her father's flat, wondering whether she had come to retaliate, reclaim, beg to be re-admitted. She paused before she pressed the bell, delicately – he is an old man, she said to herself, not to startle him. She pressed again, and again – to dent the dead silence.

She would not go. She obstinately stood her ground, the very ground where her fury was gathering force. This was her dead end, and starting point. She banged on the door with her fist, furious even at the futility of her fury.

The hum of the elevator stopped with a judder as if something were breaking to pieces. The door squealed open: and without turning she heard her father's quick presence. She turned to confront him.

What a little old man he was – her ally and enemy. Thin, unshaven. His eyes rheumy with age, wide open with confusion, and an ancient, inexplicable innocence. Her fists turned against herself before they fell limp.

"Ah! My child, here you are!" He was worried, distracted. He kept the elevator door open with his body. As Eleni walked towards him his face changed into various expressions of unsureness. His body bent down and stretched towards the interior of the elevator while one leg held the door.

"Come and help me, my child."

"My child!" No explanation, no apology. No regret, not even anger! She took a step and confronted a mountain of old suitcases held together with pieces of rope. She unclenched her hands and thoughts and helped him. One by one, together, they took the suitcases out of the elevator, which rocked and danced with relief. He counted them, seemed unsure whether they were all there, looked around in case more of them appeared as through an apocalypse, then started pulling and pushing them to the front door.

A door behind them creaked, the next-door neighbour peered through. An expression of absorbed curiosity.

"Ah! You are back, Mr Gregoriou! You daughter was looking for you."

Father and daughter nodded. Father continued nodding as if registering the various thoughts that ran through his mind as he looked through his pockets for his keys. Eleni observed him with accusing eyes as he unlocked the door, indifferently, giving no sign of even noticing the new lock.

They pushed the suitcases into the flat. He counted them again, had a moment of doubt, then accepted their number, and confident of his safe arrival took his jacket off.

She stood near the door preparing for the moment of confrontation that did not want to come. The dust had settled on floor and furniture, the silent staleness of the flat penetrated her being. He was indifferent to her presence, busying himself checking and rechecking his suitcases. He started lugging them one by one towards the locked room. She walked through the connected reception rooms of the flat and opened the balcony doors – the city traffic, fumes and business rushed in, to her relief. She stepped out onto the balcony to organize her thoughts and movements. She had come armed with righteous anger, and he presented no defence, not even an acknowledgement. He didn't even ask about the jewellery.

"Make us some coffee, my child!" He was trying his keys on the locked room.

The casual life-long authority disarmed her. Out of life-long obedience, she made the coffee – in the midst of unwashed dishes and half-eaten mouldy yoghurt tubs. Her mother's apron was on the floor, the tea towels were soiled. She heard him pottering about, took the coffee to the living room. He took his cup, oblivious, she sat opposite him. He sipped his coffee: and the innocent sipping noise was magnified into the sound of insufferable indifference, and self-gratification.

"Why did you lock me out? Why?" she shrieked – her voice cracked into fragments of hushed complaint.

He was startled. He stared, first bewildered, then angry, unsure how to deliver his paternal wrath.

She remained, confronting the domestic Pantocrator, harsh, wily, lurking behind that folded-in face and collapsed jaws, masquerading as an old man.

"Why did you lock me out?" Her voice grated with indignity – and, in spite of herself, complaint: "Why? Your own child?" And once again defeated by the native sound for child, *pethi,* and the tangle of instant and distant sentiments, she broke into tears.

He looked dazed, lost in her question. "I did? I did!" Musing with a wonder of frowning realization at anyone committing such an extraordinary act.

"You did, you locked me out, out of my own home! You cast out your own child!" Her voice had reached a pitch of young accusation: childhood broke out like an ancient disease, and she was seized by its fever.

"My mother dead only days, and you shut me out." She was on her feet. "But she is watching you!" The world her tragic stage, the domestic jumble a heap for pity and wonder; and she its high priestess and black fury, chorus and protagonist in sorrow and vengeance. She raised her arm and pointed at the innocent blue sky and at the unforgiving heaven.

She was herself subject to the spirits and powers she was calling, imprisoned in the instant domestic theology – the mixed-up

Christian and idolatrous universe of fear that had shaped her young soul. She knew the shrill thrills of the familiar rhetoric. "She sees every movement you make. Casting your child out! My mother is watching you." Her utterances were slow, each word a blow, each breath a threat. Each gesture conjuring ghosts of retribution from an ancient past.

The lids of his eyes had opened wide, his pupils retreated.

She walked to the door, sensible of her power. Out on the street she took a deep breath to centre herself, then followed the avenue, a river of business and noise that led to the sea.

Inhabitants of cities by the sea, in difficulty, naturally run to the sea front. The divide between land and water is a palpable, audible, painterly boundary – perhaps of a life, or a world, or whatever one's eyes in contemplation or despair wish it to be. The sharp mirror face of unruly thoughts.

Dwellers and frequenters of harbours may at times see themselves like small creatures living and moving on the brink of the embrace of large mysterious elements. The bay of Thermaikos had been petrified in two pointed promontories in its redoubled effort to encircle and contain the sea. But the view of that elemental lovehold, supervised by Mount Olympus and lit into dark splendour by the setting sun, was such sensational stagecraft, it made you suspect the designs of a god.

Gregoris nodded, as if in thoughtful calculation of his position, in partial cautious agreement, in dawning understanding of the world's point of view. He sat down to take stock of the situation – the lack of respect, the rebellion, the sudden fury. And from a daughter! He gathered his brow – but the face of paternal anger dissolved into tremulous bewilderment. Her words, with such ugly portent, travelled through the emptiness of the rooms filling with their intention the silence. The silence – it was full of gathering presences.

He got up and searched the room, trying to remember what

he was about to do. He walked to the table, looked, puzzled, at the dusty documents, walked to his bedroom, looked at his wife's made bed, a dressing gown on it, an old newspaper. He went to the kitchen and had a drink of water – the dirty coffee cups were on a small brass tray. On the way back to the living room he stumbled on his dishevelled suitcases, slumped mutely into their own sprawling weight outside his locked storeroom. His face brightened – he knew he had forgotten something, he couldn't remember what he had forgotten. The wreckage of leather, cardboard and rope at his feet held the answer to whatever questions worried him.

He started the routine search for his keys with new purpose: soon the excitement turned into the anxiety of a person looking for the key to life. His trouser pockets, then his jacket pockets, then his briefcase – he found his handkerchief, blew his nose with frightened fury – back to his jacket, around the flat – the keys were lying on the table.

"So here they are, the scoundrels!" He shared his relief with the keys, which, for all their misleading dead metallic inertia, became animate with benevolence and co-operative willingness. They were brought to life by the sheer desire of their owner to communicate with someone or something his short-lived triumph – in finding something. And to communicate his fear – the constant fear of losing, losing things, losing people, losing his memory, losing the very foothold on the world, the handhold of himself. He held his own, compliant and constant keys almost with paternal affection. His storeroom, and his life's contents kept in it, his mutable life and unquiet self were once again his.

Now all he had to do was unpack his suitcases – and pack them again, because he had to sell this merchandise, he had to get out, to the villages, the islands – and sell. "I have to go to Thasos," he announced decisively, to himself, as if he had not just returned from Thasos. "I'll have to re-organise the lot. Fold them up, wrap them in cellophane – presentation is all."

He started dragging the suitcases – at their last gasp – to the living room. They were heavy, he was tired. He sat down, looked around him, expecting someone to appear and give him help. He looked towards the kitchen – might someone bring him some water, or food? He made another effort, and dragged and pushed the rest of the cases. They were all there now, so he started unlocking them one by one. An outburst of plastic, cloth, age and thwarted effort. A jumble of clothes scattered and filled the floor – crumpled shirts for men, head-scarves, swimsuits for women. "We have to put these in some order," he told himself, loud and clear. "We have to put the place in order. Put our thoughts in order." We? Did he not need a companion in this difficult job? Was this the plural of loneliness? "First things first. No need to hurry." Words of advice to the man who hurried all his life. Words of perseverance, held in the light, holding the thread of his failing memory and holding together a faltering life.

The silence was palpable. So palpable, it created shapes and voices that moved and teased and tormented.

A mountain of rags had filled the room – rags he had taken hours to cram into suitcases, and days to drag to remote places to sell. How long would it take to start all over again! He sat pensively before the monument to his defeated and indomitable desires. He held his head, trying to collect his thoughts, decide on his actions. Suddenly he looked up, imploring, at someone in the room. She was there. She was there to help him.

But she was silent. Yet she was there, watchful, and silent. "She is there watching you! Locking out your child, and my mother dead only days!" His daughter's words settled like dust through the silence, clogging the mind. The room heavy with fate, alive with ghosts, dark with accusations – and from a daughter's mouth!

Why had he locked her out? He *had* locked her out, he remembered distinctly. But why? Was it her he locked out? Or was it the thieves? "There are thieves. They have their own keys, and come and go as they like, and steal things." He got up and walked decisively to the door, checked the new lock, opened it,

shut it again. He smiled mischievously. "That will teach them."
He was safe. He walked back to the living room, the dark furniture was a heavy dead mass: weighing down on him, on his
troubled mind.

His words made Anastasia's presence plausible. She was there –
or whom was he talking to? And her silence was her answer.
She would go silent when she was angry, she would sulk. A
Macedonian trait. He was not like that. He shouted, banged doors,
raised his hand. Then the storm passed, he felt good, he asked for
forgiveness, he brought her delicacies. "But, Anastasia, you sulk.
You shut yourself in the room. For days. You make me pay."

He could hear the anger in her silence, he could feel her eyes
on him. "She is angry" he mumbled, pensively. He sat down, the
jumble at his feet. The silence towered over him like an avenging
mother, its wings flapping over him protecting her child – who
is the child?

The rooms should be full of girls' voices. What happened?
Why did they grow into these women? Where are they?

He knelt down and picked up a piece of cloth – a man's tie.
He let it hang over his hand, examined it, folded it and put it
aside. He picked up another and another one. He would look at
them and fold them as he mumbled comments – "This comes
from the *Nea Smyrni* shop, this from his very first shop, this..."
He didn't remember, but his hands found comfort in the touch
of the fine cloth. And his words, translating his secret confusion
into clear sounds, helped put his thoughts in order. Slowly he
created a small neat corner in a disorderly universe. Through his
finger-tips he felt the hem of an infinite, rich and varied fabric,
weaving into itself lost lands and forgotten languages: and he
received confirmation that not all was lost. His numbers carefully
led to a sum, words followed a line of thought, a thread of life,
landed on an island of memory, startled him with a wish. They
created sounds, and alleviated the loneliness. He lay down,
dressed, on his unmade bed, and covered his eyes with his arm.

*

When he opened his eyes he couldn't tell whether he had slept, or dreamt. Fragments of a life, his own, yet distant, blinked past him – too quick for him to hold onto them. As he stretched his mind and arm, souls vanished into a surf of fantasy and wishfulness. His mother, Sophia, young and dark-skinned, (or was it his daughter?) out in the sun hanging out the washing. Sheets, pure white, flapped in the breeze; their crisp sound, each ripple a blessing, signalled unadulterated happiness. The line carrying those banners of peace continued without end – far beyond the walled courtyard, of his home in Asia Minor, which after a lifelong oblivion he recalled. The sun was blinding, the sky white with heat, bearing down on the world. Then behind him as he ran away the fire, in the cornfields, on the threshing floors, consuming bodies dead and alive, consuming the world, family, memory. The snow-flakes of ash blew up and hid the sun, leaving ineradicable black shadows on everything they touched. His horse drinking water from the village pond – the clean, starched-white merchandise danced fitfully on the animal's back, as he looked at the girls. A village in Northern Greece, yet his mother, dead, stood by him, his bride: with Anastasia's name and his daughter's, Sophia's, face. A photograph of his father with shaven head and unshaven face, ill and haggard, back from the *amele tabour* – but he never came back from the *amele tabour*. Images and more images, torn from his sight with the first trembling of his eyelids, and noise in or out of the room. He got up, stood for a few moments undecided, forgetting what he was about to do, where he was, who he was.

The sound of the doorbell was his salvation. He moved to the door – to yet another question, or to the answer to all his questions. A woman behind it, daughter, wife, mother, daughter? Regret filled his head, then the memory of a lock. And loneliness, an endless sea of loneliness rushed in washing over his life.

19

ABSOLUTION

"My child." He was surprised at her very existence.

Eleni stood as if she had come to the wrong door. The tyrant, the broker of power, had been spirited away: and all that remained in her empty hands was a small, exhausted old man, lost, amazed, at her, at the world. His hair was untidy, his clothes crumpled: his eyes, dazed behind a fine milky mist through which an intense small centre pierced. He had a look of a profound wondering sorrow – perhaps for the inexplicable cruel turns of life.

She came in, shut the door behind her, and walked through the living room to the balcony door. He followed her, undecided, but always closely watching her. He sat down, small in a large armchair, his eyes resting on her, waiting.

"I'll make us some coffee," she said, in order to escape.

"Yes, yes, a cup of coffee." He clutched on it with vehement enthusiasm. So good to have a woman around the house. "And some water, my child. A glass of cold water."

As his arms stretched towards her she tried to step away, but his arms came up to her, like the arms of a child, surrounded her waist, and kept her there. The universe seemed to fall in revulsion – and she could do nothing but fall endlessly with it. Yet she remained standing over him where he sat, his head resting on her belly. She did not know whether he felt her shudder at this unnatural embrace. Whether he understood or not, whether she misunderstood, the dreadful perception lasted a lasting moment – and then the world was restored as she felt an old father crumpling into an old child begging her, tears in his voice – "Forgive me, my child. I didn't want to shut you out. How could I have done such a thing!"

And she, weakened by this act that gave her unnatural power over her father, could not move away, although his arms now were falling from her body. She could not move away, only her soul slipped away in cold disengagement, and her mind ran to remote translations of tragedy, in a language he could not understand. The old age of King Lear had travelled lands and languages and in the body of this remote brother, ignorant of the poetry and language, was heaped at her feet.

Won over by pity, and by the betrayal of language and parent, she sat and listened, as he tried to explain what had moved him to such anger, to such an unfatherly deed. All the time staring at the pity and bitter fragility of "father".

"It was not me! My mind, my mind is so tired these days!" He held his temples, as if trying to keep his head and thoughts together.

"I have lost so many things!" He looked at her, wanting to reassure himself that she was his daughter. Then, as if only then, he remembered his wife that he had lost. "I have lost my wife, the companion of my life." She took his hands into her own, for a moment they were together in bereavement. "Do you think she is watching us?" he asked in suspicious wonder. She reflected back the question. For a moment they sat there still, under her gaze.

He felt better, got up decisively – "Time to go to business." She followed him to the next room: and there lay his fabricated shop, his portable home in tatters. The suitcases, stretched and bent and torn to accommodate his needs, greeds and eccentricities, gaped empty handed, empty headed.

She didn't know what his eyes saw. She saw dirty jumble. Pieces of cloth, remnants from his shop that he must have secretly rescued when he had to shut shop and life – and stop being a merchant. Except that he never stopped being a merchant. He was at home amongst the broken suitcases ordering and reordering his merchandise. In vain ordering and reordering his thoughts – in a universe now of permanent disorder. He was talking to himself, perhaps to her. He took out and spread on the floor beach towels, beach shoes with carnivorous flowers stuck on them, swimming caps with atrocious ornaments melting into each other. Where were the customers for this assortment of femininity?

As if he just remembered something important, he disappeared into his room, where she heard him move boxes, suitcases, furniture.

He appeared holding triumphantly a lady's swimsuit, a wire-stiffened, elasticated one-piece swimsuit, smelling of rubber, and dust.

His eyes were bright with the discovery, and with the absolution of sins. He playfully tossed the swimsuit onto her lap, as he used to when he came home from the shop with a toy for her. "A present!" he said. with playful largesse, expecting a show of thanks and cajolements. Eleni accepted with due coyness the Esther Williams relic.

He made her say how much she liked the bathing suit, and wasn't it a pity she couldn't wear it in England, but she could wear it in Greece, if she stayed till the summer. He wanted to make her say she would stay, with him, in this home that was dying before her very eyes. Stay and be a partner to a kingdom of rags! The two of them travelling over mountains and along coasts, exhibiting a merchandise of memories and thwarted wishes that no one wanted. She thought she heard him saying to her, "Stay home and be my daughter."

"Dad, you are not going out with those suitcases again?"

He rubbed his hand, permanently closed, and looked at his merchandise. "They are very heavy. But I have to work. I have to earn my bread." He shook his head again, making sure she understood the depth of meaning in these words.

"But dad, you said you'd stop." She was stopped by the utter impatience in his face and body at the degree of her ignorance and foolishness.

"No, my child. The customer doesn't come to us any longer. We have to go to the customer. If I don't go, others will."

"But your pension —"

"Too many words! Listen to me, Eleni. In this business, there's nothing like personal contact. The face speaks for itself."

"At your age!" she could only say.

"I can't let them down. They've been my customers for years. They wait for me to come. And anyway that's how I started, that's how I'll end. I was known — up to the Bulgarian border!" His spirits revived, there was a sing-song in his voice, and a smile of mischievous satisfaction on his face. "I was known, especially to the housewives!" The liquid in his eyes seemed momentarily like the sparkle of youth.

"You promised to get your pension. You don't need to drag all these things from village to village. Businessmen's pensions are very good these days, dad."

He got up. "Let us not discuss foolish things. I have work to do."

"Dad, you will take your pension. You will still travel, visit your old customers and friends. But with money in your pocket, like a gentleman."

"We have talked too much. About matters that do not concern us. We have work to do."

She recognized the accusatory plural of paternal anger.

He walked away, she followed him. She followed him to his store room — the door unlocked, negligently open, exposing its moth-eaten time-eaten secrets to the world. Its dark mouth, artificially lit by a naked light-bulb, revealed impotent desires buried in the silence of dust. The moth had inherited the earth, and in his dark kingdom was feasting on her father's life.

As he rummaged, its entrails were spilling out, and soon the place was transformed into the dirty ghost of a bazaar.

"About that land, my child" – his eyes bright again with greed and bewilderment, his gaze fixed on beauties outside that room.

"Land, what land, Dad?"

"Our land, my child. The land that I had bought, on the island."

Eleni felt him tip-toeing around her once more, sniffing the air for the main chance. His hungry being was lithe and alert, testing the ground, watching for her responses. His eyes had recovered their youthful, transparent, almost innocent shrewdness. His thin body was stretching towards an object of desire, he flexed his damaged hand. She recognised her eternal father in this obsessed old man. His regrets and new promises of love were real. His selfishness and greed were also real, and they restored the shrewd unpredictable merchant she had always known him to be. They also restored the traits she might share with him. She would join him in this bartering game over sorrows and delusions.

She stared back innocently, uncomprehending, letting him spell out his meaning.

"That piece of land I gave you. Didn't we say? It is necessary now for those plans I have ..." He shook his head repeatedly to avoid further awkward explanations, and to settle the issue.

"Ah, the land you gave me. Of course, you want it back."

He nodded. "We said. It is necessary, my child. And once that land realizes its value, then both of us will be in profit."

She didn't say no, or yes.

He cleared his throat, stayed silent. And so did she.

She attended to other things while he paced nervously. She knew he wanted that land badly. She occupied herself with the washing up while he opened old folders on the dining table and started studying them absent-mindedly. He cleared his throat again, with meaning and with growing irritation. She took him a glass of water, to re-establish a contact, perhaps give him a chance to state his terms. He thanked her, busily, then attempted to say something, but stopped and went back to his papers. She started cleaning the rest of the flat, he followed her pretending he was looking for a handkerchief, a biro. She switched on the radio, after a while he switched it off.

"I'll have to go to Thasos, soon." He reminded himself – or was he talking to her?

"Why?" She wanted an opening.

"Business. I can't just sit around! There is work to be done. And there are those papers I need for the land." His voice faded into her silence. He waited, she let him wait.

"What papers?"

"The contract, my child. We had signed it, all three of us, you remember." He was unsure how to approach her.

She recognised his confused embarrassment, his transparency, his bewildered deviousness. The familiar doubting slyness. She observed his young, delicate uncertainty as to how far to go, how far to cheat himself and those he probably loved: how far to love.

"Why do you need the contract?"

The directness made him pause. "Didn't we say we would go to the solicitor?"

"Of course, of course we will."

He was relieved – but not completely. She was not forthcoming, and he was too ashamed to spell out what he wanted from her. Anastasia would not have approved of this. "Children returning their parents' gifts! Old men inheriting from daughters! This is unnatural," she would say. "And what schemes do you, an old man, have for the land, what new madness is this?" Still, he was going to insist, he knew better, and it was going to be for the good of all.

"That land.You'll only give it to me temporarily." He waited to see her reaction.

"What do you mean temporarily? You mean you'll give it back to me? Next year, or the year after?" She resumed the dusting, to seem unconcerned. She was not sure who was the cat and who the mouse in this bartering: she was not sure what the full bargain was, or might be. She would give him the land – and in return? He would retire and get his pension. He should be the winner. And herself? She could leave with good conscience. Was good conscience enough? What material thing would he give her in return? This new bait disturbed the precarious peace of duty and altruism. How come he did not miss the jewellery? Did he remember the jewellery?

"In my will I will leave it all to you! Your land, and my land, and your mother's land, and everything else!" He finally said it. It was difficult, he thought he could never utter these words but he did, and felt relieved. Merely mentioning the word "will" doesn't mean you will die tomorrow. He expected her to jump with joy. Give him the land and say thank you, thank you very much, dad. And the will? By that time – who knows … God will put out his hand. After all she is my daughter! And I cannot take it with me.

"You! A will! You will never make a will in your life. You wouldn't make a will for mother's sake. When she begged you, for her own sake and for ours – little did she know it would be useless. Dad, you are not going to make a will." But he had whetted her appetite.

"I swear on your mother's memory! Because that's what she would want me to do!"

They both almost believed his words. In any case, she shouldn't miss this opportunity. Her sisters had so much!

"So I give you the land, for now, but you retire and take your pension."

"I'll get my pension and leave everything to you in my will," he declared, with the autocrat's large gesture. Under his breath he secured the one valuable thing he wanted. "We can go to the solicitor tomorrow to get things started." His voice tired under the strain.

"I'll get the pension procedures started then." Quietly, not to disturb the temporary truce.

He did not answer.

20

PAPER DOMINION

The pension and social services offices lay at the far end of the old market centre. Eleni followed side roads leading her through the heart of the city, damaged, changed, alive. Dotted with monuments with Islamic and Hebrew and Christian Greek names, it had the pang of history and familiarity.

She followed the patterns of lives, and the rhythms of an older familiar Greece – suspecting that pieces of herself were embedded beneath those ageing buildings. She looked for the *hamam* where she went with her mother every Saturday, wondering whether it had become a theatre, a restaurant, a rubble of stones? It used to be in the middle of the market yet it was a place that allowed no noise. A place of nakedness: simple, willing or reluctant, nakedness. Of dedicated cleanliness. And a steamy watery silence.

It was still there, forgotten, keeping its water-and-light history locked away. Behind it was the Caravanserai, that used to be an inn where travellers and their horses stayed for the night, a big noisy place smelling of humanity and animals, food, and wine. Now it had become the municipal offices, a huge concrete warehouse in whose entrails the history of the city and the separate histories of each of her citizens lay hidden in countless unaccountable volumes.

She entered the dark damp labyrinths of the paper dominion of her city. With her lawyer's instructions she would have to go from office to office to secure his pension. She needed to get proofs of her father's life, his work, identity, existence. Obscurely, her own existence depended on it.

Histories were written in ancient, slowly fading ink. This was the kingdom of records: of all deaths and all lives, christenings and births, marriages and divorces. Wills, just or not, contested or forgotten, that made or destroyed lives; wills prepared in wisdom, or with envy or selfish carelessness. Wills that bestowed grudgingly. Unwilling wills as if they were willing life away. And here were buried all the debts and fines. The deeds of justice and injustice, the crimes of the state and of its citizens, punished or neglected or forgiven. Innumerable sentences passing sentence on innumerable lives. Citizens, needing a certificate of birth or faith, a proof of marital status, a stamp of political uprightness, a passport or an identity card, walked endlessly like lost souls through the arbitrary empire of paper.

With the list of tasks and documents from her lawyer, she prepared to thread the fabrics of legality, to unravel the knots and ties of her family. Starting with her father: she had to search for his identity. His actions and transactions, relatives, religion, origins.

On both sides of the entrance to the building scribes in dark threadbare suits sat upright behind their little tables, writing out application forms. They were the self-appointed guardians and morticians of an archaic language, which they had pared down to a few dead formulae that might open the gates of legitimacy. Queues of bewildered citizens waited respectfully for their turn.

She waited outside lifeless windows in long immobile queues; she waited while middle-aged, indifferent women clerks took their time measuring her up with tired curiosity; waited, while boxes of chocolates and name-day wishes were passed around; waited as the young square-shouldered and square-hipped woman got up with unwilling effort and walked with bored almost seductive slowness to the vast volumes on the shelves, with her finger traced down long lists, finally found the name, then told Eleni she needed to go back to a scribe at the entrance of the building to fill an application form requesting the said certificate.

She went down the sunless and airless stairs and joined a queue. The scribe, the great interpreter, and keeper of the immense edifice of civil life, was scholastic with the sycophantic bows of the purified Greek "obediently begging". And he was obliging as he accepted the fee and kept the change. The important paper in hand, she returned to the office, and the back of that queue. As clerks and citizens had quietly given in to the power of paper, a tired informality was settling in the room. The secretaries let their eyes follow the lists of meaningless names with somnambulist indifference, their nameless clients, defeated by too much meaning, slumped with fatalism on any available seats. An elderly, portly gentleman started delivering without warning an account of his life, the tyranny of bureaucracy, the treachery of lawyers, the frivolity of judges. He concluded with the ills of society and arbitrariness of laws. Some of the listeners shook their heads in tired agreement, or dulled amazement; another citizen took up some of the themes, with his own observations.

The room was coming to life with argument; and the discussion between the two portly philosophers reached heights and depths of meaning. But the room was silenced for the unsolvable riddles of marriage and family – as a handsome, broad-hipped woman stormed into the room. Armed with a bundle of files, she inspected the crowds waiting around desks loaded with bursting folders, and quickly homed in on a desk innocently despised by paper and people. With irresistible force the woman heaped volumes of paper and words onto the dazzled tired old lady sitting behind the desk. She talked with gesticulations accompanying the volume of voice. The explanations were lucid but the life behind them – which involved the legitimacy of her second marriage and therefore of the children from that marriage and therefore the ensuing alimony or alimonies – was much too complicated for the lady behind the desk who looked appealingly around the room. The room was hushed with attention, while the woman talked and remonstrated, and at long last waited for an answer.

The lady behind the desk finally exploded: "Ask them. How would I know? I've been waiting all day for my case, a simple certificate for my son who is in the army, and they cannot even find him in their books."

"You are not a clerk? Why didn't you tell me? Wasting my time!" The tall woman bawled her indignation to the woman behind the desk, then turned in frustration to the rest of the room and the world. "You let me give you my whole life history, to entertain you, and you finally tell me you don't even work here." She looked round the desks, shoved the papers savagely into her shopping bag and marched to her legitimate victim.

She almost tripped over three new visitors – two men and one slim tall woman between them – who ambled into the room, with slow elegant steps, as if onto a stage. The woman – in a minute mini skirt and bright make up – smiled right and left as if to a crowd of admirers, in rhythm with her studiedly sensuous movements. The air became heavy with exaggerated femininity, superfluous sexuality and cheap perfume. They asked, addressing the public in general, who was in charge of change of identity. With a coy giggle, that made her perfectly round breasts tremble, the woman added to the upright citizens' puzzled faces, "sexual identity." Her features did seem curiously large, her skin rough under the thick make-up, her large bottom provocative, as she sailed towards the far desk where a young woman clerk prepared to help. The said person, registered as Stelios, was applying – with all the necessary birth, christening and health certificates and a batch of extra documents, to be registered as Stella.

In the course of the afternoon, the public, absorbed by the physical presence of Stella, assertive and questionable, forgot their own, ordinary cases. None of the problems of life were solved, but life had taken an interesting turn: most of them would have to come back for further episodes.

Eleni finally left the building without final proof of her father's existence.

21

NEGOTIATING

She persevered, because his pension was the document on which all the other negotiations would depend. She and her father had agreed – he would get his pension and she would give him back her piece of land in Thasos. Also, it would make him independent, and his other daughters might not insist on sending him to an old people's home.

So she moved back in with him, and persevered. For days she walked up and down dead-end streets, went up and down innumerable dirty marble stairs, stumbled on bags of garbage, zigzagged round motorcycles parked on pavements – in search of a ghost. The men and women behind the desks behaved according to the whim of the moment and the mood of the day. Everything mattered and anything might make a difference. Her appearance, the expression on her face, the look of determination or of humility; whether sunlight came in through the window or not; whether the clerk behind the desk had a good or bad night. Would they play the master today, would they be the faceless face of authority, the benevolent dictator, the bent bureaucrat, the leering male, the domineering female, the macho man, the flirt? Barricaded behind desks, they dealt out indignities heaped by others onto themselves, whether in office, home, or love-nest. In this world of arbitrariness her own will and wishes did not matter: and she felt light, almost liberated, by this realization.

She told herself that she was in the world of Kafka, but without the nightmare, of Dickens without the exuberance: and this resort to fiction made her predicament bearable and universal. So she accumulated certificates, which engendered further certificates, which needed to be signed and countersigned. So that her father's life, and work, and perhaps also her own, might in the end gain legality and authenticity; and fit neatly into her handbag.

But in her travels within that melancholy geography, through the city of dead ends, the meaning of family became indistinct. She tried to re-draw its clear lines, its natural geometry. Words like father and mother and sisters must have a meaning. They must belong to a natural order and must follow laws of love, loyalty, and obedience; they must dictate duties. But that syntax of feeling, which had once been unquestioned, with her mother's death lost coherence. What are the duties to the dead, what to the living?

She planned escapes, once again, looking for refuge: into foreign lands and languages, into landscapes that would touch her more intimately even than a mother's hand or a lover's lips. There might be an anonymous, impersonal salvation in an olive grove, or endless terraces of vines; the solitary pine tree on a rock by the sea, its tortuous trunk a surviving relic of the intricacies of the wind, its roots feeding on stone and brine. The minute changes on the surface of a boundless sea. Were these the wordless call of some ancient religion, or of the unacknowledged desire to die?

Or were they images that stood out and beyond tongues; that drew her back and relieved her from foreign and native sounds? The fragments of her own native silent landscape drew her back, even from the fraught pains of the family tongue, cleansing or obliterating the long hardening familiarity. Those dreaded, obscurely loved familiars dwelling in words learned on mother's knee.

One morning she caught the bus to the cemetery – one of those ideal mornings when the sun is bright and hot, yet the breeze is fresh. She got off at the terminus, just where the countryside started, near the cemetery gates. She spent a long time by the flower stalls: scent and sight might come up with answers and decisions. At least they offered refuge, even escape. She bought a small orange tree: she had thought of buying an olive tree, symbol of peace, but the scent of the orange tree won. She would like to keep it for herself, but she did not have a home for it here. Her father would not water it after she went, because – she was registering – she was leaving, soon. She had been secretly planning it and yet she was now surprised by her decision. And once she knew it she was already leaping over boundaries, barbed wire, thousands of miles. And the small orange tree was an offering to her mother, a dedication, a gesture of regret, a sweet-scented goodbye. Hidden in its roots was a complaint.

She borrowed tools from the cemetery shed, and started working the earth. Her mind busy with explanations, with unsettled accounts, cluttered with the undistributed household and the undispensed jewellery. She put the fork aside and dug the soft earth with her hands: her fingers burrowing their way to her mother's heart speaking to her, explaining, demanding justice. With the sign language of the deaf and dumb – atoning. With fingernails full of earth spelling her penance. With her body she wanted her mother's body.

Lifting the plant, she shallowly scratched the soil to free its pot-bound roots, placed it in the hole and gently brought the earth around it. She watered the tree, then stood and admired her work. This was her libation – an amateur gardener's work offered to her life's perennial gardener. Doing penance perhaps for wanting to leave – yet she was clinging; for not wanting to mourn – yet she mourned; for stealing her jewellery, always stealing away, for letting her mother die, for surviving. She was also accusing and complaining: why did she die and leave her, in this bereavement that was eating her life? Never having now the opportunity to confront her and complain – to complain of indifferences and injustices, and of never hearing from her lips an apology or forgiveness.

A plump young priest approached and, without asking her, chanted a hasty service. He admired the newly planted tree, talked about the weather and the strikes. "Only the priests don't strike! And the dead. It would be good if the dead were on strike, but then how would we live!" He slipped the tip into his pocket and hurried towards a newly-arrived group of mourners.

She crouched at the grave's edge, her lips moving and betraying her secret thoughts. Then she wandered through the familiar labyrinths of the dead where mounds of discarded flowers and wreaths were fast wilting in the sun. Photographs of young faces smiled negligently at the black figures slumped on the ground.

The nights gave no rest. Wakeful, she was cocooned by a darkness that was alive with smells and whispers of parents. Asleep, she allowed – even invited? – dreams, endless landscapes of dreams that vanished in the daytime. But she chased them and retrieved fragments, and listened, for their life-or-death message.

She found herself lying at night on a mattress on the floor of an empty room in a strange country, which was meant to be home. She lay, watching and waiting for the door to open and her mother to walk in. Her longing was the longing for a lover, but deeper. Her mother appeared, flanked by her other two daughters, but hardly paid attention to the third daughter who lay there waiting for her mother to come. She asked her mother to lie down with her, but her mother said she was in a hurry. Then she looked at Eleni, on the floor, and hesitated, trying to remember her name. She tried Sophia, Kaliopi, till Eleni finally had to say "My name is Eleni. The name you gave me is Eleni." Her mother nodded her head in acknowledgement and walked to the end of the room and disappeared through a door that had just appeared.

In the daylight she tried to think and enumerate to herself

what crimes she must have committed to make her mother forget her own daughter's name. Acts and words she had forgotten or neglected or betrayed. She spelled out to herself her wordless confessions and locked them into the box with the jewellery. Yet no theft and no betrayal could merit such punishment.

At least there was true negotiation here. She did not lose all arguments to the total silence, the eternal righteousness of the dead. And Eleni, in a language foreign to these ancient quarrels, in a language innocent and intact, which had taken liberties with her very name – Helen it tacitly corrects, not Eleni – answered her. In a language her mother could not ever understand, the daughter answered back and accused and complained. But she was perpetually, keenly alive to the knowledge that in death her mother no longer knew her.

She carried that knowledge with her for the next days while she made plans and preparations. For her father's future, for her own departure. She was secretly saying good-bye to city and people, to her home, childhood, her own self. She spent time walking along the sea-front, entrusting her thoughts to premeditated steps. The waves carried the flotsam of the city and monotonously let it slap against the wall. Yet by some conspiracy of light that bay had the capacity to transform itself back into early ghosts of itself. In instant shots of sea-scape idylls, Eleni leaned back on embroidered cushions, rocking with the boat – her lover leaving the oars to come and sit near her, the two shapes blending in one, the warm breeze assuring them of eternal happiness. She saw herself, swinging her straw bag, taking elegant, balanced steps on the plank – knowing admiring eyes watched. The boat, taking them to the beach across the bay, was blazing with music, youth and love. She saw herself, too little to jump into the boat, holding a hand, lifted up by her father, with ease and gusto, and exuberant cries of triumphant play and fear, and deposited in the boat that threatened to turn over yet never did. The sea had a way of washing clean the memories of that city.

It had a way of soothing and comforting, and smoothing the edges of her decisions. She would settle affairs, and say good-bye without regrets – it was time to go.

In the small hours of the night, and out of the blue, the blue of the sea and of the early day, another dream wrapped her in its misty impossibilities. The bay was receding, and the sea, that nurtures memories and wishes, was advancing inland, reaching her, reaching her and the bed she was lying on, and the child – how was this possible? – she was holding in her arms. She was holding a young girl, swaddling her securely and thoroughly till she was an immobile little doll of a girl, whom she held up and was ready to throw into the sea. At the last moment she thought she would undo the end of the band that wound round the young body, to allow her to swim. It might be her daughter, it might be herself. And as the dream concurred with the dreamer, and turned into a good dream, the little girl called back from the sea – wasn't she too young to talk? "I'll get rid of these swaddling bands, and swim, and when I reach the shore I'll go for a run and I'll be free from you." The young girl swam and freely ran out on the other shore, and out of the dream, and that was her revenge against the dreamer. And out of the story, and that was her revenge against the storyteller.

She was not sure who the girl was, who the dreamer, both of them negotiating their freedom from different shores. The sight and sound of scissors cutting the swaddling band, and the feeling that something had been cut off, held her.

Eleni lay in the dark. The dreamer would not give up. The obstinate imagination sought the illusive object of the dream, and found her, in the shallows where water is moving sunlight, her body naked and made of light, only a little denser, submerged but not drowned, waving like sea-weed – fish of all sizes swimming in elegant symmetry like a moving scintillating frame to this curious, alive and fortunate sea-vessel.

The naked girl half in half out of the water, part flesh part light, moved and danced in the iridescent liquid surface stretching her arms up in the air embracing a body, of a man or a woman, it was not clear, that vanished into thin sun-lit air. Did she, in the dark wordless depths of her being, wish, now that her mother was dead, to die? Or was this – something she did not dare acknowledge – the sight of freedom and an unacknowledged happiness?

22

BARTERING OF SOULS

She spread an array of documents on the table – her father paid scant attention. All they needed was his signature, and the pension would start next month. He nodded, cleared his throat and disappeared into his room. He came and went without touching them, hardly looking at them. Eleni waited, as the world closed in on both of them. They watched each other's movements with apprehension, each trying to outguess and outwit the other. Sophia and Kaliopi had temporarily withdrawn, Eleni tried to guess what their new tactic might be. Sophia had probably bought off Kaliopi, or they might be talking to the relatives? It wouldn't be difficult for Sophia to persuade them. Gregoris was no blood relative after all, a refugee, and anyway he was getting old – a problem. Eleni rehearsed the family conspiracy that might decide her father's fate. The thought that the relatives, greedy and superstitious, might have power over her father's life was intolerable to her.

And who gave her the right to be sole arbiter? But she feared her sisters and she feared their silence; and the documents on the table gathered dust. She decided to approach the relatives.

Her father came unwillingly. His wife's sister was a good woman, but her husband! "Rodolfo Valentino!" He spat the words with an explosion of contempt.

Aunt and uncle were welcoming, Eleni was the good niece, Father shook his head with sour acknowledgement. These people had been his courtiers when he was rich, and now the bank clerk poses in his silk pyjamas and velvet housecoat. Father spat in his handkerchief, which he folded and put in his pocket.

Uncle was sitting in his armchair, placed next to the balcony doors so that he could both enjoy the view of the Trade Fair and also face the elderly lady sitting primly on the divan. Aunt Lefki attended busily to her husband and her guest. Uncle stayed sitting when the new guests appeared, indicating both superiority and indisposition. He carried his laziness with grandeur, and enacted his perennial indefinite invalidity with well-groomed, well-fed aloofness. He explained that it was rather chilly on the balcony, but he could not part from this privileged view of the Fair. He was privileged, and he was fortunate. The elderly lady duly agreed. Aunt Lefki sweetly explained that he felt chilly because he led a sedentary life.

"It is all your fault for spoiling me."

The elderly lady smiled obligingly at the coy endearments.

Father raised his brows to Eleni, he looked around the room, bored and irritated.

Uncle had been the *jeune premier* in his youth. The brillantined hair glued to his scalp, the swooning eyes, the *carte postale* smile and coy slant of the head. A priest's son, he was ever ready to expound on family morality, always presenting his own family as the prime example. His best moments were when he chanted in his father's church: all eyes fed on his beauty, all ears on his nasal music. He liked to describe how enthralled his wife had been. "And she was speechless when she first set eyes on me in my naval uniform!" His eyes became liquid with the contemplation of his beauty and youth. Now his body had thickened, his stomach and belly were big, his complexion sallow, his eyes apathetic. His hair was thin and grey, but still all the hairs were in place for the afternoon visits. Today the atmosphere was primly moral, since the other visitor, uncle's sister, was a leading light in the Christian Circle.

"So how is Sunday school, Mrs Violeta?" Father asked with playful sarcasm. She was a slim elegantly dressed woman with faded blue eyes and grey blond hair.

Everyone in the room, even Eleni, knew of Mrs Violeta's legendary youth. "Lively!" The less lively and less beautiful wives raised eye-brows over their embroideries or a good hand of cards. "First that Italian, what was his name, Paolo. Then the Greek officer, then ... how can we remember them all!" The stitches were counted, eyes were raised, the embroidery was put aside, and the details of Violeta's life were rehearsed and recounted.

Eleni remembered her as a beautiful young woman, elegant, flirtatious, surrounded by admirers, invited to dances. Then she got married, to a much older rich man, who died. Violeta forsook the merry world and became a Christian. She was beautiful still in her widow's black, Bible in hand, money in the bank, and a serious, modest expression on her face. "Saint Violeta!" the embroiderers remarked, as they pushed the needle into the cloth. "A merry widow!" the bridge-players intoned.

Violeta's social life broadened as she organized Christian Circle meetings, visits to the city's Sunday schools and hospitals, charity balls. Uncle, her elder brother, approved, was almost inspired.

"Sunday schools are thriving, Mr Gregori. But I have a complaint against you, because you haven't shown up at any of our bereavement meetings." She was coy, flirtatious.

Father shook his head dismissively. "With my loss and sorrow, you think I have time for your 'circles'!"

"But that's what our bereavement sessions are for." Violeta was fired with enthusiasm.

Father looked at her in utter incomprehension. He shook his head as if contemplating with pity the extent of her folly. "I have a lot of business. Too much on my plate. Too much sorrow, too much loss."

Uncle looked at his sister with shared agreement that Gregoris was beyond salvation. She smiled back with tolerant benevolence.

"But my heart is at peace that we were there during Anastasia's illness and talked to her about the Kingdom of Heaven and God's glorious welcome for her soul."

Father shook his head at her, threateningly. Eleni thought, mother dribbled out your holy communion because she could not swallow. And she could not hear or speak, or know, and that was a blessing.

Eleni had witnessed that preposterous communion. She remembered her father being elbowed aside by the saintly women breaking into the quiet despair of this room of interminable illness, interrupting the long wordless interminable pleas of a wife, and mother barely – of a bare soul.

Eleni had retreated to a corner of the hospital room, away from the evangelical invasion. Without permission her body trembled, her face fell into a spasm of smiling, she coughed into a laugh. She was shaken by involuntary laughter at the desperate futility, the pretence that what remained of her mother understood, or responded to the mysteries enacted for her sake. Her mother, Eleni knew, had not wanted – while she still held onto anything resembling a will or wish – salvation. Because in the depths of her heart – while that heart knew why it still was beating – she did not want to die. She had not wanted those standing helplessly around her to save her soul, but to heal her body and take her home. She wanted home. And the last words she could utter before she stopped speaking altogether was home, take me home. When she could utter no words, and all night and all day she simply moaned, and no one knew why, Eleni knew that she was trying to moan her way home.

That laughter was her own body's convulsive revulsion against death, which had only half appropriated the living body lying before her – having smothered mind, nerves, faculties, but still allowing a heart to beat. And still allowing the terrifying question

in everyone's mind: Is there a consciousness within that immobile, unable body? Does she feel pain under that flesh that
doctors and nurses, discarding painkillers and anaesthetics, treated
as if already dead and unfeeling? Did her mother know death
was daily devouring her body?

While the ritual of salvation proceeded, Eleni dragged her
steps outside the room, and, leaning helpless against the wall, to
the bewilderment of nurses or wandering patients, she laughed.
Sophia came out and scolded her with contempt, then horror,
and Eleni didn't know how the laughter turned to a quiet stifled
wail – the sound of her own feeble frightened heart. So she
never took her mother home. Instead she whispered her good-
byes early one dark morning, and flew home.

"I'm sure our words spoke to her heart," Violeta insisted, her
brother with a benevolent nod gave her his blessing.

Gregoris blew his nose. "I say let people die in peace."

Aunt Lefki brightly changed the subject.

"We haven't even told them the news about our grandson,
Anaximenis!"

"Ah! The pride of the family!" Uncle appropriated the subject for himself, because all matters pertaining to family
achievements and morals, or cultural issues, were his domain, and
Aunt Lefki, who like her sister Anastasia had not even finished
the Demotikon School, always deferred to her husband's superior education and upbringing.

"He is of such superior mind and ability, and especially moral
standing, that we will send him to study in England! You hear,
Eleni, we are sending you our Menis, and we expect you to provide guidance!" Uncle had launched into a eulogizing delivery
in purified, *katharevousa* Greek. He gave them the scholastic history of the family's "rare offspring", his teachers' panegyric.
Greek universities were not good enough, and indeed had
proved their short-sightedness in not opening their wide
embrace to him.

"Good-bye." Father was already at the door, and before

anyone could say "good-bye" or "stay", without rancour or impatience, he shut it behind him. Eleni knew her father's sudden exits. When he wanted to go he went, when his brother-in-law bored him he went, when his son-in-law repulsed him he went, when he wanted to avoid something he went, or simply when he preferred to be somewhere else, he went.

Eleni stayed, and with sinking heart she listened to her uncle's peroration. She had taken relatives and relatives of relatives to hospitals around England, for heart troubles, stomach troubles, hair transplants, prostate operations, infertility. She had been asked to translate, justify and give hope to doctors' reports; to have long telephone conversations with total strangers, patients recuperating lonely and bewildered in English hospitals, who needed to complain about the English weather, the English accent, English prices: and who, in the anonymity of a foreign land and the meaningless hum of the foreign tongue, needed to open their hearts to a stranger in the healing music of the mother tongue.

"Where is he going?" She asked as flatly as she could.

"Precisely!" Her uncle was triumphant. "That is where the good Lord has intervened! It is, my beloved niece, your duty to your beloved aunt and uncle to expend your good will and warm interest, to introduce our grandson to the most distinguished school for the science of tourism."

She thought, and wondered, and finally admitted she didn't know any universities that taught tourism – but she promised to look into it.

Indefinitely, vaguely, she made gestures, half-hearted noises, she said no to nothing, nor a definite yes to anything. She waited for her chance.

She stayed till the elegant Mrs Violeta left, then went straight to the point.

"Sophia is trying to put Father under court order." She waited to see their reaction. They did not seem shocked, or even surprised. She wondered if Sophia had already talked to them,

secured their agreement. "She is trying to declare him senile –
she has already taken him to a doctor, a friend of theirs – and
with the court order she proposes to handle his property and
income herself."

They made small noises of acceptance, or disapproval. "Of
course, he is not a hundred per cent –" her aunt murmured.

"And who is a hundred per cent!" Eleni retorted.

"Well, he was always a rather *sui generis* person," Uncle made
his pronouncement. Aunt Lefki looked at him, evidently not
understanding the words. He did not bother to explain.

"But you do not put somebody under court order because he
is *sui generis*." Eleni was losing her temper.

They shook their heads in vague agreement. For now, she
would have to believe, or pretend to believe, they meant it.

"For the sake of my mother, for my father's sake, we cannot
let this happen. If it is at all in our hands we will not let it
happen. It would be worse than death." She implored, they sym-
pathised, perhaps they were moved.

The rest of the evening was quiet. She stayed, in order to
strengthen their insecure alliance, and to further their bartering.
As she left she promised to look into universities of tourism, they
promised to stand by her and her father. She wondered what
they said to each other after she had gone.

23

THE BENEFITS OF DEATH

By the time she woke, her father, in suit and tie, was already pacing in and out of rooms, putting his papers in order, rearranging his briefcase. She sprang up in primordial alarm – the familiar fear and excitement that he always caused in wife and daughters. Without quite knowing for what purpose, she tried to catch up with the day. He gave an impression of natural elegance, and style. His silver grey hair carefully combed back, his suit dark with a subtle stripe, although the fabric had a shine that showed its age. His body was lean, his gait generous, his face bright with conspiracy. This was the smiling face of God, and since she was a child she was taken in by it.

He had already been out and bought fresh bread and yoghurt. He rearranged his jacket in front of the mirror, he brought his hands together in a mutual embrace of determination, or prayer. In bleary blindness, Eleni hastened to live up to whatever her part in his schemes might be. She got dressed, with some formality for an unknown occasion, made coffee, set breakfast on the balcony, which had the morning sun. It was a warm, fresh April sun, and Thessaloniki was once again her own home town. In the distance a tower crane played lego with it.

He ate his bread and yoghurt with appetite, sipped his coffee with noisy relish, then sprang up and slapped his hands on his thighs.

"We're going!"

"Where?" Even as she uttered the question, the answer was blindingly obvious.

"To the solicitor!" She heard the hairline crack in his confidence.

"When? You didn't tell me anything."

"Didn't we agree, my child, about that land!" Having to spell it out made him impatient.

She didn't want him to lose his good mood, the few moments of sunny peace. "Of course, Dad, of course we agreed. But I didn't know it was today!" She wondered at his secret efficiency. "Did you make an appointment with the solicitor? Has he prepared the documents?"

"I made the appointment, the papers have arrived from Thasos, he has prepared the contract, all we need to do is go!" Impatience and greed gave him back the zest of his youth.

"Good!" she confirmed as she tried to gain time. "I'll be ready in a few minutes." She collected the pension documents lying neglected on the table – this was the chance for her bargain. "And while we're at it we can deal with these papers. You sign these and I'll sign yours." She tried to sound casual, but her jaw clenched in anxious stubbornness. He might shout her back into her dark childhood corner. She was realizing and registering, coolly, that all her life she had been followed by the sightless wings of his anger. The startled falls in her sleep were falls from his furious winged grace. She slowly turned and faced him. He was working the muscles of his face in secret calculations between anger and diplomacy, his eyes looking for prey.

"All right," he said in a matter-of-fact voice.

She put the sheaf of papers into her handbag, and climbed into her high heels ready to face the day.

They walked along the waterfront, good-spirited in their

separate worlds and schemes. As always he hurried ahead, she ran after him, unstable on her heels but determined. At the end of the waterfront he turned into the dark streets of the market. With practised agility he walked round stationary vehicles, fruit carts, garbage bags. He was indifferent to the pedestrians, but inspected the inanimate presences on the street with proprietorial alertness. He moved as if in his kingdom – the merchant's ancient familiar home – acknowledging his past victories and defeats, the devious bargains.

He disappeared into a doorway without turning back to see she was following. The elevator came grinding down towards him as he ran up the pitch-dark stairs. She switched on a light and caught up with him.

Through the dust of time she recognized the solicitor. Mists of stale tobacco stretching back into infinity clung on all living and dead things. Every movement in the room, every word, gesture or sentiment, raised a new concentration of dead tobacco, nauseous breaths of fragile pleasure. He used to be a young man, she used to be a child. He looked at her with curiosity, vague recognition, she tried to remember his name. Her father filled the gaps of memory with quick affability and pride. He was the good father, proud of his good-looking daughter, educated abroad; he was the good businessman, the important client, the shrewd entrepreneur.

"Andoni, my daughter! The youngest, my Benjamin." She had not heard that name for a long time, yet it used to be his favourite name for her.

The solicitor remembered her, she was only a child when he worked almost full-time for her father. He asked about England, the rain, the recession. Without waiting he proceeded to praise Greece, its weather, its sun, its sea – "But the Greeks! They never learn! How do they expect to be full members of Europe without discipline, without punctuality.

Father interrupted him impatiently – "Andoni, we've come for the contracts."

"The contracts?" The solicitor was gaining time, trying to

guess what contracts he was supposed to have prepared. With so little work he could not have forgotten the one and only deed for days. He opened his drawer, took out some papers to give the impression of business and control.

"The contracts for the land I was telling you about. On Thasos. My property, which I must now redeem, and restore to its true value..." Words could not express the life-and-death importance of this deed.

"Of course, the land on Thasos! I was wondering why you had delayed in bringing those documents."

Kyr Gregoris was relieved. "My daughter will be my partner. My sole partner, and after a while the manager." The relief became triumph – "And one day the landlord." He liked the word. "The landlady!" he corrected himself and liked it even better.

Eleni recognized the bribery, and perhaps the embarrassment, but mostly the largesse her father had with words and illusions. She even shared his pleasure in his easy crescendo of generosity, the music of promises, and the pretence of giving all instead of taking back the gift already given.

"My father wants to take back the piece of land he had given me, and I am prepared to return it." "In exchange for what?" was the harsh question suspended in the stale air of the room.

The solicitor looked amazed, Father a little embarrassed.

"It's all for her anyway. What difference does it make?"

"At your age, Kyr Gregori, you should give your property to your children, not take it back! What will you do with it at your age?"

"It will all be hers, anyway. When I die it will all be hers, but now I need it. I have my plans." He took out documents from his battered suitcase, brusquely. "I haven't got all day."

The lawyer looked at father and daughter, not understanding the transaction. "You should think about it seriously, Kyr Gregori. You are not young any longer. You should put your affairs in order, make arrangement for your daughters. I have seen such tragedies!"

Father looked at him suspiciously. He looked at his daughter, without love. Words of old age, hints of death were not acceptable, not tolerable. "Arrangements! Daughters!" He was rubbishing the words under his breath. "I have work to do before I make arrangements for my daughters." He was closing his mind and closing himself into old ineffable agonies, as he used to close himself into his shop, his warehouse, surrounded by lengths of fabric and fabrication, their dust clogging his lungs. And hers.

"My father is already putting his affairs in order." She proceeded without thinking whether this was the right moment or not. "We would like to conclude the issue of his pension. We have also brought these documents with us." She took them out of her handbag. "Only a few signatures are needed." She spread out the documents, and with them she decided to put the rest of her cards on the table. "If my father signs these documents and applies for his pension, and stops work, then I will gladly sign the contract giving him back this piece of land to do with as he likes." She took an official tone, to conclude the trade between them and rubber-stamp their unwritten contract.

Her father understood and shook his head in agreement.

The solicitor looked at his old client in hazy bewilderment. He had just remembered that this old man had still not consented to have a pension given to him because he still was not prepared to give up work, youth, and life. For him there was no life after retirement, the old man knew it, his daughter perhaps knew it, yet …

"You should have retired years ago, Kyr Gregori. It is a good pension. You will live royally."

The old man flexed his face muscles.

"And with that money you could do something with the land. Build something. I will give you the land, Dad." The difficulty of her generosity was dissolving in the emotion of her deed.

"Of course it's not strictly legal to do business after retirement —" The solicitor's words weakened under the caustic stare of the old businessman who knew and despised laws.

The daughter shook her head in acknowledgement, yet put her hand on her father's shoulder. "We'll do great things with that land, Dad. We'll build your hotel, the best in the village, the biggest on the island." She had entered his desperate world of illusion. Perhaps she had never left it, never left her corner in his shop where she watched him measure and put in order his beautiful fabrics, forgetful of her and of the world.

The solicitor glanced at the mass of documents before him, trying to find a family compromise. He made his secret calculations of costs – in money, perhaps in heartache. "The tax for the transaction will be – considerable, quite high.

Eleni looked at her father, his face hanging in agony on the feared figure. He was so near having what he wanted, only to see it vanish. His face looked gaunt and hungry, his eyes were red with sleeplessness and want. He looked imploringly at the solicitor, at his daughter: his body tensed, caught in the impotence of poverty.

Eleni was filled with sorrow for him. She would have preferred him to be the tyrant – unreasonable, capricious, but powerful. That was the father she always knew, that was the presence that all her life filled her with the secure familiarity of fear. The man, who might, undeservedly, heap wealth on her, and on the spur of his anger withdraw it, was himself now at the mercy of life's merciless rules and regulations.

"There is a different way – much cheaper and fairer." The solicitor had gained power over both of them. "You could keep possession, Kyr Gregori, and all the rights of use and income of this land, while you are alive: but make over the ownership to your daughter now. "The tax is negligible, and your beneficiary – or beneficiaries – will be saved inheritance tax."

Gregoris was caught by a new bewilderment.

"The land, and everything else, everything you own will be yours. While you are alive you will have possession, and sole right to use it as you like, let it, get the income. After your death – we cannot take them with us, Kyr Gregori!"

Death, beneficiaries, retirement, death. The words sat upon his euphoria like tombstones. Beneficiaries! The thought that anyone – even his own daughters – would benefit from his death was unbearable to him. But it was a solution. And it was cheap.

"Can I sell it?"

"Yes, with her permission. The land will be hers, but she will take possession only after your death. While you are alive it is all yours."

Death, he was not prepared to contemplate death.

"It's cheap." The solicitor worked on him. "And it's fair."

Fair! Life was slipping through his arthritic fingers, his visions of wealth and power were blurred and lopsided, his memory could not hold sums and decisions and events and people together. And Anastasia was no longer there to remember for him, and put his thoughts in order, scold him when he lost his temper or his briefcase, remind him of what was fair and unfair. Fair! While events were piling up, and people, these women, daughters, wanted wanted wanted from him.

Eleni leaned forward. "How much would this deed cost?" This was the moment. The chance to secure the written proof that she was the one and only, the beloved, the favourite daughter. She would pay for this deed, and give up the little her father had given her, for the secret knowledge that one day she would be repaid with her father's written, stated, signed, rubber-stamped will, and proof of love. Her avarice grew with the melancholy thought of yet another death and yet another loss. And also her need to keep hold of him, his scrawny hands, his fragile body, his clothes, his ugly habits, his possessions, his knowledge, his fainting memories, his sufferings, his passions. The need to take material possession of this father she had never possessed, to fill her hands and arms, head and eyes and mouth with father, and mother, parent and author. The ritual metaphors of the Church that had bred her and had touched her spirit and body were coming to life. This was the meaning, the greedy pleasure of the Eucharist. The invented moment of matter and of spirit, of

standing before the priest – beautiful in his embroidered splendid vestments – waiting to be given the holy communion –
"This is the body and this the blood of our Saviour." The incense
and chanting made her soul and body hungry for that mystery
fabricated for her sake.

"I will be glad to pay for it. How soon can you prepare the
papers? Can we sign a draft agreement today? Now?"

Perhaps moved by her sudden efficiency, perhaps because she
was present and the other daughters absent, perhaps because he
wanted something from her – she was after all his favourite until
she went away and froze his heart – for whatever reason, he once
again forgot the slow and difficult duties of father. "Very well, I
will sign, anything you want. Let her inherit – all. The rascal!"

He consented to give, in order to take, probably scheming
escapes and petty deceptions. She consented to give in order to
take, knowing this was an unnatural reversal. The solicitor, having
seen worse things, set out to prepare the papers.

24

EXPULSION

They both had a fragile euphoria as they left the lawyer's office. After all that talk of death, father was full of hectic life. He walked with distracted energy, his body thin but coordinated, not stooping; his hand, pulled shut by shrinking tendons, in a half-closed position of querying or begging; his eyes bright and hollow. She wondered where he was taking her, she would lose him and wonder whether he was lost in the labyrinth of the market alleys. Yet she followed loyally and insecurely.

At this unstable moment of promise and loss he must revisit his empire, material proof of new possibilities of wealth. Of course he knew it was no longer his empire but that was immaterial: he made his way – which he had never lost – towards his building. He had sold it piece by piece and he was left now with a small percentage. But it was still his building: this was where his shop had been, the big splendid department store, this was where his success still dwelt, this was his home. His face was glowing with the fever of possession.

Buildings stood tall and tired in their dirty grey modernity. But Gregoris' building – in God's eyes, his – still stood in their midst, a dignified old aristocrat under preservation order. It was losing its plaster ornaments, its fluted pilasters; its walls were blackened by traffic fumes, the wooden shutters of the upper floors were bleached, dusty — slats or whole panels missing. Yet people still knew the building with the name he, Gregorios Gregoriou, had given it: Nea Smyrni — a name with history, a name to tell the world his own history.

He had stopped, to admire it and feel a father's pride: in spite of its size, and neglect, it had elegance, it had grace. With a care he had not shown to his children he examined the destruction of time: the upper stories looked empty, the small iron-laced balconies forlorn. On the lower floors, instead of intimations of old grandeur and civilization, a violence of sound, colour, and youth. In the relentless rock-and-roll rhythm fleshless mannequins attacked you with gloomy aggression. Everything half price. Father shook his head mournfully at the sight of a foreign world.

They went in. Father made the introductions with false affability. The shopkeeper, well fed and well groomed, asked Eleni about England and without waiting for an answer proceeded to tell her, with breezy worldliness, about London, the stock market, the recession. Father started searching his pockets.

"So, Kyr Gregori, have you thought about my offer? Now your daughter is here perhaps you can discuss it with her."

Father looked puzzled. "What offer?"

"The offer for your percentage of the building. Considering the market, it is, I think, a generous offer."

Father did not remember.

Eleni asked what the offer was, the shop keeper gave a figure.

"That's why I forgot it!" Father jumped in with triumphant sarcasm. "Because it is contemptible."

They were ready to go. Father tightened the muscles of his face, blew his nose. "I was wondering about this month's rent", he mumbled.

"Weren't you here two days ago, Kyr Gregori, and didn't I pay for this and the following month?" He opened his drawer. "Here are the receipts!"

Father looked embarrassed, tried to remember, gave up, and

laughed it away. "With all these worries and preoccupations, I forgot! This mind, how can it cope with so much business!"

"He is here every day – aren't you, Kyr Gregori? He forgets, Miss Eleni, he comes first thing in the morning, as if he's got the keys to the shop, and asks for the rent. We are pleased to see him, we are always pleased to see Kyr Gregori, but... he is getting old." A group of schoolgirls walked in noisily, he extended his hand to say good-bye, Eleni and her father took their leave.

"How could I have forgotten!" Father kept exclaiming to himself.

What he always forgot was that this was not his shop any longer. Eleni could see him going to the shop first thing in the morning in order to open it. He would look through his pockets for the keys, then perhaps remember, then ask these unlikely shopkeepers for the rent, not to leave empty-handed.

The shop next door was different in style and atmosphere. It seemed to be an unsold remnant from the past. No mannequins, no music, no "decor". Pieces of material, folded or rolled, lay dully on benches; others were thrown in baskets in disarray. A short dark man stood at the entrance – his hair and moustache an unnatural opaque black – inviting with depressed indifference lady clients into the shop. In the dim background the owners slumped over benches staring at the entrance with inanimate expectation.

Father, having already shelved his disappointment, entered the shop with the air of a benevolent owner and important long-awaited guest. He extended both hands for greetings or general congratulations. He knew he would have a better reception here. That other man was young, not even born when Gregorios Gregoriou was a known businessman of this city. That's why he doesn't show proper respect. But these lads – they knew him when he was rich and powerful. They were his errand boys, he taught them the trade, and let this shop to them for "a piece of bread", they should be grateful. But it's true they had done nothing with the shop. For twenty years now, the same old furniture, the same dowdy stock.

The two owners, still preserving their Mediterranean good looks, were pleased to see their old boss. Almost affectionate. They offered seats, ordered coffee immediately. They made small talk with Eleni, flirtatious in a tired routine way. Then to her father they complained about the poor business, the recession, high taxes. "It's dead, Kyr Gregori, the market is dead."

When a middle-aged woman walked into the shop they both sprang up in sudden theatrical animation, competing in courtesies and gallantries. She looked dryly at the folded materials, unfolded a few, threw them on the bench contemptuously, walked out. They slumped sourly over the benches continuing their complaints.

Father shook his head with little sympathy. "That's business – it has its ups and it has its downs. But obligations are obligations, my lads."

"Things are very bad, Kyr Gregori, very bad! I hardly make a living," the older one murmured.

"And I need my rents, Niko! How will I live? At my age!"

"Didn't we tell you, come next week, Kyr Gregori? You come every day asking for these rents"

"You owe me three months rent!" Father's anger was sudden, and it was fragile – an old man's anger. He wrestled with the key of his briefcase, and finally produced a stack of papers, some fell on the floor.

"I know we owe you three months, Kyr Gregori! You tell us every day. We are glad to see you, to remember the good old days, but the rents will have to wait. Look, look, not one customer. In any case" – he turned towards Eleni – "you should live on your pension, Kyr Gregori." The man pursued the diversion with energy. "At your age, you shouldn't need to depend on these rents. Visit your daughter in England! Visit your other daughters, enjoy your grandchildren, as old people do. It's not for your age, trailing from shop to shop every day of the week, asking – for what? Peanuts! You've been working all your life. Now rest."

Father shoved his papers into his briefcase with impotent anger . "The bums!" he murmured as they left the shop. "They are not businessmen, they are bums, beggars, impostors."

Eleni passed her arm protectively through his arm, and tried to direct their steps away from this fatal building. But her father insisted on visiting another tenant who owed him rents not for months, for years.

"Tsikotis, I have to find Tsikotis. And if he doesn't pay I swear I'll send him to prison." He started swearing in Turkish, in impotent thwarted anger.

Father talked to the woman who had gradually installed an entire shop of haberdashery in one of the side entrances. Steps, niches, alcoves were filled with underwear. She had started a few years ago with a basket of lace. No one paid much attention. Hardly worth the rent, what rent! Then she put shelves up, then a bench in the corner alcove, now she has taken possession of the entrance, and sits in her winter coat and shawl, in the middle of her thriving business. Rent free.

Father glowered at her, she just lodged her stocky body firmly in her chair and gazed at the street. Her answer to any demands for rent was "Sue me!" And no one did. The same with Tsikotis. He started with a corner in the mezzanine floor. A handicraft studio. Then he spread out. Gradually he occupied the entire mezzanine. He spent the whole day up there, in a vast storeroom. He shouted at intruders from behind locked doors.

They went up cluttered dark stairs looking for new enemies. The noise of a soft footed army reached them distantly. It was not a march but a delicate tapping of thousands of dancers, each one following their own invented rhythm. The windows on the stairs faced a wall which allowed hardly any light. Most of them were broken and brought in sudden draughts; the remaining glass was opaque with grime. Corridors crammed with stacked boxes, crates, broken furniture. They pushed a glass door and entered a dark passage – on both sides iron bars, wrought-iron railings, iron gates were carefully propped against the wall.

They pushed a door and saw what looked like a mass grave of babies, of broken bodies of pink-fleshed babies. Eleni touched a shiny hard surface with her shoe: they were broken dolls, hundreds of broken, crippled, naked dolls. Some without eyes, some without legs, some headless. They gazed vacantly into this travesty in plastic of the world's so many tragedies. Who populated this ghastly domain? The soft dance overhead of the tireless invisible population never stopped.

A door creaked open and a shadow appeared at the far end of the corridor. A man in working clothes and a dishevelled grey beard stood in the meagre light of a half-opened door, watching them.

"What do you want?"

"I want you, Tsikoti." Father walked towards the man.

The other man stayed still and silent. As they approached, Eleni saw animosity furrowing his face, but a glint of irony played in his small hooded eyes. He was older than he looked at a distance.

"And what can we do for the boss?"

"You can give me the years of rent you owe me. In cash and with interest." There was a curious equality and directness between the two men.

"When you and the other landlords repair this wreck, then you can have the face to ask for rent."

"Your rent – which you don't pay – is nothing, crumbs, chickenfeed. It's a pre-war rent and you don't even pay that. I told you, Tsikoti, my patience has a limit. Year after year after year."

"Get out of here, Gregoriou. You are owner of nothing now, you are no landlord. Five, ten per cent of this wreck? Big shit! And you come asking for rent!"

"I did you a favour, Tsikoti, to let you move in here. I gave you a corner, and you took over the place, filling the world with your garbage." The two men stood opposite each other, old and ravaged by time, but stubborn and belligerent.

"Big favour! Landlord Gregoriou! When you owned all this you gave me a corner – to keep an eye on the building, and on the other tenants. That's what you said then, Gregoriou." He stabbed his finger at him.

"I don't know what I said then, now I am poor. As poor as you are, poorer. And I am an old man, and I need this rent."

"What are your daughters for?"

Father was pushed into a dead end. He wanted no mention of daughters.

"You gave them dowries, didn't you? Now they should look after you." He stopped and gazed at him. "Poor Gregoriou. The sly bird is caught by its beak. You were lucky, Gregoriou, weren't you? Out of all of us refugees, you were shrewd. When we worked at the tobacco factory for crumbs, you owned one and two shops. When we lived still in the shanty town, you lived at the waterfront, opposite the White Tower. And like a *budala* you lost it, you were robbed in your sleep, and you didn't even wake up."

Father was weakening. The past, and the follies of the past, the sheer thought of them weakened him. "Enough. Give me my money, Tsikoti."

The other man just stood, saying nothing. He looked appraisingly at the enemy. Onetime friend, compatriot. Then, quietly, without animosity, he said. "Don't waste your time, Gregoriou. You will not see any money from me. I don't sell anything, I don't make anything. I am old, like you."

Father only waved his finger at him. "In court, then, Tsikoti." His words came in a hoarse whisper, he was ready to go, yet he was staying.

After a pause, Tsikotis said quietly, a friend confiding to friend: "I want to show you something, Gregori. You and your daughter – she's the youngest, is she?"

Father hesitated for a moment, then when the other man moved and said again, "Come, come this way, Miss," both father and daughter followed him. He seemed the guardian and ruler of the place. He led them up a narrow back staircase through deep darkness. Father objected, questioned, but followed. As they ascended blindly, one storey after another, the dark was filled with the sound of a multitude of feathery dancing steps accompanied by an excited susurration. So soft, so feathery, so quick and alarming in their unruly movements, like uninvited, unprepared-for thoughts at moments of wakefulness.

A ray of light finally came under a door, but when the tenant, and host, with quiet reverence pushed the door open, his guests stopped still at the noise and the sight. Hundreds, perhaps thousands, of what looked like doves were flying in circles and spirals, swooping down or staying suspended with spread white wings in the light. Sunbeams descended through the broken roof, tending towards a secret mysterious place within the playful geography of light and spirit. It might have been a revelation of the Holy Spirit, multiplied into a multitude – to feed all humankind? A noisy, active, busy Holy Spirit, a population of holy spirits, of both sexes and all ages, feeding and playing, throbbing and cooing flirtatiously over each other, performing gyrations of seduction, or flying in circles and spirals of contemplation. The vast room, half covered by tall rafters meeting in elegant arches, was a church flooded by the light and spirit of God, and by the presence of an ancient and great forest. The floor was strewn with the leavings of holy and earthly activities.

"That's your property, Gregoriou. The pigeons will inherit the earth. Starting with your building. Who are you to ask for rent? Will they pay rent? Will you kick them out? Will you plug the holes and mend the roof? When you do, come and ask for rent."

The pigeons continued their life, some flew out and many flew in. Eleni thought she saw something greening in a far corner, like the small beginning of a garden – from seeds the birds had brought in, she speculated. She imagined the countryside slowly flying in, seed by seed, and reclaiming its ground. She walked into the room stepping on soft layers of bird-shit and stood calm and erect within the brightness and warmth, and, as if rooted in the long past knowledge of that ground, prayed for the place – this place and her whole city – to turn into a vast garden.

Her father, she knew, was mourning the wreckage of his building, his own private church built with the sweat of many hard working years. She took his hand, cold and permanently closed, and blindly descended the stairs – wishing the country-side to return and reclaim the ground and air, freeing this place and its inhabitants from all family enthralments, the houses and households, the furniture, the utensils, the clutter of doubted love – and all the words that tied her to them.

Hand in hand they took their solitary way through the iron-mongery, and abandoned carpentry, and crates – the remains of generations of tenants. Like the angry soul of the dying building, a seraph with flaming sword, the tenant pursued them to the exit, and beyond.

25

TRANSIENCE

Ready to leave, she stopped and gazed at the old iron patches on the inside of the door. They had been added in the years of occupation and war, to make the door safe and strong, and they were still there in the years of peace. They had kept the enemy out and the three daughters in. The heavy iron bar, the *ambara*, rested against the wall, the thick iron hooks on either side waited for it. The small window in the door was covered with an iron shutter. She ran her finger around its edges, measuring the pain it caused her when, as a child, she squeezed through it. The smaller the opening the more she had wanted to escape, in the middle of the night, to run to the park to play with the children. To play, and to see what enemies waited behind the double-locked door.

She found no children, and there were no games. Only dark guilty shadows coming together entangled in – to her unspeakable – acts of love. The dry-mouthed taste of fear, the persistent effort to make out the dark movements, to hear and discover the words that might uncover everything: that forbidden gaze through the night contained the dark wish of exile and expulsion.

The taste of fear would return, together with the accompanying nausea, when she caught glimpses, through a half-opened door, of couples bringing faces and bodies together when they thought no one was looking. The taste and the nausea took her back to the sound of the parental bed, at daybreak, feeling under tired restless eyelids the whispers of acts to a young mind unbearable.

Years later she crawled through that iron window again. Her body was formed, the pain deeper, the bruises ugly. And the dark was dense and seductive like the thrill of meeting her lover in a guilty tangle of shadows.

She opened the door, and went out. She had decided to leave – to leave this city and fly home. She would walk along the waterfront to the Olympic Airways office at the end of the bay, to confirm her flight. At least to confirm it, and know there was a date. Knowing there was an escape she felt less hurried – especially in that bright clear light. She would have time to say her long goodbye. She stopped at the park by the White Tower, as always expecting more than she found. She wandered along its paths and looked through the dusty green foliage. Children were playing, young mothers chatting, two lovers kissing, an old gentleman gazing and reminiscing. Out at sea a freighter sat still and tired, small waves brought all kinds of garbage. She half-looked for pleasure-boats coming and going, taking people off and bringing them back. Like them she would go, and one day come back. But those boats had vanished long ago.

She looked at the people strolling by the sea: they belonged to this city and the city belonged to them, she envied their assurance and comfort. Her own city was a vessel floating on the sea. Made up of old memories, long absences, historians' and poets' impressions, a child's uncomprehending glance, an errant imagination.

But she knew the dense night in the past of this place, the shadows that came together to love or to kill. Abominable acts had desecrated the streets. The violated ancient temples and churches, the violently blinded icons, fortress city walls, spoke of invasions, lootings, rapes, massacres. Goths, Slavs, Saracen pirates, Crusaders from the North, Venetians, Turks, Bulgarians, Germans.

Terrified peasants ran for refuge inside the walls, citizens ran for escape to the hills and to the sea. Running back and forth is the movement of this city, as inescapable as the movements of the sea. The very soil – she knew this from her city's poet – is not the good earth where trees and flowers grow: but minute fragments of shattered households, temples, statues, religions, civilizations.

What was it about this place that gathered people from so far afield? Refugees from Armenia, the Black Sea, the depths of Anatolia, Judea, Spain and Portugal arrived here escaping from pogroms and expulsions. Herself a child of refugees, she feels scattered by the sweep of this Diaspora, ready to migrate. Moved, it seems to her, by a wish to re-discover, or exorcise, the violations and favours those foreign names had done to her tongue. Or by sheer curiosity, because it is no longer those foreign demons she fears, but the familiar ones.

But she always returns, because she also returns to an ancient legend enduring, for her, beneath other stories: that King Solomon had built this beautiful city, and lived in it with all the people, and all the spirits, with the birds, the nymphs and the demons. She had an unspoken belief that if she dug deep enough into the lifeless crumble of broken civilizations, she would find vestiges of Solomon's ancient city.

She paused on the waterfront, then with decisiveness entered the Olympic Airways office. But she could not decide on a date, the clerk was busy, politely impatient, she hastily named a day, then changed it, then postponed the decision, and asked for a few days grace.

But she stayed in the Olympic office – neither here nor there. She let her body in transit sink into the luxurious armchair: the smell of new leather was the smell of transience. Its seductive softness preparing for the flight's feathery suspense between sky and earth, the proximity of death, the noiseless changing formations of cloud, the wordless cheating of one's fated life.

She left the Olympic terminal without deciding on a date. In the meantime, the nearest thing to flying out of Greece was to hide in a telephone booth and let her foreign words and sounds travel abroad taking part of her soul with them. If someone, who had patience, and who knew about exiles, looked at her, he might see her face transformed as it concentrated and poured its meaning into the inanimate receptacle. She stayed on the phone for a long time, trying to put into foreign sounds the native tangles. Through the foreign rhythms she might hear and locate the family hiatus. In translation she might understand it. Distanced, it might be harmless. She talked, and laughed, had tears in her eyes, and sent kisses to remote presences who were not allowed a voice.

The man waiting outside asked where she was ringing, she said England.

"I've been there myself."

Back in her native tongue and her double and divided life, she was soon giving kisses to another – compatriot, playmate, constant brother and lover, and, with her, inhabitant of the underground story of this city. These might be their last kisses for a long time, or simply their last kisses. But they said nothing yet. They avoided thoughts of endings or divisions or betrayals – as if the first crossing of borders of land and language had made all other transgressions inevitable, and forgivable. The original transgression eclipsed all.

She was now another person, in another story, uttering other words of love. Or keeping a warm silence through the prolonged siesta. Tangled together in body and thought, falling in and out of sleep. At moments she was surprised by the permanent tan of his body, that made her own body look pale, and sunless. She had undergone a palpable change. The sunlessness of her skin went deep, she felt, into the layers of her body and spirit. That was the price of her escapes and betrayals. She kissed and kissed his body, drinking the sun she had longed for, for many years.

They went out, to catch the April sun, and catch their city in a brief moment of lazy afternoon inertia, a momentary pause from the constant mutability. They walked uphill to the walls of the city, following the Byzantine and Roman avenues that gave onto labyrinths of Turkish alleys – familiar escapes and hideouts of love. Love that was without home and furnished comforts crept for protection against walls – soft warm walls, protected by the protruding bay window on top, walls that were hollow inside from damp and age, and crumbled easily under the soft pressure of their bodies, walls of gardens suffocated by the jasmine scratching their arms, but healing everything with its scent. Walls and alcoves of the small Byzantine churches, or sanctuaries behind the shrubs, or corners in cemeteries, filled with the smell of mortality from the cut flowers resting on graves. They were rarely disturbed – by solitary steps, or the sound of unstable high heels, or the loud voices from legitimate couples. Because secret lovers – like themselves – only whispered, rarely interrupting the eternally absorbing voiceless kissing.

In the winter they used to frequent small furtive cafés and taverns, looking in them for the ancient legendary inns, where travelling merchants stopped and spent the night drinking, and where, according to travel writers, clowns and singers and foul-mouthed men, and also poets and men of letters, and dandies, and those in love, rested, any time of the day and night. They would have liked to join that caravanserai of sensation, greed, and imagination – and the dance of whirling dervishes, caftans, turbans, long *kelebias*, or native Macedonian gold-embroidered skirts.

But, underneath, the austere ascetic saints of Byzantium waited and watched. These lovers' ultimate refuge had always been the underground arcades and Saints' crypts, the secret churches of the early, persecuted Christians, the excavated foundations of temples and the Roman Hippodrome. The spirit of this city was underground, where it was damp and warm, and where unforeseen organisms grew. The icons on the dark walls, the ancient scratched messages from huddling congregations and secret, whispered baptisms, the ghostly presence of an embracing Love, which might forgive and cleanse their young and unruly bodies.

They had remained locked in each other's arms, confronted by the dark Byzantine faces tremulous like the flame of the oil-lamp. But the incense and scent of beeswax, and the memories of chanting and the frescoed dome descending and surrounding them – that beauty of the house of God – embraced them and their fugitive love. They remained locked, refugees in a perennial city of refugees, and made this their first and last home. It had been a kind of marriage, although they uttered not a word, not even to each other.

They walked now, trying to relive that fugitive furtive love, homeless and open-air, that thrives in parks and cemeteries and churches, grateful for protection from the cold and from curious eyes.

Now the world was open, and changed, and sunny, although the sky was deep blue, and the sun across the bay blood red.

It had all changed, and they said nothing. Because they had no story. They both knew that their plot was in the past. Their words then had wounded each other and wounded their lives for ever. Now, in this interlude, they were gentle to each other because they knew they had no future together. They were not sure why they met again, what they wanted from each other, what they could offer. Their feelings were suspended in a no man's land between his life unknown to her, and her life kept secret and foreign to him. The ending did not belong to them, their script would not affect any one's destiny, so they sat at a café and said little. In the dark, they returned to his flat and, surrounded by comforts, they made love. And again they made love.

26

LOVED BY WOMEN

Father decided to take Eleni to Thasos for Easter, to show her the land. He made plans. Every morning he announced the trip with fresh enthusiasm, extolling his island as if she had no knowledge of it, but by the middle of the day urgent business intervened, and he had forgotten.

And she – before going back to England – she would go with him to Thasos, to do him this last favour; she would finalize the land deeds and secure her future possession, settle the pension – then leave.

Perhaps he knew that soon he would lose her, perhaps he did not mind. She knew she was losing him. He shut himself into his storeroom for hours, she heard him drag boxes, shut suitcases. A noise of things falling. He reappeared covered in dust, his soul still in the double-locked room. A sharp alertness in his eyes, a cold calculation of her movements. She caught him looking at her as if he wondered what she was doing in his home.

She wanted to get away, yet she kept postponing her flight. At night she was afraid she would stay imprisoned with him for ever. She dreamt her body was paralysed and she was unable to move.

She received a phone-call from her father's solicitor. They had an appointment, he said, but her father did not show up. "He wants me to tear up the pension deeds, didn't he tell you?" No, he hadn't, and she didn't mention it to her father.

She received another phone-call, very early one morning. It was her Aunt Lefki, for her father. On the phone he was cautious, then suspicious, then he said no, he was busy, finally he said "all right".

He put on a clean shirt, his suit, asked her to polish his shoes. She didn't want to ask him where he was going, or what her aunt had said, and he didn't say. He was thoughtful, preoccupied.

"We are going to the cemetery." He said. She took this to be an order.

When her aunt appeared at the door and pulled him to her with crude endearment, he looked at his daughter expecting her to come.

"You will not lose her," Aunt Lefki ordered. "Let her have a day free – anyway there's no room in the car." Aunt Lefki played mother, there was no disobeying her. Father followed her meekly, Eleni, relieved, and suspicious, went out on the balcony to look.

Gregoris was puzzled, and a little flattered by this sudden attention. He inspected himself in the mirror of the elevator. He stopped, threatened and belligerent, when he saw the Mercedes in front of the building. It was his son-in-law's trophy – the proof of his success, and wealth. The constant reminder that while his father-in-law was getting old and poor, Tryphon was reaching the summit – of his professional success, and of his manhood. The old man made a sour face. His tongue played with his false teeth nervously, he stared hard through the smoky glass of the car. Kaliopi came out first – a middle aged woman, he noticed. Well dressed and well groomed, but she was getting fat. That's what the good life does to them.

Sophia, in the driver's seat, stayed in the car, and her father noticed. He disliked – always and especially now – he disliked her coldness and negligence. He stopped, ready to turn back. He himself had never learned how to drive, and became irritated seeing her in control. She had a way of lording it over child, husband, sisters, even her old father.

Lefki pulled him towards the car with loud maternal ownership: he gave in to her. He gave in to plump women – their flesh filled him with a warm comfort. From Lefki's strong arm, he was passed into Kaliopi's deep and slow daughterly embrace. She kissed him on both cheeks and left on him the lingering sensation of a soft womanly undaughterly body.

Sophia finally got out of the car. Thin, elegant, hard. He didn't like her smile and didn't believe her kiss. But he did get into the car. He was offered the seat next to her, he said he preferred to sit at the back. Kaliopi got in next to Sophia, and instantly, temporarily, was her ally. His sister-in-law with some upheaval made herself comfortable next to him, her noise and weight muffled the currents of irritability.

Sophia had never shown a proper fear of her father, Gregoris thought with displeasure. Kaliopi was softer. When he raised his voice, she cringed. Not Sophia. Her tongue had poison, her eyes contempt. That's what happens when they get educated. And yet, when she had her first case in court, and only a woman! He was proud. And Eleni – he heard her lecture once in a foreign language, English. He didn't understand a word, but he was proud. Eh, at such moments, he did think, with such daughters who wants sons! But the world was changing and women forgot their place. And Eleni had gone. Kaliopi was here, and she was a good housewife, like her mother.

"What is this? Where are you taking me?" Gregoris tried to establish some authority.

"Just wait and see." Lefki assumed the role of mother. "A picnic. We are going out, on an excursion. So, be patient."

"We are visiting Mother, Dad!" Kaliopi turned round and smiled at him with sad sweetness. She stretched her hand and took his half-closed fist and pressed it with sympathy, and trust. Sophia revved the engine, to silence words and tender communications, and to demand her passengers' attentive support in her battle with the city traffic.

Kaliopi was not going to be bullied by the elder sister. "All together, we will spend some time with Mother – her soul will be contented."

Father shook his head, uncertain. Sophia drove with the appropriate contempt for all smaller or slower vehicles, voicing recriminations and insults. The passengers sat still and silent as if her attacks were directed at them.

Father sat back and concentrated on his thoughts. Lefki was talking to him in whispers. He was not listening, she was probably advising him about his diet and his clothes and the household. He was absorbed in his own worries. His poor wife Anastasia! She did not have enough trust in his projects, not enough optimism. Perhaps he should talk to Kaliopi, she has a know-how in these matters, and she might want to invest. They certainly have the money – the dowries he gave them to start with. They might want to repay their poor father now.

They came to the outskirts of the city, Sophia stopped hating streets, cars, people. Mount Hortiatis, a comfortable humped body, grew beside them. He thought of his land on the island, saw it covered with pine forests and olive groves, rolling to the edge of the sea. He saw it developed – a modern hotel with bright-lit rooms. "I want to have a word with you, my child," he announced to Kaliopi, and she smiled obligingly. "Later."

Sophia gave Kaliopi a sidelong glance. Father returned to his doubts. "Not Sophia," he thought, "she will spoil everything." Then suddenly "everything" slipped away, and left a blank. What "everything"? What would he tell Kaliopi? He tried to remember what he wanted to tell Kaliopi, he panicked. Then the hotel's hundred lights twinkled like so many eyes winking at him, and his land, a real paradise, glided back into his failing sight.

Lefki was telling him, in loud ingratiating whispers, how lucky he was to have such daughters, who took him to places and looked after him. They would look after him from now on, put his affairs in order, he would have nothing to worry about.

Father felt optimistic, perhaps the world was good to him this morning. Lefki always saw the bright side of things. She might even persuade that tight-fisted dandy of a husband to invest some capital in his hotel venture. He had given her a dowry when she married her Rodolfo, now they could do a bit of repaying. And anyway, it was a good investment. It was not really the money he cared about. No. It was those beautiful buildings, modern and international, on that green land that grew larger and greener as it stretched down mountain-slopes to the edge of the sea.

She used to be beautiful, Lefki. In her youth, she was the most beautiful girl in the village. More beautiful than Anastasia. And jollier. But he had chosen Anastasia and at heart he remained faithful to her. She was his wife, and the mother of his children. She was a good woman, Anastasia – but Lefki was the beauty.

"How come you left your husband all by himself?"

She heard his irony and dislike. "He is with his sister. Talking about Sunday schools. I thought I would have a break from Christianity!" She laughed, her belly trembled, everyone laughed, Father laughed louder. Her generous flesh was close to him. The car was warm, and heavy with the smell of women – a mixture of perfumes, soaps and bodies. He sat back, looked at his sister-in-law with familiarity, his land now following the large curves of a woman's body.

He was surprised when they arrived at the cemetery. They bought flowers, gave him a bunch – he looked for his wallet, it must be in his other jacket. Then he realized he was wearing his good suit. Eleni was not here, where was she? But Anastasia would like this gathering, she was fond of her sister. Sophia, Kaliopi, but where is Eleni? He repeated their names, all three names, and kept hold of his mind. He looked at his suit and searched his pockets. No wallet, no keys. He was lost – his hands and his mind reached out and hung onto things, tangible things and words. He spelt out in intimate whispers, names, plans, intentions, duties – not to forget, not to die.

They stood by Mother's grave. He mused at her picture. A plump, stubborn face. That he wouldn't forget. She had been a good wife.

"What Anastasia would really like you to do is take your pension and leave all worries to your daughters." Lefki separated her words with maternal didacticism.

Sophia agreed with matter of fact certainty. "Father has finally understood that. Haven't you, Dad? Now you will let us settle your affairs. I am a lawyer, Tryphon is a lawyer, you need not run around paying lawyers, begging your tenants for rent."

"I am not a lawyer, Dad, but I love you, and I will look after you." Kaliopi would not be excluded. She gave him a tight embrace, which worked better than all words. Her father needed the touch of hands and warm women's bodies. But they were too strong, these women. He was lost, bewildered. This sudden love, and attention – "What affairs? They are my affairs, stay out of my affairs." He wished he was left alone, to collect his mind and rest and look after his affairs. He needed to collect himself.

They did not stay long. Sophia complained about the traffic, and her maid. She didn't dare leave her alone. Efterpi was probably spending the day ambling along from the balcony to the fridge, from the fridge to the television.

The journey back was scattering before his eyes. What did they want from him? Where were they taking him? Why couldn't they stay a little longer at his wife's grave? She was the only one he trusted. Poor Anastasia. If she were with him, she might save him from all these women. Telling him what to do and what not to do. That is not how he had raised them. What happened to the fear of father and mother? The respect, the timidity. Where was the fear?

They took him to Sophia's apartment, the maid made coffee, Sophia harried her over the housework she had not done. Lefki took her shoes off and loosened her corset. Kaliopi was trying to ring her husband in Athens, Sophia reminded her that long-distance calls cost money. Father sipped his coffee on the balcony, his mind suspended over the city traffic and the distant sea. The women were busy, the telephone didn't stop ringing, they were in constant whispered arguments – he stayed out of it. He needed rest, and silence. He needed to go to the island. Tomorrow he would go to the island. He would climb up on the mountain, survey his land, and the lands below and beyond, admire the view. Admire the world.

The bell rang, his brother-in law-arrived, the handkerchief in his pocket, the perfume, the smile. Gregoris looked him up and down, he couldn't remember seeing him wear anything other than his pyjamas for years.

The brother-in-law joined Gregori on the balcony and let the women pamper him. He already missed the view from his own balcony, but the coffee was good, yet not as good as his wife's. And the smell? Of dolmathes? "Mm... Enticing! But nothing like the heavenly delight of my wife's."

Father removed himself to distant lands and islands. Too tired to be annoyed by his brother-in-law.

The bell rang again, another woman arrived. A familiar face and voice. She seemed to know him, very well. He pretended he knew her. A nice woman, younger than Sophia. And kinder. She asked him questions, about his health, the island, his land. She talked about her own father, also from Asia Minor. Now dead. She had her mother live with her – a good daughter. Nice woman, plain.

Then she mentioned she was a solicitor. And she would be very glad to help him with his affairs. She had settled her mother's affairs when her father died. Old people should not have to worry about these things. He gave her a hard measuring look.

Lunch was good. And rich. There was Naoussa wine for the occasion, probably expensive. And he was made to sit at the head of the table, as was fitting. The young solicitor – they called her Annoula – was solicitous, like a daughter, better than a daughter.

They talked about money and what money could buy – trips and good dinners, and sitting back and not having a worry in the world. They talked about pensions, and what security a pension could bring. Still, why were they all full of advice? But he liked the care, he needed the care.

Perhaps he would let this young solicitor, this Miss – or Mrs – Annoula, look after his affairs? She would probably come up with some clever idea about the development. The development – that's what mattered. They can keep the dinners for themselves, what he needed was someone to show interest in the development.

After dinner he talked to her about himself: and she seemed interested. He felt assured, relaxed. All he needed to do, she said, was sign a power of attorney to her, or to his daughters and her – it didn't matter, it was all the same – and she would do all the running and organizing.

Why? Why a power of attorney? What was all this bureaucracy? He got up, giving her a searching look. She reassured him. All she needed was a signature – and she would do the rest. She took his hand with both her hands, she was so warm and forthcoming – as girls should be.

When they went into the living room, and she put a document before him, he held it at a distance and peered frowningly at it. He put it back on the table. "I haven't got my glasses with me. Another time." His brother-in-law offered him his own glasses, Gregoris held them in his hand, then put them down and pushed them away from him. "This will have to wait. I will speak to my lawyer." He got up, undecided what to do next. The young solicitor simply put the paper away. His daughters and relatives stood still and quiet.

"I think you need some rest, Dad." Sophia was, with some effort, gentle. Both daughters led him to Alexis' bedroom and helped him with his jacket.

He lay half dressed staring at the ceiling. Soft whispers came through the door.

He needed sleep.

His eyes, reddened, hot, wide-open, stared at the ceiling. He wanted rest.

He appeared barefoot and dishevelled at the door of the living room, pursued, haunted. The gathering fell silent as he gazed at them. They couldn't tell what he wanted from them.

"Let me have that paper." The order was given with a finality that reduced the room to silence. It was either a moment of total victory or total defeat. He asked for a pair of glasses and put them on carefully. He held the paper with ceremony, did not read it. He was given a biro, he held it up and looked at it with the largesse of a patriarch – some blue ink bled through its cracked casing smudging what it touched.

His signature had the familiar flourishes of calligraphy that betrayed confidence and style, but ended in a faint, protracted line. The relatives waiting round him in a circle remained grave, silent – the silence was as cold as death.

"Now I have to lie down. It's been a long day, and I am tired."

27

NO MAN'S LAND

He gave his storeroom a last thorough inspection before he locked it. She secured the shutters, drew the curtains – the flat had a hushed Easter neatness. She took her shoulder bag, he had prepared three large, bulging, battered suitcases. He secured them with string, and with her help he pushed and dragged them to the lift. She gave a last glance at the family repository and closed the door gently, not to disturb the secure silence. He tried the door again, it was locked, he double locked it just in case. The lift rocked violently as she pushed in two of the suitcases, it shuddered into motion, and with an infernal groan plunged down the abyss till with repeated jolts it tumbled to a protracted stop. Eleni pushed out the suitcases, which threatened to fall apart. As soon as the door shut it jumped upwards to her father's call upstairs. It reappeared below with a similar paroxysm, and after her father had pushed out the third suitcase, it subsided into terminal subterranean rest.

They had agreed with the lawyer, Mr Tastsidis, that they would bring back from Thasos official copies of the deeds and the surveyor's map of the land, and any existing documents of its previous history. Those tasks felt quick and easy as the taxi carried them away through a quiet, still unawakened city. Buildings interrupted by streets played a fast game of hide and seek.

Eleni at the edge of a bounded country, spirit, and language. Yet that narrow world looked beautiful and adequate.

At noon they sat in the sun at Panayiota's taverna waiting for her bean soup. She only allowed fasting food during Holy Week: meat, eggs, butter were forbidden in those days of grief. With the scalding hot soup she brought olives from her own trees, salad made of young tender bracken, still curled into a ball, and mountain herbs for which she had been climbing the mountain slopes since dawn. Only she knew the places. She sat with the visitors with crossed arms to hear praises. Her taverna would open only for the Resurrection, but she gave to the visitors from her own family's food – because after all they were visitors, brave souls to come up here in the wilderness. And the visitors ate gratefully, following her orders and the spirit of Holy Week.

A young woman called Iphigenia, timid and quiet, helped with the serving. Her husband, Michalis, a good-looking Turk from Thrace, sat around talking about the non-existent tourism.

"The tourists don't bother to leave the beach and come up the mountain. They don't even know about this village."

"Advertise!" Was her father's advice. "Drive around the resorts with a loud-speaker. Put the place on the map."

The priest of the village appeared from the kitchen, in his plain black cassock, carrying his bean soup. He was a short, plump, smiling man with mischievous black eyes. He seemed to be an old friend of her father's. He was sorry to hear of Kyra Anastasia's death, he promised to give her a memorial service. "But life must go on, Kyr Gregori." He was so glad to see him in church and hoped that they would both come to the evening liturgy. "There are no young women remaining in the village, and a young face would be good for the faith of the congregation, in these cold days." Then he turned to Michalis and scolded him for not showing up in church that morning.

He poured some ouzo into Michalis' glass. Ouzo was just grapes after all, and Jesus had blessed the grapes. And it was a good way of winning souls. If he made Michalis the Turk come to church, what greater miracle!

The men of the village slowly joined them – serious, taciturn men who carried on their shoulders the destiny of the village. They gathered in Panayiota's taverna every evening, because there was nowhere else to go, and drank with fortitude when they were treated. Today they were louder in their pronouncements and freer with the rounds of ouzo ordered by Kyr Gregoris. They seldom left the village, and almost never left the island – only for serious illnesses, touch wood. As for Europe – Europe was a word, a power that was good when it paid subsidies, and bad when it passed regulations.

The setting of the sun brought a chill to the air and a bleakness to the mountain. The company moved indoors and stayed there to discuss the issues of the village till it was time to go back for vespers.

The issue of the day was the water. The lower village wanted their water. "They got the road, they got the tourists. Now they want our gift from God – our pure, ice cold water."

Then there were the goats. "They jump into the vineyards and olive groves," murmured the growers, "and make straight for the top branches. They don't leave a green sprig. What destruction! Sarajevo!"

"Mend your fences," grumbled the shepherds. And Cain and Abel are still at war.

Gregoris too talked about his land. He described his plans, and made mad promises to bring them tourists and make them all rich. Michalis joined him in his enthusiasm, in flattery or sympathy, or hazy alcoholic euphoria. The others listened quietly.

"Your land... Why don't you go and have a look at your land!" Margaritis, a small wily-looking man, mumbled, but his words were lost in the general conviviality.

The following morning father and daughter set out to visit the land. They walked hardly a kilometre east of the village, to the point where the view took in the entire bay, flanked by slopes covered with pines and olives. Father's step was light and secure – as if the mountain were his home and he its shepherd all his life. Eleni kept up, elated by the sunlight that revealed such a good bright world. The contours of mountains and valleys were clearly defined, and the olive trees exposed their naked history and torments of age in the knots and twists and bifurcations and reunions of their much-suffering trunks. Yet the silvery grey of their foliage against the rusty brown of the earth were whisperings of untroubled peace, and of light-spirited constant youth. The long history of the plane trees was finely drawn in the elbows of their branches, slow elaborate journeys through the years down towards the ground – perhaps to make new roots – only to change their mind and direction on touching the soil, and leap upwards to new foliage and shade. In that clear-aired sunlight, shapes and shades and destinies appeared in true clarity, and the world had a lucidity of beauty and purpose. She desired with all her imagination to belong to this world of this moment.

She stopped. He hardly paused – at the sight of the large wound that had uprooted the life of the mountain. Rocks and earth had been dug out by the gigantic iron claw of some mythical god in a rage of greed and envy. It was an earthquake, restricted, in meanness, to this particular, most beautiful spot on earth. A mass of red dead soil haemorrhaged down the mountain. Straight, tall pine trees lay at all angles, ready to slide further, or roll, or tumble – their dead roots, still buried under clinging petrified earth, stretched dried-up tangles of arms to the sky. Naked rocks, loose stones, dead branches, mounds of dried up mud, and loose rootless soil perpetually and purposelessly slipped away.

They saw the compressed beginning of a road. A narrow strip of levelled ground with destruction above and destruction below. An unmanned excavator sat in the middle. Small mounds of rubble stood neatly at the edges. The world was turned inside out, its entrails dying in the sun.

Eleni lost her orientation in this new geography. In the monstrous bite out of the mountain, the gentle forested slope of her father's land had disappeared. It had been devoured, together with the life that grew on it. She didn't utter a word: only gazed at the disfigured landscape, waiting for her father's despair to pile upon her. He too remained silent, but she felt his body twitch as if missing a heartbeat, or waking up from a feeling of falling, or the feeling of a mysterious loss of life – an inexplicable lessening of stamina, or will. An interrupted breath.

His bad hand shut into itself. His good hand shut and opened, caught in a spasmodic survival. His face danced with a confusion of ugly thoughts and torments of belief and disbelief. His false teeth were gyrating in his mouth in panic.

"They are making a road!" he declared in a non-committal, diagnostic tone. And after a long silence: "Well, that will be convenient. They have brought the road straight to our door."

"How? What do you mean?"

"There, you see?" He pointed at the forested land just above the destruction. "The road comes just below our land."

"Where is our land?"

"Just above the road. Can't you see? The slope with the pine trees. And the open plateau in the middle is just right for building." He pointed at the entire forested mountain.

His piece of land appeared to his ageing eyes an entire forest, a mountain. A seat of power, a vantage point of beauty. An old man's home.

She did not argue. And she followed him up the mountain to the higher, untouched slopes where the air was even purer, the sun nearer, and the view had a large, world-sized embrace. They clambered on the slopes, his strides quick and nimble, the compass of his inordinate wishes defining new and wider boundaries of a land populated only by his hectic imagination. She followed and agreed, and thought – "What does it matter?" She watched him to see how much of this Zeus-like stagecraft he believed. Or was all this for her sake?

But, as if to stop the tilt and the slip, or to stop reality from intruding, he paused. He had enough of building skyscrapers on mountain tops, he tripped down the slope, half slipping, half running and skipping, bringing down with him loose earth and stones.

That evening at the taverna there was a strange silence about the new road. The locals, citizens of the mountain, were ashamed to admit that they took his land to make a road. Because it suited them, or because he was after all ... not one of them. And he kept quiet, perhaps because he could not fight all of them, because he did not want to lose his last friends and compatriots. And because his stubborn aged mind was not willing to believe that he had yet again lost his land. In any case, in the feverish euphoria of approaching death, he possessed whatever lands of whatever inestimable beauty he desired.

The following day they visited the sea – in case it was kinder to them. The day was warm, but his body shuddered from sudden draughts of icy thought. His face was pale and old, his eyes, filmy, looked up at the mountains with an old man's complaint.

They walked along the harbour and sat at the taverna of his old friend and compatriot Vangelis. He needed friends, and he needed a home, and the island offered to lost travellers countless instant homes in the green plane-tree shade of its kafeneia, and tavernas. Father was friendly, talkative, but he did not talk about the mountain. His body and voice were weak, as if they had suffered a blow in a secret unknown part from which they could not recover.

Vangelis gave his condolences. He was a proud-looking handsome man, of few words – younger that Gregoris. His own father, who had started the shop, was sitting by himself against the wall where it was warm – blind and silent. He had not taken root in this land, he had not forgotten his village in Asia Minor.

"So the shepherds took your land." Vangelis sat down with his friend.

"They didn't take my land. My land is higher up."

"They took your land, Gregori, to make their road. That's them, that's how they are."

"You are making a mistake, Vangeli. My land is higher up. What they took is not my land, it is no man's land."

Vangelis sighed with resignation, banged his hand on the table. "Right you are Kyr Gregori, let's have something to drink." They ate and drank and did not mention the land. They reminisced.

"Miss Eleni, your father and I have eaten bread and olives together. We have eaten fresh fish together. We have ploughed the seas. Those were the days, eh, Kyr Gregori?"

Eleni did not ask what seas they had ploughed. Father drank with his friend to their young and wild days, and to their compatriots, dead or alive, and to their old home – but his heart was not in it.

28

THE SLAUGHTER
OF THE INNOCENTS

Eleni and her father spent a day at Thasos town, completing the paperwork for the land on the mountain of Sotiros. They visited the registry office and got the official copies of the necessary documents, they visited the topographer, they visited the land with him. He looked at the dug mountain, then at the description of the land in the contract, then walked around the vast mounds, mountains, of debris of the destroyed forest. He turned to Gregoris and Eleni: "Your land is – this. They destroyed it to make a road. But I can make a map of the site. You can take them to court – but it will take years."

They went to see the president of the village. He shrugged his shoulders. "Did you look after your land? Did you even care?" Then he gave them an application form: "Write here your complaint." Eleni stated their case, her father was not interested, he was impatient, displeased. Eleni rang her father's lawyer in Thessaloniki, he told her they should start a court case, her father did not want to know. He was angry yet did not say what made him angry. He would take them to court, yes, he would destroy them – yet he insisted that his land was higher up the mountain, beautiful and untouched.

Having voiced his threats he cheered up, and so did Eleni. And in any case Easter embraced them within its cruel mysteries. Gregoris took his briefcase under his arm, let Eleni embrace his other arm and together they walked away from the wreckage of their property schemes. Slowly they took the path back to the square where the whole village had gathered. They were over-taken by goats gathering from near and far slopes for the night, and were soon left behind. Goat-bells filled the mountains with multiple, distinct, un-synchronized notes, each reverberating to the whim of appetite, the momentary curiosity of the moment. They made up the familiar music of daily life.

Demetra, the widow, had taken to the mountains looking for her one and only goat – spoilt and stubborn – wailing like a for-lorn mother. The dogs barked with lazy self-importance from habitual early evening excitement. In the village they were flanked by the goats which ran unfettered, dislodging stones on the already dilapidated paths. The villagers were out calling to them, with threats and cajoleries.

The following morning Eleni was woken by a havoc of voices and barks and distant truck noises, cut through by high-pitched brittle bleating. Her father was already up and out. She was sent by Panayiota to the barns at the edge of the village where "the whole world was".

The whole world of this village was now to her an enemy world. Yet she did not know who the real enemy was: who took the decision to destroy the land, who gave the order, who car-ried it out.

Trucks and vans were parked at the edge of the mountain plateau. The villagers, and many new faces, stood in a circle waiting. The wooden troughs had been pushed aside, people stood staring at the empty circle of land with horrified curios-ity and anticipation. The young goats were restless, their eyes aimlessly searching.

They waited while the place became alive with communal appetite, like a bazaar in the early hours of the day when new merchandise is brought out, or like a church preparing to receive a needy congregation. Some of the women spread their blankets under the trees, as if for an all-night vigil. Eleni saw her father gaze un-lovingly round the gathering.

There was a frozen silence, the forested mountain remained unmoved but the singing of a bird was distinct and isolated. Then the bleating started, and soon became shrill and panicked as the herdsmen shoved and tugged the animals un-tenderly – some very young, babies – into the circle.

This was the moment of the sacrifice. Eleni knew it, but in any case the woman next to her volunteered in a reverent mutter, "It's the Easter slaughter!"

The yearly drama was soon enacted. The men tried to separate the kids – some newly born – from their mothers. The mothers were obstreperous and unruly, the men hauled them away, with curses and sticks they tried to push them to the upper pastures. The mothers escaped and returned, the men, swearing, grabbed them and carried them up the mountain, the animals leapt out of their arms again. Their bleating turned ugly and long-drawn-out, the mountain, sun-blessed, echoed with war and pain. Only a few of the bigger goats took their usual path to the mountain, obediently and indifferently. They delayed at each opportunity, chewing on any possible green on their way. "They are lucky, they are the barren ones," the woman explained.

The small kids were kept together, restless and bewildered, their cries weak and piercing. A lean handsome man with a thin moustache was preparing with serious attention the instruments of slaughter. The hooks were hanging from the trees, the men briskly sharpened their knives, the butchers haggled over prices, the tanner shouted an offer for the skins rejected by the shep-herds. "This is no price, its rubbish. You'll get a fortune for each skin from the tourist shops."

The spectators from this and the other villages waited to buy their own Easter kid, some of them bought two – they were so small. The selling had begun, those who wanted them alive pulled them – unwilling but weak – by a rope, or held them tightly in their laps as the small animals struggled.

The slaughterer worked with quick elegant movements: the small animals were quietened by the confident stab. The skinning was quick, dexterous, clean. Then the long tear along the thin belly, and the entire delicate network of innards, liver, kidneys, fine intestines, heart, were pulled out still warm, still alive.

"Not much meat here, but so tender! Loukoumi!"

The mound of skins built up. The tanner looked at it pensively. He made his calculations. They would soon hang outside the tourist shops. They were too small for rugs, but bags and purses, and patchwork? Two local men were discussing prices. They had sold a lot but they were depressed. The bloody stain under the carob trees was spreading and deepening.

Eleni pulled her father away. She didn't know what he felt, nor did she ask. Was he even attending?

A young man was pushing small goats, confused and desperate, into a truck.

"They are lucky and they don't even know it." He slapped them with amusement as he forced them to make room for new company. "We sold them for breeding and for milk."

Loud wild howls came from the mountain slopes, and the kids, unmindful of their good luck, only knew their mothers were calling, and bleated back to them in thin weak cries, milling around in the truck, climbing up on the sides wanting to leap or fall. The man moved right and left grabbing and pulling and scolding, like a harsh angry mother.

The truck drove away on the winding dirt road through the olive grove that was being torn by the voice of young terror.

29

UNKNOWN, MY OWN

They went back to the president of the village. "I don't know about contracts and papers. I told you — if this land was yours, why didn't you mark it? Where is your fence? Where are your trees?"

He sent them to the Forestry Office. "This is forest, mountain forest. You cannot fence it."

They went to the police. The officer ignored the old man, measured the woman with sexual interest. "Go and see the president. Tell him I sent you. He is my cousin."

Tired, dejected, quarrelsome, they sat over their ouzo and olives at Vangelis' café by the harbour. In his friend's company, Gregoris recovered his exasperated male authority.

"I told you my child, our land is higher up. You are wasting our time, dragging me from office to office, an old man. This is not how you do things."

Vangelis raised his glass. "Let's forget the land. Let's drink to our health, and the memory of Kyra Anastasia."

Eleni clinked glasses with the two old men, and got up. The island was a small tight place.

She walked away and along the waterfront, which was already decked out brightly with flimsy kaftans and seashell ornaments. She browsed at the windows, went into dark cool interiors of souvenir shops to try clothes and silver jewellery. The tourist's Greece, of trinkets and chimes, was an easier bargain.

She returned near sunset. The two men still sat where she had left them, their backs to her, whiling the time away on the desolate beach, fingering the past with old appetite and quirky memory.

A young girl sat on the beach with her back to them, contemplating, perhaps enjoying, the sea view.

Eleni stopped a short distance behind them. She saw her father lean forward inclining his head towards the girl – as if to see her better, or to make himself audible to her.

She remained still and watched.

"Eleni, my child, why do you sit there all alone?"

Eleni was not sure whether he was talking to her, or not. But his body and head did not turn to her, the tenderness and love in his questioning was not directed to her.

He was tending and attending to that young girl on the beach. But the girl did not turn around. She may not have realized he was talking to her.

How did he know her, how did he know her name, why give this stranger her own name! The tenderness and love! – such as she could not remember hearing in his voice! And to a stranger? Eleni was shut out.

Her father called out to her, to the girl, again. "Eleni, my child, come and sit with us. Why do you sit all alone?"

"Who do you think she is, Kyr Gregori?" His friend was puzzled, amused.

Gregoris turned to him with indignation. "What do you mean who she is!"

Only then Eleni knew that her father mistook that girl for her. He did not know his own child? Yet it was his own child he thought he saw in that particular girl on the beach. Eleni looked at the young girl. Brown straight hair, small body, it could be herself at seventeen.

"You are getting old, Gregori. Is that your daughter?"

Father looked better at the girl, then at Vangelis with disbelief. Vangelis shook his head, observed the beautiful, rounded bay in resignation.

Eleni knew that she should run to him and stop this mistake which was hurting her – because her father preferred another daughter, even if he thought it was her. Yet that young body and that head bent in contemplation, her thoughts, innocent, perhaps of love: there was a time when this could be her.

This girl was her ghost, and her own father stretched his arms and his words to the ghost of her youth. Not to her, not to this woman standing behind him spying on his thoughts and feelings and his straying hurt memory. She was that age when she left – when she decided to stop being a daughter, and packed up her bags and left.

He got up and walked towards the girl. Slowly and awkwardly, because the sand held his feet, making his body heavy and slow. He approached the girl furtively, bending towards her, examining her features as if spying through a keyhole – yet making a spectacle of an old man creeping up on a young girl on a deserted beach. The girl turned towards him alarmed, Eleni saw her disturbed expression. The old man was not dangerous, he just looked at her face, searching for who knows what half-forgotten feelings and losses.

Eleni saw fragments of fatherhood she had not known.

He straightened his body and took the difficult journey back, thoughtful, confused – suddenly facing his daughter, standing still.

His friend Vangelis turned and only then saw Eleni, petrified somewhere between past and present.

"There is your daughter, Kyr Gregori! Telling me that girl is your daughter!"

Father looked at his daughter in confusion, unable to deny that this woman was his daughter and unable to abandon the image of the young girl. Eleni thought she could see his undecided, divided mind being pulled in different directions, yet trying to keep the world together. "Ah, my child, Eleni, here you are!" Unconvinced, disappointed, guilty. "And I thought you were sitting there all alone." He looked back at the girl, who remained unperturbed by the family drama in which she was innocently participating. "I must have been wrong... because – here you are!" The little false triumph of discovery revealed all the sorrow.

"Here I am, dad!"

Her father still looked, now at the girl now at the woman, trying to take in the two Elenis. Perhaps it was the wish to hold onto a large and embracing feeling – of paternal, and larger than paternal, love. It was also the effort of a mind falling, fast falling to pieces, and seeing the world around it splintering into so many shards, blindingly bright and sharp.

"She is not you, but, nevertheless, she is a person dear to us." He spoke contemplatively, and this contemplation was a most valuable thing. She was moved with pity and respect for him, for managing to keep something of his heart together. And by the formality of his language, which had the dignity of his sorrow and paternal authority. "But she is beloved of us." She mused on his words, which did not want to abandon this girl on the beach or that other girl stranded on the tide-washed sands of the past. Beloved of us? Did that plural include her? She was glad to share in whatever obscure love he dictated. Or was that "us" simply the plural of majesty? The royal we – which at that moment she granted him. An old king, without a kingdom, translated to a remote island. With all her heart, and in confirmation, she gave him a strong and long embrace.

She sat down and shed some secret tears, for the childhood she lost and for the father she was quickly losing.

The girl on the beach had quietly disappeared.

30

MOUTHFULS OF GOD

By the morning of Good Friday the small carcasses hung in cellars while their forlorn mothers wandered in disarray around the mountain, dislodging rocks or standing still on stony hilltops examining the changed landscape. The father and pantocrator of all goats, the hefty billy-goat that belonged to the Vardas family, the big family of the village, was tied securely under an old olive tree whose lower branches he had already devoured. He was ruminating on his territory.

All day the church bells were ringing death through mountain and valley. The women had spent the day in the church ornamenting the Tomb of Christ with flowers from their gardens. The men stood in the churchyard, serious and dignified, discussing sales. Eleni and her father entered the church, Eleni with the women on the left side, Father on the right with the men. The smell of death was the familiar, dizzying scent of flowers mixed with candle-wax and incense.

With chants of lamentation the congregation prepared for the Epitaphios procession. The priest, solemn and dignified, holding the icon of Christ to his chest, led the procession from the church – yet his eyes sparkled with fervour and lascivious mischief. Behind him the strongest and youngest men of the village carried on their shoulders the Sacred Tomb, drowned in flowers, and rocking with slow seductiveness, like an oriental sedan carrying not a dead god but some mythical potentate or legendary beauty. Then the congregation followed, hesitant on the stony paths, with cupped hands protecting their lit candles from the breeze. Like a long incandescent snake entering the hidden recesses of the mountain, the procession carried with reverence their God, dead, through their slowly dying village. The flowery edifice and the lengthening and thinning line of candles trembled on the thin lip of the ravine: its dark depth waited in silence – broken only by an isolated bleating or goat-bell.

Then all perfumes, of candles and of spring flowers and of the intoxicating incense, all were drowned in stench: the ugly familiar stench of the Vardas' billy-goat, in heat.

A goat in heat out of season! Was this some kind of rude miracle? The divine prank travelled through the men and women in the congregation – even the priest was distracted. Old Aristides Vardas, the owner of the village's one and only billy-goat, walked proud, his moustache bristled with sudden virility. "This time of the year!" Kyra Varda exclaimed to the women next to her in shamefaced whispers. "With all this trafficking of the goats, there's no restraining him." Her hushed excitement and mischief, and a wish to laugh and be merry, passed like an invisible current through the female congregation, who kept their flighty eyes on the flame of their candles. The wild flame imprinted an unceasing dance on their faces.

Eleni too accepted the message from the mountain, nature's carnal miracle, the bewildering moment of strife between lust and death. On the remote mountain in the cold dark of the night, the war or communion of "eros" and "thanatos" was re-enacted. The Christian god dying; the pagan animal god, all of his babies dead, yet triumphant in the lustful stench of his flesh. Words, native words, shone full of meaning in the dark. She could see now, and even smell, why "tragos", the native word for billy-goat, was the father of Tragedy and all tragedy. In the cold night of bereavement he reigned, seducing with his stench congregations, out-stinking rituals, and announcing to the world that he was uncontrollably and unashamedly on heat. One god is dead and another god, hoofed and horned, descends from the mountain tops bringing to young and old a whiff of new lust.

Saturday was the last day of the fast. And the fast of the truly faithful was total: no food, none of the pleasures of life until the Resurrection. The mournful melodies from the church spilled over into the expectant silence of the village. The bereaved goats scattered aimlessly on the mountains, the baby carcasses hung prepared, the Christian souls preparing. The billy-goat killed time in the shade of the old olive tree, unmindful of the tragedies of mountains and of communities – only in the early evening he went again into a frenzy when the goats came home.

But the needs and pleasures of life were already anticipated. The women would pause in their laments and run to their kitchens. With slippery hands they handled and untangled and turned inside out the delicate innards of new-born kids to make "magiritsa", the soup of the Resurrection. In good time, long before midnight, their minds turned to spiritual thoughts. Clean and properly dressed, their clean white handkerchief and candle in their handbags, they took again the dark paths to the church. The chanting resounded with grief in that forgotten village, the two aged church-wardens were that evening the stars of the community. But the priest, dressed in gold-woven splendour, sur-rounded by candle light and incense, and surrounded by his timid congregation, was a Byzantine Patriarch or Emperor, who in his happy plumpness kept strange company with the ascetic saints in the church's frescoes. He gave a scented hand to all the women to kiss, a special smile, a twinkle in his eye. Iphigenia was graceful, her eyes shone in the candle light. And even Michalis, the Turk, had been persuaded to come. He would make a splen-did Christian, so handsome and well groomed, so respectful. They were all there, a community waiting for the Holy Com-munion. Even the strangers, the merchant from Thessaloniki and his daughter, whose souls were rootless, and their spirits restless and wounded, on that evening belonged to the congregation. And even the mountain, with its pagan smells and bewildering gods and rituals, huddled in with them.

As the melodies quickened with the Resurrection, the congregation chanted with vigour, candles appeared from pockets and handbags, they all pushed for the holy light coming from the priest, who at that moment was transformed into the giver of light and love. The congregation moved forward preparing for the Holy Communion. Closer and closer round the priest, expectant, fighting, greedy for the flesh and blood of their God. They accepted it with a hunger on their faces that was not only spiritual. And as Eleni and her father approached, and she tasted the bread and the wine, she thought of her mother's dead body and her father's dying body: she wished she could contain in her mouth, in those two simple flavours, all the loves she was losing. Households and native land, and lover's body, and all material consumable things, desired – with such need desired! – were concentrated and consecrated into that mouthful of transubstantiated bread and wine, flesh and blood of gods and earthly souls.

They all went home, hosts and guests, in a communal effort to keep the candle flames out of the wind, and bring the holy light into their homes. Then they ate: on that night, the animals' innards, livers, guts, hearts and all. The following day they ate the rest – with songs and dances, and tokens of love. Michalis the Turk called the Christians brothers; and the priest, divested of his Byzantine splendours, admired the nun of the village who had taken her glasses off and revealed her handsome, cold face. Father and daughter momentarily paused in their grudges and searches, and partook of the food and the celebrations: Gregoris released for a little his wounded mind from his wounded land. And Eleni – her belly full of food, her heart full of love-making and death – conjured up visions of the stinking billy-goat, presiding demon of the feast.

The following morning they said good-bye. They promised to come back, and caught the boat for home.

31

AND THE MOTHS
SHALL INHERIT THE EARTH

The door of the flat was half open, as if they were expected.

"Who is it? Who is here?" Gregoris hid his alarm behind the staccato commands.

Eleni pushed the door quietly, but did not enter.

Gregoris took out his keys, and contemplated their uselessness. He put them back in his pocket. He rang the bell, as if this were not his home. "Is anyone here?" His anger echoed in the empty stairwell.

The noise of their puzzled fear gave them enough courage to push the door wide, and step in. A cloud of sun-lit dust travelled slowly through the flat, propelled erratically by a draught of air. Motes were lit by sun-beams in their slight movements of balance and suspense.

Through open doors they saw empty rooms, large – larger than they remembered. The curtains had been removed and the light came in freely, exposing the stained, pock-marked walls. Furniture and rugs were missing, the marked floors were covered with a film of dust and littered with the scattered household – stacks of plates, folded tablecloths, a plastic basin containing an assortment of bric-a-brac. A saucepan on top of a pile of blankets, like a madman's crown; a vacuum-cleaner in the corner. Yet the place had a freedom and bright lightness.

In the middle of the cluttered floor two women crouched – it took Eleni a few seconds to recognize her sisters under the film of dust covering their hair and faces. Her eyes witnessed, stunned, this aftermath of a sandstorm, or premature hoariness of old age. One of the women still held a coin. In the distributed piles around them, and in their postures opposite each other, Eleni saw them tossing a coin for the division of the household. She saw the coin – she was sure – in her sister's tightening fist, and saw in them not sisters but soldiers casting the dice over Christ's garments. The scene, cocooned in a halo of translucent dust, seemed constant and constantly repeated.

They stood up, saying nothing. Father looked before him at his absent home, and beyond it through the glass door at the sunlit world; he paused and closed the front door behind him to protect perhaps the remaining home. Then with raised hand he strode to them and struck, and cursed, crying with tears and anger. "Children. Dogs. I have no children. May your children do to you as you do to me." Sophia and Kaliopi stood in terror, protecting their heads and faces from his blows and curses. A cloud of dust, pain and fear travelled in large movements round the room. When he finally crumpled on the floor and held his head between his hands, the daughters crawled near him, no doubt sharing in pity and self-pity. "We had to do this. There is no other way. We found a new home for you – you cannot, cannot live alone any longer." Their heads were lowered, as if it was not they but fate who had willed these events.

It was not fate, it was his own daughters who were killing him. Eleni blamed her sisters, they blamed her, rage swept away words and reasoning, and, like a blind savage child, she ran at them, and lashed out and tore and kicked and struck.

The old father sat resigned in the corner of the room. With tired tearful eyes he watched, as if on a stage, his daughters savaging each other with their bare hands. He watched with drowsy mind the hideous scene – and never said "Stop."

Indifferently he stood up and went to his room. The door was still locked, and he gave a sigh – audible only to him – of relief. He produced his keys, without fumbling, and unlocked it. His room was still there. He switched on the light and disappeared into the remains of his kingdom. He moved through the years of clutter, oblivious of the hate and damage outside. Untouched boxes piled ceiling high, old wardrobes bursting with ancient merchandise – the dust choked his lungs. He pushed deeper through the mountain, into the belly of his trade: boxes that had not moved for years fell over him and burst apart, letting their life pour out, and with it dust, more dust, and – like souls, tiny winged souls imprisoned for eternities, or snowflakes flying upwards with gusts of wind – insects, thick swarms of tiny insects flew out in fear, or freedom. Blinded by them he opened more boxes, frantically looking for something, releasing more and more swarms of moths that were now pouring out of the room. His hands dug into dark places, interrupting feasts, clasping materials devoured and hanging in rags, clinging on him, crumbling into dust.

He found what he was looking for. In a hazy swarm of moths he appeared at the door – cobwebs, woven through with dust and moths, clinging on him like unwanted memories. He was holding thick wads of money, large, colourful, exotic-looking paper money, which he stuffed into his pockets.

"Its pre-war money," Sophia mumbled in pity and resignation.

He gazed at the space. His daughters were there, alive, but hardly visible to him through the cloud of moths pouring from the room, and from room to room, darkening the place, and soon populating and darkening the sunlit world. The hour had come for the moths to fly free and inherit the earth.

Eleni pored over the document signed by her father. It gave her sisters power of attorney to dispose of all his income and property as they wished and thought fit. The date was recent, two days before they had left for Thasos.

It could be revoked, it could all be revoked – Eleni mused at the fragments of a scene flying dishevelled in different directions.

Sophia put the document back into her handbag. Kaliopi was making arrangements over the phone for the phone to be cut off. Her father was stuffing the useless money into his briefcase. Eleni let the fragments become smaller and smaller as they flew away to distant lands.

The few days before her flight she spent at a hotel, in transit between lives. Her mind was abandoned to the currents of immediate emotion, her body already caught in the movement of escape. And in the meantime rights and wrongs, debts and benefits and duties of life and death remained in suspense in a no-man's language and land.

Eleni walked round the ailing city, its body like her mother's body, bloated, dead to her. As war stalked its walls, the city huddled inside its noisy tavernas gorging itself to silence and forgetfulness on its sorrows and fears.

She noticed the garbage was being cleared up. The strike must have ended, yet she smelled the pollution.

She met her sisters briefly. They were dressed formally, ill at ease. Kaliopi had prepared the ritual memorial food – boiled wheat with nuts and icing sugar. She passed them the bowls of the food of remembrance with dignity; and the shared flavour brought back to them the family's litany of deaths.

Sophia recited her responsibilities for their father's life. She was willing to show the accounts to the other two, she was willing to hear of any other solutions. The other two were silent. Having asserted the authority of the eldest child, she folded the documents before her and took off her glasses. She was at ease with power; but, unexpectedly, looked defeated by its burden.

If Sophia now took the place of Father, Kaliopi played Mother. She asked her sisters caringly if they wanted more "kollyva", and once she felt she had fed them she was overcome by emotion, perhaps at her own motherly kindness. With tears in her eyes she announced with a quiet confidential voice that she had been praying for them.

"I dreamt of mother." Eleni's voice was hard. "She was angry. She told me she has been waiting at the dinner table for us to sit with her and eat."

There was silence in the room. In silence the dream effortlessly slipped back and removed in slow motion everything it contained: her mother, blind to her, and the table she was sitting at, the empty chairs, the entire room, and the house that embraced all. Her own dream left her outside, looking through the steamed window at her home and the life in it.

Kaliopi offered her sisters more "kolyva", material and spiritual food of comfort. They ate, wiping the tears from their eyes and the icing sugar from their lips. Perhaps, separately, they each thought of their father. They knew this was no reconciliation and no restoration.

They agreed to share out the furniture some other time – it was for the time being in store. The household had lost its hold on her, it was so much dead weight.

She took out of her handbag a small evening bag made of black and red beads. There was a slight start in her sisters' faces.

She put it on the table. "Here is the jewellery."

No one wanted or dared to open the bag – as if the world's evils would all over again fly from it and darken the day. They agreed to place it in the bank till a better day.

"I will keep this ring," Eleni said, the other two noticed it was already round her finger.

Their material world, that had shaped their souls, was quietly falling away in so many tatters, leaving them amazed, and free. Leaving them with a deep endless shared guilt for their mother's death and their father's life: and an unspoken fear for themselves.

Eleni's last nights were crowded with dreams. A man unknown to her, perhaps a lover with an anonymous face, gave her a parcel of letters to read. He took them out of his breast pocket: the gesture, his hand moving so near his heart, and the gift of words, even unread words, was a rare gesture of love in her dark slumber.

She visited her lover in his flat in Vyzantion. The place seemed inhabited by other lives. She sat on the downy sofa and over a drink attempted to tell him about the island. She heard herself telling him of a voyage that had been taken by someone else, leaving out the meaning of it. One day she would work this meaning out – but for now she kept the island to herself.

They lay together on the marital bed – already separated. The telephone rang, he let it ring and ring, the ringing stubbornly and wilfully drilled a hole straight through their love. Their minds and bodies already ran ahead to negotiate their separated lives, promising to each other with loving words to meet again, knowing probably they would not.

As she lay next to him she thought of her mother dead, and knew that their love would always be touched by death. Their last love-making was gripped by the unacknowledged icy pain of brevity. The unrelieved sigh of an erotic moment expiring.

She also knew that now and in the years to come she would think of her mother's death with the tinge, the taint, of a momentary blushing pain of erotic pleasure. Inexplicable.

As they separated their mouths silently came together and naturally contained each other in a kiss that was all silence, and enduring, eternal immobility. During that kiss which was not going to end, her unspoken words gave him form, her breath from mouth to mouth brought him to life, he was made no longer of flesh but of her language. A sculpture of her native sounds and meanings.

She visited her father at the Home to say good-bye. The old men and women in their dressing gowns, sitting lined around the wall, remained indifferent. Indifferent to the stinging smell of urine and disinfectant, indifferently staring at the soundless pictures on the television smoothly and silently moving from violence to violence.

Her father was concentrating hard on keeping busy, and alive. He rehearsed for himself every single simple activity: getting up, sitting down, losing his handkerchief, finding his handkerchief.

He mumbled to himself an uninterrupted stream of words: directions for life, snatches of a world. Eleni caught fragments. "My jacket? I am wearing my jacket. Where is my handkerchief? Here is my handkerchief. Where is my money? I have no money." He slowly looked to her. "Eleni, I want to go home."

"I am going home, dad."

He liked the candy she brought him, gave her one, signalled to her not to give any to the other old men and women staring at them. The television picture changed to an ad, a happy family in a green meadow – but no music, no sound. Only a heartbreaking shriek from one of the rooms, which startled none of the inmates.

"It's the Greek-American," the gigantic nurse explained. "He is just yawning, bored." She was tying a bib round an old lady. "He has no one in this country so he wants attention."

A small, very old man, much older than her father, declared to the room that he had fought in the Asia Minor expedition, in 1922. The audience remained uninterested.

Her father said he too came from Asia Minor.

"I don't remember you," the older man said and spat into a dirty handkerchief.

Her father put another sweet into his mouth. Then started searching his pockets.

A brief animation in the room. The dinner trolley, and the medicine: the sweet sedative syrup that they all liked, that brought them peace and quiet in the daytime, and the other sweet syrup that brought them deep dreamless sleep. Oblivion and slow death. The television images changed silently, indifferently, to the desiccated insect-like black figures slowly crawling on arid African earth.

Like good children the old men and women opened their toothless mouths and waited.

Time to say their good-byes. Hers was tearful, regretful. His was tired, distracted.   ·

She promised they would go back to the island, she saw a

violent gleam in his eyes, then he concentrated on tying his bib round his neck.

Without tenderness he watched her walk towards the door.

On her last night she dreamt of an execution. Of herself. By two – men? Women? A couple? She couldn't see them, they stayed behind her, in the dark. She had a choice – she saw the knife but chose the bullet. So she prayed, and the prayer was interrupted by the bullet entering her head, making her head explode and open like a flower.

"No, this is wrong," she could hear her voice in her sleep, in her mother tongue, in the empty hotel room, as she died: but those very words stopped her from dying.

So, with the courage of her words, in the sequel of the dream, she travelled around her native city with a bullet in her head, telling its amazed citizens she had a bullet in her head.

32

THE ISLAND OF
THE RESURRECTION

The official searched her face, then glanced at the passport photograph, then studied her again – unable to place his suspicion on any single sign.

Her handbag was emptied, turned inside out – nothing of significance. Curious hands fingered her body reaching into her mind. They let her pass into the waiting room – her original guilt nestling in dark recesses feeding on the familiar unspoken thoughts.

There were delays. A flight for Mytilene was cancelled because it was overweight – the plane was small, with propellers. The three heaviest passengers were asked to dismount, she saw a fat woman cross the runway blushing with anger and shame.

The passengers around her spoke foreign languages. She only now noticed how unnaturally many there were. Some of them seemed from their tired faces and slumped bodies as if they had been waiting for a long time. They must be asylum seekers, she conjectured, Greeks from Eastern Europe, or Russia, the former Soviet Union. Were they waiting to enter Greece, or were they being sent back? Perhaps they were tourists?

It was all a conjecture. In this waiting place her story began to lose its dimensions. And as recent events became suspended in a land of half-translation, and remained amongst other ghosts "in transit", the invisible serpent fed like sin on the unacknowledged regrets. For escape, her mind circled round texts in foreign languages. Tragedy had enacted itself, within the stench of the billy-goat king of foreign and native tragedies. An ordinary and humdrum tragedy, with the butchery, though without the poetry. And its randy stench would always be mixed with the smell of homelessness, of urine and disinfectant.

Her mind, in idle retreat and escape, circled above other places. Colonus, the enclosed green land of eternal rest and translation. The beauty of the place hurt – because her father could see and feel and know the ugly terror of his end. A terror which was cosily curled inside her with dear intimacy. The stench of ammonia that made her eyes water would outlive her father and linger, clinging to particles of the air – of whatever green shady wood – she breathed.

She turned to Medea – that other Asiatic woman escaping westwards, betraying father and homeland, casting in the sea her brother torn in pieces, arriving in the new land a foreigner and a barbarian. In the contemplation of that trail of horrors her mind rested.

At Heathrow, she abandoned herself to the scrutiny of the country's keepers. Like a person who has committed a family crime and is now pursued by the Furies, with lowered eyes she sought asylum.

The official asked what she did, she said she was a translator. He nodded unwilling approval, and she re-entered her quiet exile from the mother tongue.

Behind her, behind the glass doors, her mother tongue, embodied and divided into a mother and child, was talking to her, incessantly, yelling, shrieking at her, streams of words, feared and loved words, a river, a waterfall of words, whose lashings would always distract.

She turned away, and in smiling silence she walked towards her life. She saw a man holding a child by the hand: her home, foreign and intimate, intact: her family, her loves, needing no translation. She walked to them, and out of a story.

She walked confidently into the embrace of home and of exile – except for a fragment of her, a passage of story, a ghostly shadow, a rag that escaped from the Fates' weave, that strayed and journeyed back to her father's island of the resurrection. She climbed through pine forests and olive groves and reached the terraces of vines hanging between heaven and earth. Below her, a world of orderly patterns of sun and shadow, a divine geometry out of this world, a mother's embroidery. There, in that sun-lit silent solitude, seized by the ceaseless wordless song of the cicadas, she stopped.